Price scratched his head. Why would he have written to Lenore and offered her employment when he obviously had no use for a paid companion? He had no female relatives, or a wife, either.

She caught his eye. "Could we talk today, after you change perhaps?"

He nodded slowly and glanced outside. Yes, it was definitely afternoon, and judging by the increased traffic of elegant carriages heading toward Hyde Park, it was almost time for the promenade. He'd lost track of another day. But he'd also lost track of his reason for writing to Lenore, and that seemed the more pressing problem. "I didn't realize it was so late."

"You've slept the day away, but I'm glad you're finally awake to sort things out." She grinned. "Do you think... Would you mind very much putting some trousers on while we discuss my new duties?"

Heather Boyd

USAT BESTSELLING AUTHOR

Romancing the Earl

Distinguished Rogues

12

Dedication

For my very first hero.
Tall, handsome and a damn funny man.
Rest in peace Dad.

Chapter One

London
Autumn, 1815

In Madam Bradshaw's House of Pleasure, a gentleman could buy practically anything and anybody for the right price. This was no penny amusement. A man paid a premium for the pleasures offered here.

Price only came here to drown his sorrows.

The light was low in his corner, but the footmen knew to freshen his glass with cider brandy as soon as he drained it. His nearby friends indulged their own vices in a different manner. They took lovers, gambled, and argued their points of view vigorously as if the world turned only for them.

Price, however, kept his opinions to himself these days. He took nothing for granted now, when once he would have been in the thick of any debate, freely expressing his opinions as he'd once thought his right to do so as the Earl of Carmichael. He'd risked his fortune on the turn of a dice many a night and offered his heart for the thrill of loving women, especially one in particular.

He knew better now. Money and position did not guarantee happiness. Pleasure was fleeting but not to be forgotten. Every moment he drew breath was precious to him, as was the happiness of others.

But he freely admitted he had no power to make others happy anymore, nor desire to try.

Price appreciated the sanctuary this place offered to someone who did not wish to be jollied into a better mood. His heart was broken—never to feel the indescribable joy of holding the one person who'd meant the world to him ever again. He embraced his solitary existence, relished it in a way he never had before.

But that loss did not decree that he must hide.

Madam Bradshaw prowled through the room, an empress of her decadent domain. Said to have been a duke's mistress once upon a time, Madam had become infamous since going into business for herself. Past her prime now, she had opened this establishment and employed others to offer a level of attention most gentlemen of the *ton* craved but said they never found at home. The establishment had thrived these past years, and the waitlist for admittance was said to be long.

Price had applied for membership on a lark years ago, never meaning to come here but once. For the fun of it. Lately, though, he came each night to indulge his current vice—drink.

Madam Bradshaw's pretty temptresses came by every once in a while, attempting to bolster Price's ego as they slid onto his knees and purred seductions into his ear. However, he was sure they all knew by now that he wasn't interested in more than a brief conversation. Madam Bradshaw probably insisted they at least try to flirt with him once a night so he did not look like he was being neglected.

Price didn't feel neglected. He was happy here. He only came to drink in the company of others who would not criticize or try to reform him. He detested drinking alone at home, and his friends came here, so he did, too. If they thought he drank too much, they kept that opinion to themselves.

He glanced about the room again and squinted at his surroundings. Madam Bradshaw's was a place quite unlike anywhere he'd visited before. The opulence of the furnishings was a touch overblown for his taste. The women who passed by wearing very little to suggest modesty reminded him of a painting he'd once glimpsed of Roman times—even down to the gold-leaf coronets adorning their heads.

Not that he was at all interested. The only woman he wanted was dead, and he mourned her still.

Price finished his glass, pushing away his despair, and was grateful when a footman instantly appeared by his side balancing a full glass on a small gold tray on his hand. "For you, my lord," he murmured.

"Thank you," he murmured with a nod, taking another sip and eying the temptations on display dispassionately.

Of the women Madam employed to give men pleasure, there were currently any number to choose from if he was so inclined. One or a dozen would join him in bed if he wished for it on any night. Their limbs were fleshy and firm, young, their faces artfully painted with cosmetics that emphasized their eyes. If the eye was supposed to be the window to the soul, then those ladies suggested desire when they looked him over.

Price wasn't the only gentleman in the room watching the pretty parade pass him by in the dim light tonight. To his right, several gentlemen friends reclined on chaise lounges like his, glass in hand, too, jaded eyes lingering on Bradshaw's offerings. One beckoned a fair lady onto his lap, and when she sat astride him, Price turned his attention back to his glass lest he saw more than he really wanted of their exchange.

A few other gentlemen on the far side of the room had women sitting over their hips, too, in various stages of making love to them regardless of their audience. They'd go soon, find a room to make love in. They were free with their affections in a way Price could not be anymore.

Price turned his attention to the other side of him, where the door was located. The card room across the hall was better lit and brimming with hardened gamblers, but he knew better than to play a hand when he was so deep in his cups.

He could feel the tension rising in this room, though, smell the scent of arousal in the air, but was not affected by it in the least. He was almost too drunk to feel any discomfort, too. The room, the people also, began to take on a soft glow as if he were seeing them through a dirty window. That made him happy. He saw none of their flaws under the influence of spirits. The world was a beautiful place when he was in this condition. Just as he preferred to imagine it.

He took another drink, tilted his head back, and closed his eyes. He had but one lovely memory to savor during the long hours of the night. He and Angela Berry, the young woman he'd loved and meant to marry, hiding together behind a crimson drape in a room slightly less opulent than this. Hands fumbling, lips meeting, tongues tangling. Breathless with anticipation. Angela had been inexperienced but very eager. He'd been eager, too, but with the experience to enjoy the anticipation of teasing her until aroused, but never going further.

He should have married her after their first kiss. Taken her away to Gretna Green and forgotten about trying to win over her family before they married. He should have—

Hands, soft and gentle, slithered over his shoulders, pulling him from his regrets. "You shouldn't be alone, my lord," a sultry voice whispered in his ear before he sensed her moving to sit at his side.

Price opened his eyes slowly. "Not…"

The words in his throat died as he blinked in surprise, and then he came to his senses fully.

The woman in front of him bore a striking resemblance to an old acquaintance. But that was impossible. Lenore Griffin was miles away in the country acting as a lady's companion, and she would never throw away her good reputation in this sordid place.

He blinked quickly, and that slight confusion disappeared. The whore might have the same abundant chestnut hair spilling around her pretty face, but that was where the similarities thankfully ended. It was just a trick of the weak light and of the drink.

"Not tonight, my dear," he stated, turning his face away.

The woman took his drink from his hand and out of the corner of his eye, he saw her sample some before speaking again. "Not any night, I hear. Madam is becoming worried about you, my lord. Why do you shun our company?"

He smiled at her as he retrieved his glass. "Madam only worries about money, and what I do shouldn't be of interest to anyone. I pay her well to be left in peace."

A faint smile tugged her lips. "If you're trying not to be noticed, you are failing horribly, my lord. We find your disinterest even more challenging the longer you remain alone."

He shook his head. "I'm sorry. I've no room in my heart for women."

"I don't want your heart, my lord." She winced. "If I might be entirely honest, I don't really want *you*, either. But Madam expects us to entertain someone, and there is a wager worth winning over you. I thought perhaps you'd help me win it by making it seem as if you like me more than the others."

Whores wagered on him? Price found that sad. Angela had often made ridiculous wagers with her friends. He'd helped her win a few, too. Their laughter when she won seemed so long ago. Price did appreciate the whore's honesty about her reason for approaching him, though. What could be the harm so long as he only had to pretend? "Join me then, and we'll pretend together."

Her smile was utterly delighted. "Gladly, my lord."

She swung her feet onto the chaise and wiggled around until she was in his arms. He pulled her close against his body but kept her facing away from him. He didn't want to kiss her or take her to bed. Her company was all he would tolerate.

After a time, the woman stirred in his arms to look back at him. "My lord?"

"What is your name?"

"Angie, my lord."

He startled. A variation of the name of his true love was not what he had expected to hear. He darted a quick glance beyond Angie, searching for the abbess. Madam Bradshaw was known to go to extraordinary lengths to fulfill her clientele's unasked desires. He wouldn't put it past her to have dug into his life a little and found a woman specifically for him. "Is that your real name?"

"Yes, my lord. Madam wanted to change it to Celeste but that were my mother's name and I thought taking it up disrespectful."

He calmed himself, believing Angie was telling the truth about her name. Women with daughters of marriageable age had been known to push their offspring at him all his life. Avoiding romantic entanglements was one of the reasons he had avoided many of this year's parties and amusements. There was no scheme or contrivance here.

He looked at the woman beside him again. Her hair had a dark reddish tone to it, her lips pink and smiling. Her eyes were blue, but cold and calculating in a way that unsettled him as he looked at her longer.

Lenore Griffin had blue eyes but soft, and often sad. She'd hardly ever smiled, which wasn't surprising given her station in life.

He exhaled slowly. "How long have you been here?"

"Not very long, really," she murmured then looked over her shoulder again. "But every day feels an eternity."

"I know the feeling." He moved her hair aside when it began to tickle his nose, and then lifted his glass to his lips for another sip of the cider. He leaned his head back again, feeling the effect of the spirits dragging him down toward unconsciousness.

The woman turned over and faced him, lying half across him. Her limbs tangled about his, and he felt not the slightest pleasure in it.

She put her hand to his cheek softly.

"I'm not asleep yet," he promised.

"But you soon will be. The wager cannot be won this way. You should come with me, my lord, and we will find a room together. I'll let you sleep, but everyone will think otherwise," she whispered, trailing her fingers down his chest. He grabbed her hand before it could wander too far. "Unless you've changed your mind and want something more," she purred.

"No. On second thought, I *have* changed my mind. I'd rather be alone here."

"I'll look after you better tonight than anyone ever has before," Angie whispered.

Despite his disinterest, he couldn't help but smile at her claim. She was a determined one. "That is not possible. Find someone else."

Angie flounced off in a huff, and Price finished his drink in peace. He did not wish to become involved with bothersome, demanding women.

He set his head back on the cushions and thought of Angela, or tried to.

Instead, he found himself thinking of quiet Lenore Griffin and wondered if her new situation suited her as well as the last. Her previous employer had passed away suddenly, and she'd been taken in by a respectable widow in the same town. It had been a while since he'd heard from her. He should write and make good on the promise he'd made long ago to keep in touch.

"I say, Carmichael, are you asleep, old man?"

He opened one eye to find Marquess Wharton standing over him. "Not with you shouting at me."

"Good. We're done here."

Price refocused his gaze, noticing his party had shrunk down to just three. "Where's Sullivan?"

"Gone off hours ago," Scarsdale, a lanky man of similar age, said with a scowl. "You know he disapproves of these places."

"He could just drink like I do and ignore the rest," Price suggested.

"No one drinks the way you do and hopes to live very long," Wharton complained. He got hold of Price under the arm and hauled him up to his feet. "Good grief, you're heavier than you appear."

Price wobbled a bit as he straightened his coat and tugged down his waistcoat. "I didn't need help."

Wharton scowled. "You certainly *do* need someone's help."

"Come on," Scarsdale said as he grabbed Price by his other arm, and the three of them weaved their way toward the entrance hall and the newly rising sun outside.

Price stumbled into the carriage, taking up one whole bench while his friends sat side by side opposite him. He ran a hand over his jaw, covering a yawn and the beard he'd grown since he'd stopped caring about trying to impress society.

"You'll ruin yourself with the drink, you know," Wharton started before they'd gone too far along. "And that beard has to go soon."

Price shrugged away the criticism. "What does it matter what I look like to you?"

"Well, the ladies don't much care for beards, I've noticed."

He grabbed the bench as the carriage lurched into motion. "I'm not interested in women."

"You can't be in mourning forever," Wharton protested. "You weren't even engaged to the girl. It's been months now. Time to look to the future."

"I'll never love another," Price warned, wishing his friend would understand and quit pestering him about Angela. He knew the state of his own heart.

Scarsdale laughed softly. "Who's talking about love?"

Wharton silenced Scarsdale and sat forward. "Listen, I understand what you're doing, but Angela Berry wasn't the only pretty woman in society who could have made you a good wife. There are many keen to catch your notice. Why, just the other day, I heard a pair of ladies speaking of you."

"Indeed." Price shifted in his seat. "Protesting that I could hardly have suspected my godmother was a murderess, I suppose."

Wharton nodded. "No one blames you."

"No one talks about anything else. That is why I started avoiding certain hostesses and still do. The ones who leap to my defense are the worst because they never let the matter rest. I'd rather be alone."

Wharton sighed. "Surely there's something better than spending every night of your life in this state."

"I'm not a drunk," Price promised.

"No. No. But you are not acting like the man we admired," Scarsdale complained. "First month after Angela died, you hardly ate, then you dine lavishly every night as if it was your last meal, and now you're drinking constantly and moping."

"You forgot the month he could not stand to be still," Wharton complained. "Damned if I had the stamina to keep up with him."

"The point is, you can't keep this up much longer without it affecting your health. It's time to put your grief aside and think of the future."

Price scowled at them. "You are trying to marry me off."

"He means you should live as you did before. As a gentleman. As the earl you were before Angela died," Wharton said. "You used to be fun to be around. Reliable. You have responsibilities. You were a voice in the House of Lords once. People looked to you to know how to vote."

"How dull that sounds."

"And you must marry, too," Scarsdale noted. "We have to face that at some point, don't we?"

Wharton nodded emphatically. "If you want the best, to make your own choice rather than stumble into a situation not of your own making, you'd better face the world clear-headed."

"What are you saying?"

"We can't always be watching out for you. As drunk as you are, you'd be an easy fellow to capture by a husband-hunting shrew."

"I *had* the best," Price promised, thinking of sweet, perfect Angela. The love of his life. They would have been happy together. He'd lost that hope for the future, and he couldn't imagine making love to someone else.

"So you can't have her. Just pick any woman you can tolerate and marry them. At least then, we can stop worrying that some woman is going to trap you and make your life even more miserable than it already is."

Price sighed deeply. His friends had a point. He'd loved Angela with all his heart, and the chances of feeling that way again were remote. He'd be wise to take matters into his own hands eventually. "I suppose there is no sense in delaying anymore."

Wharton slapped his knee. "Just make sure she's a pretty face, and you'll be fine when it comes time to bed her."

"She'll need a dowry and impeccable connections," Scarsdale added.

Money wasn't a driving need for Price. He'd wealth enough to value other qualities. "Discretion. Kindness. Loyalty," he murmured. "A lady who doesn't demand the world be given to them."

Scarsdale burst out laughing. "Is there any lady you know who doesn't have their own agenda when they choose a husband? They all want something from us."

"Usually they want a man with the highest title," Wharton added. "Thankfully the Earl of Carmichael was a popular devil, and will be again. Still, it is a tricky proposition, choosing the right wife from within the *ton*. There are definite advantages to taking the reins early."

Price held Wharton's stare. "What do you know about courtship or marriage?"

"Not much, but I've never dismissed the idea out of hand the way you have been lately." Wharton leaned forward suddenly. "Would Angela really expect you to live your whole life alone?"

Price stilled, and thankfully saw that the carriage was drawing up to his home. He got out before he had to answer Wharton and only said goodbye.

Love might be out of the question for him, but he was expected to marry, unfortunately, for the sake of the title. He had a duty, and Angela would have understood that, too. She'd been like many women in the *ton*. She'd had her pick of the field, and had chosen him, an earl she'd fallen in love with.

There was no lady Price knew who could equal her in the *ton*. Any marriage he made would have to be an arrangement. Since adoration was no longer a factor, he was free to marry anyone he chose, as long as they never expected him to fall in love.

Chapter Two

"Lady Kelly!" Lenore Griffin cried out in terror as the phaeton she was traveling in veered wildly toward the pavement, where innocent townsfolk could be trampled.

She shut her eyes instinctively until she finally felt the phaeton jerk, and then slow. Cautiously, she risked a peek at where they were, and then glanced to the far side of the seat.

Lord Thorne, her employer's new beau, had the reins in hand now, and Lady Kelly was grinning. "I was getting the hang of it," she promised.

"You did admirably for a first go, my dear lady," Lord Thorne enthused. "It is my turn now. It is a true honor to drive you and your companion about Town."

Lenore leaned forward. "I do appreciate it."

It may have been disloyal to her employer to prefer Lord Thorne's skill at the reins, but Lenore had one life, and she was truly quite fond of living it. She felt infinitely safer with Lady Kelly's beau driving them about instead of her recently erratically behaved employer.

Lady Kelly gave Lenore a quelling look, and Lenore quickly stared straight ahead again, shrinking into her seat a little. Lady Kelly, an at-first-glance respectable pillar of their small community, had been giving Lenore that look ever since Lord Thorne had started coming around. The lady had started acting more boldly, too, and had become less concerned with the happiness of others, especially those in her employ. Why, just last week, she had slapped a maid because of a harmless remark about needing to let out a seam in Lady Kelly's best gown.

Lord Thorne had been courting Lady Kelly for a few months now, and this wasn't the first time she had done something reckless in his company. Was the lady trying to impress him with her daring so he would think her more appealing?

Lady Kelly was the latest in a long line of demanding employers who expected their companions to meet high standards of deportment and agreeableness at all times. Lenore found that last expectation the hardest to meet. Lady Kelly was exceedingly contrary in conversation. Lenore never quite knew which opinion she wanted to hear agreed with first.

But Lenore had grown comfortable with the baron, and she expected a match to be made any day now. An older man, Lord Thorne had deep pockets, impeccable connections and spoke intelligently on any number of topics. He had no vices Lady Kelly disapproved of. Although experience had shown Lenore that gentlemen were not to be relied upon in general, especially men courting her wealthy employers, she felt his addresses were sincere. He seemed quite determined to make a good impression with all of Lady Kelly's friends, too.

When it came right down to it, all that mattered was that he made Lady Kelly happy. Lenore had already started discreetly considering where she might find a new situation for herself. There were not many women in need of companionship in the village so she had taken to reading the newssheet for opportunities farther afield.

However, Lenore was not at all desperate that she might be cast out straight away. She had built up a little money of her own for just such situations, and those funds would support her for a few months should she fail to find a new situation immediately.

Lord Thorne and Lady Kelly exchanged a loving look as he

explained the difficulty of handling his high-spirited team as they drove along. Lenore kept her gaze forward, wishing she could make herself disappear rather than hear them fall in love.

Lenore's whole life had revolved around making herself invisible. First as a child and later as a companion. Keeping her employers calm and happy had always been her goal. She couldn't have refused to take this drive with them even if she'd wanted to.

"I received a letter from my elder sister, Lady Bedwell, today," Lord Thorne announced. "She has invited me to spend Christmas with her in Cornwall."

Lenore had not met this particular sister of Lord Thorne's, but she'd heard much about the woman over tea in the drawing room. The lady had practically raised Lord Thorne in the place of a mother, he'd said, and she was essential to please, Lady Kelly had confided to Lenore later.

Lady Kelly gasped. "You wouldn't really go away so soon, would you?"

"I'm not sure I can refuse. She has been very good to me through the years, and she's all alone now since her husband passed. I fear she's become lonely."

"We'd be lonely without you, too." Lady Kelly blushed. "Wouldn't we, Lenore?"

Lenore made a sound of consent because Lady Kelly had been much happier these past months with Lord Thorne around. She dreaded the tears that would flow on the day of his departure. Lady Kelly was an emotional creature. It was Lenore's job to listen to her woes, sympathize and bring her cool cloths to soothe her puffy eyes. But Lord Thorne's consideration of the feelings of his female relations only improved her opinion of his character as a contender for Lady Kelly's hand.

Lenore leaned forward. "She must miss her husband terribly."

"Indeed, she does." Lord Thorne's smile fell upon Lenore. "Never fear, I won't have to make any decision for a week or so yet."

Lady Kelly fell silent, but she had her bottom lip between her teeth as she looked ahead. That was never a good sign. Lenore could almost hear her worrying about spending Christmas alone without him.

He smiled. "Did you have any plans for the coming holiday, Lady Kelly?"

"None." She sighed. "We'll most likely stay home, as we always do."

Lenore had been with Lady Kelly for almost a year but had spent the last three years in the area. Three dull and uneventful Christmases spent looking out at white nothingness with only old women for company. The prospect of another year of it lowered her spirits.

"Ah," he murmured. "Your home is quite a lovely, quiet little place."

"It is," Lady Kelly agreed. "However, I have for some time been considering a holiday, too."

Lenore was surprised by that. Lenore's last employer had claimed Lady Kelly had put down roots and settled like a pig in mud. Until Lord Thorne had started coming around, Lady Kelly's only interest had been in criticizing the behavior of her nearest neighbors. But the prospects of travel to new surroundings appealed to Lenore very much.

She risked asking a question. "What is Christmas like in Cornwall?"

"Dull and gloomy," he answered with a grin. "But my sister sets a good table, and there's the shooting, of course. She entertains often."

"I suppose you've many friends there?" Lady Kelly asked in a worried voice.

"Some, but none as lovely as you," he promised grinning down at Lady Kelly. His gaze flickered to Lenore, and she blushed and looked away quickly. She shouldn't have noticed their affectionate exchange.

Lenore stifled a sigh. How long before he proposed marriage? She wished there was some way to know when it would occur before her need for new employment, and a roof over her head, became immediately pressing.

She was very glad when he turned the carriage for home at last and she could escape the close confines with the prospective couple.

"Home" was almost a little farm, with cows in the green meadows, chickens scratching about in the garden, and a few servants in the fields picking fruit in the orchard. The land had belonged to Lady Kelly's late husband's family, though a neighbor had taken over the managing of most of it recently.

It had a pretty patch of grass to one side of the main house, in which they sat on warmer days, watching the clouds scuttle by overheard and allowing Lenore's dog, her best friend in the world, run about herding the chickens.

When the weather was drear, they sat inside in the study and read anything in the lady's small library, or simply stared out at nothing.

At the house, a gardener rushed out to hold the horses of the fine phaeton. Lord Thorne climbed down, turned to help Lady Kelly, and then, to her surprise, offered to help Lenore down, too.

His fingers were firm around her waist, and she floated to earth with a soft laugh and breathless thank you. That was all the adventure she ever got in her life.

She followed them inside, taking Lady Kelly's bonnet and shawl when it was handed to her. Lady Kelly turned for the drawing room on Lord Thorne's arm, and Lenore was relieved to see the back of them. "Miss Griffin, please have tea brought into the drawing room," Lady Kelly called over her shoulder.

Lenore curtsied. "Yes, my lady."

"And fetch me my summer shawl, too."

"I'll return as quick as I can," she promised without meaning a word.

As Lady Kelly was a widow, and did not technically require a chaperone, there was no impropriety for her to entertain Lord Thorne alone in her own drawing room for a little while. Perhaps while Lenore was gone, Lady Kelly might be proposed to.

Lenore refolded the shawl she'd been given and turned for the stairs.

A heavy step sounded behind her. "Wait a moment, Miss Griffin."

She turned in surprise. "Lord Thorne?"

"Might I have a word in private?"

A movement caught her eye, and she saw a footman had come into the hall, holding letters against his chest. He signaled her that he would wait in a nearby room until she was finished with her conversation.

"Yes, of course," she agreed, looking up at him. "What can I do for you?"

Lord Thorne gestured her toward a shadowed corner beneath the staircase. Lenore hesitated, but then dismissed her concern about any impropriety. Lord Thorne was a gentleman, and it was very clear that his sole focus was courting Lady Kelly. There could be no harm in his request, surely.

"I wonder if I might have the comfort of your opinion," he whispered.

"On what, my lord?"

He drew closer, his lips curving into a smile. "You're a very unusual companion with strong opinions."

Compliments usually unsettled Lenore, but she reveled in this one. She preferred to know how people saw her. She hated when people assumed she hadn't any wits or her own opinions. "Thank you," she answered. "What do you need my opinion on today?"

"I have a gift. I was hoping to hear your thoughts about its suitability." From his pocket, he removed a long gold chain with a locket hanging from it.

Lenore lifted the piece to look at it better. She thought it very nice, but doubted Lady Kelly would consider it worthy of her. Lenore wondered how to delicately dissuade him from offering it to her employer. Lady Kelly possessed a small collection of beautiful gold and gemstone pieces upstairs. This necklace hardly compared. She would rather not have him embarrassed when it could be rejected outright. "I suppose this is for a niece of yours for Christmas?"

"You don't like it?"

"I like it quite well," she hastened to assure him. "Very pretty for a young woman to wear." As a companion, she had no jewelry. She was never meant to outshine her employer in any way or draw attention to herself. Lenore wore restrained gowns in colors that did not dazzle anyone and kept her hair neat and tidy. Thankfully, she did not have a disposition that coveted her employers' possessions.

"Good," he said, stepping back. Lenore held the necklace out to him but he shook his head. "Keep it."

The hair at her nape started to prickle, and she held it out farther from her body. "I cannot accept a gift from you. Take it back, please."

His eyes twinkled. "I'm sure you'll enjoy all the delights Cornwall has to offer as much as your employer."

She stilled. "What do you mean?"

"I will be inviting Lady Kelly to spend Christmas with my sister."

Lenore beamed. "I'm sure Lady Kelly will be overjoyed to hear such an invitation."

"You will come with her, too."

Lenore frowned, drawing back from him a little. "I go where Lady Kelly commands until she has no use for me, and then I will find other employment."

"She's an exceptionally accommodating woman, and I am a busy man," he assured Lenore. "I'm certain I can persuade her to keep a companion after we marry. You will be a great comfort to both of us."

Lenore tried very hard to dismiss the feeling of dread growing inside her as he drew closer. She wanted to believe she'd misunderstood Lord Thorne's offer of a gift, but the longer she looked at him, the stronger her fear of him became.

He touched her arm, tried to walk his fingers up to her shoulder.

She flinched away and heard him laugh softly. "There's no reason to be afraid."

There was every reason.

Clearly, Lord Thorne was a scoundrel who was attempting to seduce her *and* her employer, and believed he would have both of them in his power when they reached Cornwall.

She tossed the gift back at him. "Isn't there?"

He laughed softly again, flicking the chain around his fingers. "We'll discuss the matter further another time, one way or another."

"There is nothing you could say or do that would alter my opinion of you now," Lenore stated, but Lord Thorne only grinned wider at her warning.

"Unspoiled and full of promise, despite your age. How little you know of the world beyond this dreary backwater. I mean to educate you properly, and I'm a patient man who always gets what I want. She'll never suspect or believe I'd give you a second glance, so don't go bleating to her about this or you'll find yourself in peril and unemployable."

She gulped. "Lady Kelly is expecting you to propose to her."

His smile was triumphant. "I know, and of course, even after we wed, she'll still need her proper companion. I will insist upon keeping you on."

Lenore tried not to gape—shocked that she'd underestimated him so badly. "Lady Kelly is waiting for you in the drawing room, my lord. I'm sure you can find your way there."

His smile slipped. "When Lady Kelly invites me to stay for dinner, I expect you to join us afterward in the drawing room and sit beside me when she plays the harp."

For a moment, she imagined a glint of fierce excitement in his eyes, and she was afraid. Lady Kelly played the harp with her eyes closed and would see nothing of any impropriety.

Lenore forced herself to hold his gaze, becoming angry that he would put her in an impossible situation. "I am not sure what my lady's plans are for dinner, my lord. Excuse me."

"Yes, do hurry back with her summer shawl."

Lenore strode into the adjoining room, chin high but

quaking inside. What the devil was she to do tonight? Lady Kelly would never take her side, not against Lord Thorne without proof of his unwanted pursuit.

She'd have to leave before the marriage took place—and soon. She refused to warm a scoundrel's bed. "Thank you for waiting for me," she told the waiting servant.

"Cor," he whispered. The man's eyes were a little wild with shock. "He's finally showed his true colors. Are you all right, Miss Griffin?"

"I'm fine," she promised. Though the back of her neck prickled, the sensation passed as Lord Thorne's footsteps faded away and he returned to the drawing room and Lady Kelly.

"He means to have ya," the fellow hissed.

"He will not get his way. Not with me," she promised.

Lenore had no close friends here among the servants, but they could protect her to a point. Companions were above the household staff. She could easily find herself at his mercy if he bribed a footman to look the other way.

She needed a new position, *now*, and to somehow obtain a reference from Lady Kelly, too, without Lord Thorne meddling.

She quickly flicked through the mail, glad of the excuse not to rejoin her employer until her temper had cooled. She couldn't believe Lord Thorne's nerve.

"A letter's come for you, too, Miss Griffin," the footman enthused, pointing it out. "From Miss Wagstaff in London."

She studied the letter addressed to her, squinting but hardly able to read the handwriting. It was indeed addressed to her, but very poorly done. And it was not from a woman, either, though the footman didn't realize that.

Her letter was from an earl who pretended to be a lady for the sake of Lenore's good reputation. "I'm surprised this even arrived."

"I think it must have had an interesting journey. It has a funny odor about it."

She sniffed the letter carefully. "Stale spirits. Miss Wagstaff would be horrified her letter arrived so sullied," she murmured to keep up the ruse.

"That's what I thought, too. I hope it's not bad news."

She held the letter to her chest. "I'm sure it isn't. You'd better get back to your duties."

Once the footman was on his way, Lenore hurried up to her employer's room, discarded the bonnet and swapped the shawl for another one.

Then she slipped along to her own chamber and darted inside. Her nine-year-old spaniel, Hero, had been cooped up inside while she had been out with Lady Kelly, and he was ecstatic to see her return for him at last.

She scrubbed Hero's curly black head with her bare fingers for several minutes until he calmed down. "I'm lucky to have made it back alive," she whispered. "But there are other dangers to navigate now, my friend. You were so right to be wary of him."

Hero whined, and then rushed to the closed door to scratch at it. Hero was a very well-trained dog, otherwise she'd never have been able to keep him all these years. She'd have to take him out for a walk in the grounds before she read her letter. Lady Kelly would accept that excuse for any tardiness in returning better than anything else she might say.

She headed down the servants' staircase quickly and quietly.

She felt safer outside, freer. The dog usually did his business quite quickly, and then Lenore would usually make him run about for a while so he was worn out for the evening.

Hero immediately ran off on his own, leaving Lenore to find a spot to wait for him. She chose a place out of sight of the windows of the house, to read her letter.

She'd known Lord Carmichael as a child, when she'd lived on his estate with her maternal grandmother. Though Grandmother had died many years ago, Lord Carmichael had insisted she write to him with her directions. He usually responded to her letters, but he *never* wrote to her first. She ripped open the letter, praying nothing was wrong.

When she unfolded the thick sheets, she found several pound notes tucked inside. His writing was so terrible that she had to squint until she made out a few words, then the letter finally made sense.

She raised her hand to her lips to contain her relief. She was holding a generous offer of employment from him.

He wanted her to come to London to be his new wife's paid companion. He'd sent her enough funds to make her journey very comfortable, too.

Lenore collapsed against the wall she was hiding behind. She immediately knew her virtue would be safe in his household.

She folded the letter and the money quickly, and hid them in her sleeve. After she called her dog to her, Lenore hurried back to her room to begin packing up her few belongings.

On the way there, she heard the news that Lady Kelly would marry Lord Thorne, and she smiled to herself while everyone else worried about their positions. Lenore would be long gone before that scoundrel Lord Thorne was any the wiser.

Chapter Three

Price heard a dog bark and threw a shoe across the room toward the sound. His footwear bounced against the door with less impact than he could be proud of. Unfortunately, the barking only continued unabated, and the fog of sleep lifted bit by bit.

Price felt like hell, but that was not unusual for a Tuesday morning.

He opened one bleary eye and raised his head gingerly to look around the room.

No dog stood nearby.

He must have imagined it or dreamed he still had one of his own, and he lowered his head again very gently. His dreams of late were often unsettling reminders of the past, but a dog was a welcome change.

He squeezed his eyes shut again and rolled onto his side, clutching his arms tightly to his aching head. Too much wine again last night, or not enough to last. It was always one or the other these days. In a few hours, he'd be back at Madam Bradshaw's to do it all again, though. His friends would probably complain he was drinking again, but he was learning to ignore their arguments that he had to consider the future.

The barking resumed, louder this time, nearly splitting his skull in half.

Was the creature right outside his bedchamber door?

He stretched out a hand, waved it around until it glanced off the side of his second shoe sitting on a nearby chair. Since the barking continued to torture his poor head, he made more of an effort to secure it so he could throw that one, too.

However, in doing so, he caused himself to fall. The air burst from his lungs at the force of the impact.

It was only then it occurred to him that he wasn't in his bedchamber but downstairs in the dining room. He'd been sleeping on top of the table but now lie face down over a hard chair.

He pushed himself off the chair, falling to the hard bare boards untidily. He scowled at the underside of the dining table and then shrugged. There was no one around to see him in his current state. He had no one to apologize to. Honestly, he couldn't even remember coming home, or how he'd made it this far into the house, when he tried. It wasn't the first time Price had thought better of making the trek upstairs to bed, either.

"Devil take it," he complained as his head started to throb in earnest.

A dog barked again.

Price twisted and got to his hands and knees, and then he started to crawl toward the distant door. "Someone shut that dog up. Do I have to do everything?"

He didn't expect an answer. One didn't engage in a lot of conversation when one lived more or less alone in a large house with few staff. He had driven almost all his servants to find other employment in the past months. He was happy to be spared their pitying glances in the mornings, too, and surly responses when he'd demanded they fetch him more wine.

Price crawled across the floor, an awkward thing to do when cup-shot and holding a leather shoe in one hand.

Finally at the door, he made several attempts to unlatch it before succeeding. He threw it open wide but winced at the pain a shaft of sunshine inflicted when it struck his eyes. After a moment, his sight returned, and he dragged himself up to his knees, leaning heavily on the doorframe as he looked out.

There was a dog in his house.

A black one.

He blinked in surprise. "Humphries?" he croaked, and then wet his lips to call again.

The dog barked at him, but its tail wagged back and forth in a friendly fashion.

Price called for his butler again, a little louder this time.

Still nothing, and yet more barking from this stray dog.

He put his hand to his head and scowled at the animal, noting that the barking and whining it was doing continued unabated. It was going to split his skull open at any moment, and something must be done about it.

He tried smiling at the animal. "Shh," he urged.

It whined, head lowering, but it never took its eyes from Price, and its tail continued to twitch as if waiting for a game of fetch. The animal was a few years too old to be making such a fuss, but it was clearly well cared for. Its curly black coat had been clipped short and gleamed in the sunlight. It must have been locked in by mistake. If someone didn't let the beast outside soon, Price feared his head would destroy itself.

Price managed to push up to one knee, and then he pulled himself up the rest of the way until he was standing. He immediately clutched the door as the room spun horribly.

He glanced at his front door, and the sun shining through the glass pane above. Price's dining room did not usually face the rising morning light but the afternoon's fading one. It seemed much later, now that he considered the angle of the sun.

He squinted at the dog again. Now that he was standing, it seemed a small animal for the fuss it was making. It was getting brave enough to approach him, too. It watched him with keen interest from a few feet away. "Afternoon, dog," he said.

It licked its lips.

Price lowered his hand from his head, hoping the beast would stay quiet. "Would you mind doing what you're doing someplace else, sir? I've the most horrible head right now."

The dog, however, misinterpreted his conversation to mean Price would like to hear more of his barking tale and restarted at an even louder volume.

He scowled at the dog as it really got worked up.

Afraid he'd never get any peace, and not hearing Humphries anywhere about, he left his support behind and made his way unsteadily to the front door to open it himself.

However, once Price had finally managed to unlock the bolts on the heavy oak door, the black dog started growling severely and danced backward.

He looked at it in alarm. "You can only stay if you learn to be quiet."

The dog sat on its haunches and whined. But it had stopped barking, and for that, Price was profoundly grateful.

Head spinning, Price nudged the door shut with his hip and slid down to the dog's level to sit on his bum in the hall. "Sitting is definitely preferable to standing right now, my friend. Although lying down is better than everything in the world, really, don't you think?"

The dog flattened itself on the parquetry floor. Impressed that it seemed to be copying him, Price held out his hand again. "Good dog. Come here for a pat now."

It came to him slowly, on its belly, but only close enough to sniff his fingers. Eventually, it got even braver and licked him, too.

"Aren't you a curious little thing?" Price said as he rubbed the dog about the ears, and then down its chest a bit. The dog lifted one paw, an expression of doggy bliss crossing its face as Price continued. "I had a dog like you once."

He turned the animal toward him and studied its face. "Very like you, actually. Where's your master this morning?"

"His mistress is standing right here, my lord, and I hate to be the bearer of bad news, but it is the afternoon," a female voice supplied. "I am truly sorry if he's disturbed you, Lord Carmichael. He got away from me and has led me a merry chase all over the house. It won't happen again, I swear."

Price looked up slowly and squinted.

A young woman with dark hair and thick, straight black eyebrows wearing an ugly green muslin gown and matching pelisse hovered nearby. "Is he yours?"

"Well, of course he's mine." She pointed at the animal, and then curtsied quickly to him. "This is the dog *you* gave me, Lord Carmichael."

He looked at her face more closely, and then at the dog. Recognition dawned very slowly. "Piggy? Is that you?"

She winced. "Lord Carmichael, are we not a little old for name-calling," she said curtly, and then curtsied again quickly. "A pleasure to see you at last."

Price hurried to apologize, and then pushed to stand up, or tried to. He found it took several awkward attempts before he got his feet firmly under him again. Lenore was as short as he remembered. He bowed, albeit a bit unsteadily. "Likewise. Forgive me for not recognizing you immediately. The dog distracted me. He sounded miserable out here, and I could not ignore him."

She blinked several times, and a blush crept up her cheeks as she lowered her eyes to the floor. "I apologize for the disturbance."

"Think nothing of it."

She smiled quickly, and then beckoned the dog to her with a quick movement of her hand. "He's not adjusting to his new surroundings very well, I'm afraid. I'll make sure he doesn't bother you again."

Price leaned against one wall because he felt weak, and decidedly unwell, now he was standing. "He's scared. You should stay close to him while he becomes better acquainted with the noises and smells of the city. Eventually, he'll happily go around with you."

"I should not neglect my duties." Her eyes drifted over him again. "I hope you don't mind him being here with me."

Price glanced at the dog and pulled a matching long face. "Where else could he go but with you? That was the point of my gift, don't you remember. I didn't want you to be alone."

"I remember," she whispered.

Price then tried very hard to remember why Miss Lenore Griffin could be standing in his home that afternoon. He hadn't seen her in a very long time, not since she'd gone to be a companion to a neighbor's mother some distance from his country seat. He'd remember later, no doubt, but for now, he'd pretend he wasn't an earl and she wasn't a former servant's granddaughter. "How are you?"

"Oh, as well as ever. I was very happy to receive your letter."

Price laughed softly, and then looked up quickly. "What letter?"

She frowned at him. "*Your* letter. The one that brought me here. Don't you remember?"

"Of course I do," he promised.

But he didn't. Price hadn't seen Lenore Griffin since he'd given her the puppy, Hero, as a parting gift some years ago. He was surprised he even recognized her, given how long ago that had been and how much her features had improved. But he had written to her each year in reply to her letters. Only at Christmas, though. Lenore was alone in the world now, and he'd felt an almost brotherly responsibility to keep in touch.

A pretty young lady he hardly knew really shouldn't be standing about in a bachelor's home without a chaperone right by her side. Actually, neither Lenore nor a chaperone had any business here at all.

He put one hand to the door, intending to open it up again so she could leave the house with her dog.

The dog rushed toward him, and he patted his head absently. "Hero seems well trained."

"Oh, he's impossible only occasionally but always behaves for people he likes. He must like you. He was once so fascinated by the feathers on one of my previous employers' turbans that he nearly got me fired. He was forever following the lady about and staring at her head. She, of course, made it worse by almost running from him."

Price laughed. "Dogs have a unique ability to sense kindred spirits."

"That's why you gave me Hero. You said he would warn me away from unscrupulous or cruel employers. Hero has gone everywhere with me and really is a fine judge of character. I've turned down several positions because he didn't warm to the people we met. He's been the best companion and protector a woman could ever want."

"Let us hope in your next position Hero loves everyone you meet."

She looked at him strangely for a moment. "It seems so already. Do you have as many dogs at Edenmere as you did before?"

"No. None now," Price said as Hero jumped up, putting his paws against Price's thigh. He gave the boy a good rub and then pushed him down, but the room spun. Price pressed his fingers to his temple and rubbed hard. "I never quite got around to finding replacements when the others died."

"Oh, I'm sorry. I used to be envious of how cleverly your dogs were trained. It took me two years to stop Hero from jumping up on people." She smiled quickly. "I'd happily help train more if you want another again."

Price shook his head. This was a strange conversation to be having. "When did you arrive in London?"

"Yesterday. Unfortunately, you were out at the time. My belongings are settled into the servants' quarters upstairs."

He stilled, and then looked at her quickly. "Whose servants' quarters?"

"Yours." She seemed to shrink, and her head dipped low. "I know I should have written and waited until I had a response from you, but the money you sent seemed to suggest an immediate start was preferred. The housekeeper didn't know what to do with me when I arrived, but I showed her your letter, and she, and the butler, agreed I should wait and talk to you."

Price scratched his head. Why would he have written to Lenore and offered her employment when he obviously had no use for a paid companion? He had no female relatives, or a wife, either.

She caught his eye. "Could we talk today, after you change perhaps?"

He nodded slowly and glanced outside. Yes, it was definitely afternoon, and judging by the increased traffic of elegant carriages heading toward Hyde Park, it was almost time for the promenade. He'd lost track of another day. But he'd also lost track of his reason for writing to Lenore, and that seemed the more pressing problem. "I didn't realize it was so late."

"You've slept the day away, but I'm glad you're finally awake to sort things out." She grinned. "Do you think... Would you mind very much putting some trousers on while we discuss my new duties?"

He stared at her, and then looked down. His legs were bare. "Why didn't you say something?"

Lenore's laughter followed him into the dining room while he blushed.

Price found his trousers atop the dining table, crumpled into a ball. He must have used them as a pillow. He struggled into them and snatched up his footwear.

Lenore laughed softly again, somewhere behind him. "You've still got skinny little chicken legs, my lord."

He looked back with a look he hoped would fell her where she stood. "Stop laughing, Piggy."

"It's not as if I haven't seen them before. Remember that time one of your dogs stole your breakfast one morning? You chased it down the hall, wearing even less than you are now. Just a linen shirt covering you. Still everyone at Edenmere saw more of you than we should that day." And then she schooled her features. "Sorry. I know I should never make fun of you, now you're the earl. I promise to remember my place in the future. I'm just so happy to be here."

He sighed. Lenore, despite being a servant's offspring, had been his friend for a long time, and he would forgive her for laughing today. There was no meanness in her. They had never really been master and servant to each other anyway. "Accepted, if you'll forgive me, too, for the horrible view you just had to endure."

A blush colored her cheeks. "We'll never mention it again, just like last time." And then she laughed heartily and scurried away, trying to smother the sound in her hand.

Resigned to hearing that sound for a while, Price finished dressing in peace. As he swept his hand over his coat sleeves to remove any dust, his fingers brushed over the spot where a band of mourning he wore tied over his shirt sleeve was tied. He sobered and cast a quick look toward where Lenore Griffin had recently stood.

What the hell had he be thinking to offer employment to Lenore by letter when there was no companion position here for her? He must have brought her here to be companion to someone else, though damned if he could remember whom it was now.

Price hurried back out to the hall and found Lenore waiting in the drawing room doorway. She was standing but when her dog hurried to her, she bent low to pat him. "Be good now. We can't afford to lose this position."

Price winced and gestured for her to enter the drawing room ahead of him. "Please, take a seat while we sort this out."

"I know I should have written first to accept, but there was no reason to delay. Lady Kelly was about to marry and had no further use for me."

He nodded. So Lenore was entirely without ties elsewhere. He'd find something for her to do until he remembered what he'd really summoned her for. Then he'd find her a fitting situation in a good household. "I trust the journey wasn't too arduous."

"Indeed, no. The funds you sent made everything simple." She dug in her pocket, and then held out a handful of money to him. "Your change."

He took the money and stared at his palm, confused even more by the leftover amount. Just how much had he sent her that she could return such a large sum? "I am afraid I cannot offer you a position at this time."

She gaped, obviously upset by the news. "Did you ask someone else and forget about me? Was I too slow in coming?"

He frowned. "There never was a position to fill here."

"But you sent for me. Paid for the journey to London."

Price shook his head. "Let me see that letter I sent you and we can clear this up," he demanded. "There must be a misunderstanding."

"I'd never lie about something so important. I really do need a position, my lord. I gave up everything for a fresh start here with you."

Price shook his head. "You know you can't stay."

"But I can. Once I explained my connection to your country estate and then with everything you put in the letter, they were very eager to make me welcome. They even wanted to put me in a guest room, which of course I refused to accept. I know my place in the world. I'm sure there's much I can do in so large and grand a house as this."

He took a pace toward her, and the dog was immediately between them, teeth bared and snarling.

Lenore clucked her tongue. "You shouldn't rush at me like that, my lord. Not until Hero knows you mean me no harm."

The dog started to bark again.

"Hero, sit," Price demanded, and the dog submitted, lowering his head to the floor.

"Ah, how unfortunate that he remembers you were the man who started his training," Lenore said as she looked down on her dog sourly. "He has always been my protection. But I suppose he sees no danger in you."

Price didn't believe Lenore would lie to him to get a better position somewhere else, but he wanted to read that letter to know exactly what he'd said to her that could be so persuasive she'd give up a perfectly good paid companion's position in the country. "Perhaps we should start over."

She nodded. "I think that's a good idea. Try and figure this out together."

Price agreed, seeing no other option. One thing was certain, though. He had uprooted Lenore Griffin's life. Without question, he had to see her settled again. He was responsible for her now.

"May I see the letter?"

"All right." She produced it and held it out.

Price turned it over in his hand, noting the shabby condition it was in. It was well folded and far from pristine. Something had been spilled upon the paper, blurring the letters of her mailing address.

He unfolded the sheet and noted the blurring continued on the inside, too. He barely recognized his own handwriting. It was so untidy, the letters almost illegible. But it was written by him—and very clear about his intentions.

In no uncertain terms, Price had offered, not employment, but himself in marriage.

Chapter Four

Price was rendered speechless for several minutes. He had proposed, by mail, to make Lenore his wife, countess, and mother of his children. A marriage of mutual respect and comfort, he'd claimed. He read a bit more and paled further at what he'd done to himself.

He looked at Lenore, noting her happy smile was back in place. "See. It is quite clear about the position," she said.

She'd said she had come to take up a position as a companion, not as a wife. "Did you read this? All of it?"

"As best as I could. I must say, your handwriting has declined quite markedly since last Christmas. The stain didn't help, but with the money enclosed, it was easy to catch the gist of your meaning. You'd married, or were about to, and wanted a companion for your wife. I was to come immediately to London and use the money enclosed for the fare."

Dear God, Lenore didn't even suspect the truth.

Price wiped his hand across his mouth, mind reeling at the realization that he'd chosen a bride in the last few weeks and had forgotten. Failing to remember he'd proposed made him feel quite idiotic. He hoped to God no one heard about this or he'd be the laughingstock of London.

But this could all be smoothed over and Lenore sent on her way if he acted quickly with none the wiser.

And then he remembered a few things Lenore had said earlier. "Did you say you showed my letter to my housekeeper?"

She nodded, her eyes bright. "And the butler as well. They were beside themselves with happiness that I had arrived safe and sound."

"I bet they were," he grumbled.

If his senior servants were happy about Lenore's arrival, then they both knew he had no use for a companion. They *must* have read the letter properly and seen the truth in his blurred handwriting.

Whereas Lenore had seen only what she wanted to see. What she had expected from someone like him.

An offer of employment out of the blue must have come as a surprise. That she'd traveled half the country to accept seemed a little odd, though. But then, she'd cobbled together only the words that made the most sense to her. He had, after all, been instrumental in finding her that first companion's position. She trusted him to look out for her.

Lenore hugged her pet again. He listened to her gentle promises of treats with half an ear. "I'm sorry we have to stay inside today, Hero. We'll go for a nice long walk in the square at first light tomorrow before I start my duties."

Lenore Griffin was a kind person, loyal and generous. A hard worker. They had always gotten along well.

But surely he hadn't meant to propose to her...and yet, how could he explain the letter any other way? The letter was in his handwriting. No one could make a forgery look so bad.

So he had written a proposal to Lenore Griffin, and now he had to get rid of her with as little fuss as possible.

He put his head in his hand and groaned.

"You should eat something," Lenore whispered softly. "If you don't mind me saying so, you're not looking very well today."

Why would he be after this? Price sat up and ran a hand through his hair, and then smoothed his beard. He'd made a horrible mistake in writing that letter. The housekeeper's and butler's silence could be bought, but what would Lenore think about him when she discovered the truth? It would be better if he explained the situation, the mistake, before anyone else could enlighten her.

"So about my position?"

He held up his hand. "There is a complication."

"Oh," she said, looking worried. "What's wrong?"

He considered Lenore a friend, an old, good friend, and she deserved the truth whether he liked it or not. He held out the letter to her. "You need to read this again. Properly this time."

Her brows knitted together. "What do you mean, properly? It is as clear as day you employed me to be a companion to your wife."

"I'm not married," he said.

"So, I'll work as a maid or whatever you want until you do."

He bit his lip and moved to sit beside her. "I never offered you a position as a companion, Miss Griffin."

"Certainly you did. It is there in the letter."

He swallowed hard. "I did ask you to come to London," he whispered. "To be *my* companion…for the rest of my life."

She burst to her feet. "No, you didn't!"

Her denial was music to his ears. He could most likely escape the offer with no slight given. "Oh, yes, I did." He moved toward her and showed her the letter again, using his finger to highlight certain words she'd obviously misinterpreted. He read the letter to her, word for word, until her eyes widened. "Wife."

She moved away and stared at him with huge eyes. "Why would you write that to me of all people?"

"Why indeed?" He and his friends had been talking about the necessity of choosing a bride recently. Had they goaded him into picking out a bride when he'd been drunk? He *did* vaguely remember deciding not to take a wife from within the *ton*. Choosing Lenore, a lady's companion, was as far from the *ton* as he could have picked from. She had no family, no important connections, no dowry, or funds of any significance.

Price raised his hand to his aching head, struggling with what to do. He would prefer to tell the truth, and hope she didn't attempt to hold him to his offer. He couldn't marry Lenore. "I don't recall exactly why I offered for you at the moment. I confess I might have been very deep in my cups at the time. I can only ask you for your understanding in this matter and beg that you will release me."

"You didn't mean it," she whispered, taking back his letter and ripping it up. "I suspected you might have been drinking when the letter arrived stained and boasting an odor of stale spirits. It doesn't count if you were drunk. I know men often say strange things when they've overindulged. I'd never hold you to this."

"Thank you." He breathed a sigh of relief as the pieces fell into her lap. She'd released him, destroyed his letter, and now they could both get on with their lives—separately.

The silence lengthened.

"Shall I call for tea and something for you to eat, my lord?" Lenore asked suddenly. "Perhaps when you have a full stomach, you'll help me find a situation better suited to my talents."

Price would certainly help Lenore after this. At least they agreed that her future lay elsewhere. "I remember your mother was forever suggesting food before I made important decisions. Truth to tell, I've missed your counsel as much as hers."

"I've missed yours, too," Lenore admitted shyly and then shook her head. "I am sorry that you've not found a proper wife yet."

"No, not yet." he lied easily. There was no reason for Lenore to know his heart was broken.

Lenore smiled. "Perhaps next season you'll meet someone special and you can ask them to marry you."

He studied Lenore. He remembered her sense, her humor and optimism had always cheered him from a low mood in the past. She was easy to talk to. It was that aspect of her character that made him gesture for her to sit again.

They made small talk, mostly about her pet's antics and the weather. His proposal had thankfully changed nothing between them. It truly was a shame that she had to leave. He supposed he might never see her again after this debacle, unless she took a position with a friend again.

Would it be strange to see her in society as someone else's companion? To know that she could have been his wife instead.

Price knew he would never marry for love. And he'd already decided that a dowry, connections, family were not as important to him as they'd once been. The best he could hope for when he married was to like his wife. To pick someone he could get along with. Talk to easily.

Lenore actually met every one of his requirements for a wife. But it was obvious she didn't want to be the one. Price found her response to his mistake intriguing. She acted as if his blunder had never happened already. "Why *not* marry me?"

She snorted softly. "Well, for one, I am not a lady."

He folded his arms across his chest and looked her over. Her poise was perfect, back straight, legs neatly tucked beneath her skirts. Admittedly, her gown wasn't the height of fashion but a few hours with a better dressmaker and unlimited funds would fix that problem. And if they hired a lady's maid they could do something better with her hair. She could easily pass for a proper lady. She certainly spoke like one. "You're no longer the hoyden who raced me to the kitchen, skirt hem caked with mud and six inches wet from rain-soaked fields. You've improved your mind, too, since then I expect, but you're still honest, which makes you an ideal candidate."

"Oh, please. You must still be under the influence."

"Not enough to matter," he warned, getting to his feet. He was at last steady and clearer headed. Perhaps he'd been on to something on the night he'd written to Lenore. He could marry her if he wanted to. He had no family to disapprove of her. She was already of age and didn't need anyone's permission. "I believe that my actions and behavior requires a permanent solution for both of us."

"Such as?"

"The housekeeper and butler read that letter, too, Miss Griffin. *They* are unlikely to forget what I've done, and I cannot have another word of gossip spread about me this year. We will have to marry after all."

"Well, I know what my grandmother would advise if she was alive today, my lord. She'd tell you to come to your senses. Of course you cannot marry someone like me."

Price ignored Lenore's protest for a moment as he moved to ring the bell, summoning his housekeeper, while hoping the butler would come, too.

He paced the room while he waited, keeping one eye on Lenore Griffin. She seemed uncomfortable, but he wasn't anymore. He was thinking of the future at last. He was arranging their marriage…and it was sudden and strange, and he was doing it quite coldly.

And he could see why he'd picked her out of anyone he'd known before. Loyalty, compassion, and kindness had always been part of her character. He liked her.

She was sweet, and yes, he had said nice things to her when he'd been drunk as a callow youth. Those small flatteries had washed right off her shoulders, not that he'd been serious or smitten with the woman at the time. She'd been part of the Edenmere family. One of them, and by extension of her late grandmother, part of his family already.

He'd made a surprising but entirely acceptable choice for his peace of mind.

The housekeeper arrived, followed by the butler. Their expressions openly expectant of happy news about to be delivered.

"Ah, thank heavens you have come Mrs. Baker and Mr. Humphries." Lenore gestured the servants to sit as if they were her honored guests. "As you will remember, Lord Carmichael's letter summoned me to London to take up a position as a companion."

Mrs. Baker smirked. "That's not what it said, dearie."

Lenore threw her hands up in the air. "Why didn't you say something?"

Humphries winced. "We felt the letter could be best explained by his lordship and decided not to interfere."

Lenore's eyes narrowed on them. "You tricked me into staying."

Price stifled a laugh behind his hand. She was incensed, and that *proved* she was worthy of becoming his countess there and then. She didn't crave the position, but out of anyone he knew he thought she deserved it.

The butler winced. "We felt it better for all concerned if you remained here for your safety. The city is a dangerous place for a respectable young woman alone."

"True," Price added. "Unfortunately, I do not remember writing the letter myself, or I would have said something of it to someone before now. Do either of you recall the day I wrote that letter?"

Both nodded.

"Could you please verify that I was not coerced to write it, for Miss Griffin's enlightenment only, of course?"

Mr. Humphries shifted in his seat, looking very uncomfortable, but he nodded. "I'm sure you did write to her, my lord, without any coercion. I recognize your handwriting, and the address from your prior correspondence. I did not know the contents until Miss Griffin arrived on the doorstep. Miss Griffin showed it to both Mrs. Baker and myself."

"And since everyone here is aware of the contents, there is but one course of action to take," he finished with a firm nod. "Am I right?"

Lenore turned to him, her look imploring. "We could all just pretend you never wrote it. But I still will need your help obtaining a new position. You see, I left my last place of employment without waiting to receive a reference. It might take a few weeks for my last employer's letter of recommendation to arrive."

He laughed softly, finding her lack of interest in marrying him almost funny. He'd hardly finished his proposal before Angela Berry had accepted him. Any woman of the *ton* would be shouting about this from the rooftops by now. Not Lenore, though. "You spent the night under my roof. In the eyes of many, I've already ruined you."

Her mouth opened. "You certainly did not, and I wouldn't have let you."

"I mean theoretically, not actually. I've no doubt you would have screamed murder should anyone have tried, which unfortunately would still force the same solution upon you."

Her eyes narrowed. "Don't think for one second there will ever be an *actually.*"

The housekeeper and butler exchanged an amused smile before she spoke. "Go on, luvvie. We can't have you ruined because of his absentmindedness. He's a good lad, under the right circumstances. It could only have been his idea, and he will do the right thing by you in the end. You'll make a fine countess. A real lady, too."

With that ringing endorsement hanging in the air, he caught his servants' attention and with the toss of his head, dismissed them from the room.

When he was sure they were gone, he faced Lenore. She was being unnecessarily stubborn when they both had so much to gain. He offered her a good life, free of hardship and toil, and she only had to do one little thing for him in return. It might be blunt, but he had to be sure she knew what he wanted her for. "I intend to be considerate of your feelings, but when we marry, I will want a son or two. Perhaps a few daughters as well. Would you not do your duty if you were the wife of any other man?"

Lenore's face turned bright red with a blush.

He smiled to himself. Lenore was most likely a virgin. A blush like that was all too telling. Hero had done his job well protecting Lenore from scoundrels while they'd been apart.

He called the dog to him and gave him a good rub as thanks for his devotion.

When he turned back to Lenore, she was staring at him.

She was not smiling.

He spread his hands wide. "It is the perfect solution to both our problems. I get to marry someone I trust and like, and you never have to toil in the service of another demanding employer again."

"Oh, you remind me of your father," she said, gesturing around her own face. "All smiles but seriously tricky behind a beard."

It hadn't occurred to him that he might look so much like his father. Lenore had been frightened of the late earl.

"It will be gone tomorrow," he promised. "See, I am willing to compromise to make you happy. Other than that, I don't imagine either one of us must change very much to make this marriage work."

"This is madness." Lenore nibbled on her thumb. "What about parties and dances and such? I've not had a lady's education, and you know it," she warned. "I'll trip over my own feet and be such an embarrassment, you'll wish you'd never heard of me."

He shrugged. He hadn't considered her lacking in accomplishments, but there was an easy way to manage Lenore's introduction to society—he'd keep the marriage quiet at first and, as he was avoiding most of society already, awkward introductions would be few and far between. "Everything you need to know can be learned. We can marry, take our time becoming properly acquainted, and whatever instruction you might need in deportment can be discreetly done far from the prying eyes of the *ton*."

She still looked uncertain, and he moved to sit beside her. "Would you truly remain a poorly paid companion rather than the mistress of all you survey now? And more, too? I am offering you a life of wealth and comfort in exchange for putting up with me."

Her eyes softened a little. "Surely there are better choices for a bride."

"I can't think of anyone living, and believe me, I have looked. I have offered for you now, and I think we'll do well together." He nodded. "I might have chosen to ask for your hand while in my cups, but I don't think it was ever a mistake. What do you say, Piggy?"

She bit her lip and then looked up at him. "I should like a little time to think about this."

He smiled. "Let's have tea and discuss the matter in greater detail then. Hero is looking a little hungry, don't you think?"

Lenore immediately turned to her pet and Price quickly arranged refreshments to be brought to them. They sat down at one end of the dining table, the dog between them gobbling up anything that came his way. "He's a happy dog. Would you not like children of your own for him to play with one day?"

She was quiet for a while. "To be honest, I never imagined I would have any."

"Now you could imagine anything you want. I've wealth enough to support a large family of children, and dogs, too. You do remember the size of the nursery at Edenmere, don't you?"

"It always seemed so large and lonely a place."

"The perils of being an only child. I would have a dozen children running about if I had my way, getting into the sort of mischief we sometimes did."

Her eyes narrowed on him. "*I* hardly ever got into mischief that you didn't start."

Lenore had been a reluctant playmate. He regretted each adventure that had got her into trouble enough that she'd been punished for. "I know. I was a terrible influence."

Finally a soft smile broke over her face. "You were always encouraging me to run off and play."

"I still am." She would have a position in society to take up and more responsibilities than she'd ever known but she would also have more freedom. He didn't imagine she'd become wild or reckless when his back was turned. Still, they'd only spent a few days together as an adult, and corresponded once a year by letter. There was of course the chance they would not suit as husband and wife. Only time would tell if that turned out to be true. "Only this time, it's not really play and you'll never get in trouble again. I propose an immediate marriage to protect your reputation."

Lenore looked around the room quickly and groaned. "We're alone again."

He took a quick sip of his tea to hide a grin. "Hero does make an admirable chaperone," he noted.

"No one will believe that," she grumbled, her eyes fixed on her pet. Price chose another piece of cake and broke it in half. He gave one portion to the dog and started eating the other. "At least I will never have to face your godmother now."

Price stilled. "You heard about her?"

"It was in the papers. The murders. Her name," she admitted. "I remember her visiting Edenmere Park when we were children. Forgive me for saying this, but I was always glad when she was gone. They way she looked at me sometimes made me afraid of her too."

Lenore, a servant and a friend, might have been another victim if he'd not secured Lenore a position far from him. At least there, he'd done some good. "No need to apologize. Your instincts were better than mine."

"But you loved her. She was almost a mother to you. You must be deeply troubled by her actions."

"I guess I never really knew her, did I?"

"I suspect no one did," she whispered. "I would need time to prepare before the marriage was consummated."

Now it was *his* turn to blush. He did not tell Lenore that for months now, the idea of bedding anyone but Angela had been like getting doused in very cold water. His sexual appetites had gone away the day she'd died. He would have to work himself up to sharing a bed with Lenore eventually. Marrying her was one thing, being immediately intimately acquainted quite another. "Filling the nursery is not urgent."

"Good." She looked at him shyly. "Before I do agree to anything though, I want your word that after we do marry, you will not seek to control me. That I may come and go as I please. Have my own friends and interests."

"I wouldn't have it any other way." He raised one hand. "I swear I will never be demanding of your company. I give you carte blanche. Once we marry, you may have anything you want so long as you never fall into bed with one of my friends and embroil me in your scandals."

"I don't want to be in *yours*, either. If you should ever become pestersome, I really would hate to have Hero teach you some manners," she warned with a small grin. "It could be painful for you."

He nodded, glancing at the dog, noticing his teeth were bared now. Price felt his manhood shrink in his trousers and quickly offered the dog a biscuit. "That side of our marriage can wait until you are ready."

Until they were both ready.

"Thank you."

He studied Lenore, looking for some insight into what she thought of his proposal now. A home, security, protection were hers for the taking. It was what most women wanted, he'd thought, but Lenore did not seem overwhelmed with gratitude or eagerness. "So, we are in complete agreement about everything? We will become man and wife, soon, and then we'll go our separate ways most for the time?"

"Indeed."

Lenore held out her hand, and they gripped each other, the same way they had the last time they'd said goodbye. This time, however, her grip was decisive, and slow to withdraw. Her hand was more of a match to his larger one now. Still delicate and feminine but exuding pleasing confidence in her decision. She was no retiring miss making a desperate bargain to save her reputation. "Thank you, my lord. I don't think we need ever discuss today again, or that letter. Do you think the housekeeper and butler will gossip, though?"

"Oh, they'll hold their tongue if they want to keep their positions. I'll make sure of that." He shrugged. He'd pay both his servants handsomely to forget knowing about his proposal by letter too. "I'll do my best to be a good husband to you," he promised.

"That's what they all say," she murmured. She did not look reassured, but then, she had no reason to believe otherwise. Once she got to know him better, she would understand and believe he only had her best interests at heart.

He would care for her, protect her, provide for her and their children. He'd given himself no choice but to make this match, really. He'd made a promise he couldn't break. His honor would not allow him to weasel his way out of this unplanned marriage. "I'll have marriage contracts drawn up for you to sign this afternoon."

She nodded.

"Do you have somewhere else you could stay before we wed?"

She blinked a few times. "I do have friends who live in London, though I have not seen them in some time."

"Why don't you pack most of your things and go and visit them this afternoon. If they invite you to stay, well and good. Otherwise, I shall secure lodgings for you at the best hotel money can buy."

She nodded slowly, and then she frowned again. "What about love?"

Price blinked. "I am not in love with you."

"Nor I with you. But you could still find love if we didn't marry each other."

"I have proposed, and you have accepted." Price leaned forward and touched the back of her hand where it rested on the table between them.

Hero began to growl, low and menacing. Price was unwilling to have the dog dictate his behavior. He would most likely touch Lenore's hand often even if he did not make love to her. The dog would have to learn to share his mistress. "Love isn't at all necessary in a marriage like ours."

She blinked quickly and shrugged. "I suppose it isn't."

When Lenore remained silent, staring at him with a frown, he sighed and stood. He couldn't love her, but he could give her happy memories to share with their children one day.

He rounded the table and dropped to one knee beside her. Lenore's eyes widened in surprise, and he took up her hand in his. "Lenore Griffin, would you do me the honor of becoming my wife?"

That hadn't been at all difficult to do a second time round. Quite easy, really.

"Yes," she whispered.

Price moved back to his chair and took another sip of his tea, pleased that he had done the right thing. "Good. Very good."

Since he had the marriage side of his life once more decided, he supposed he really should take more of an interest in world affairs, starting by showing his face in the House of Lords again perhaps.

Chapter Five

———◆———

Lenore had only a few close friends, but the ones who were living in London happened to be the most dear. She hoped they were home. The Hillcrest women, all cousins, had moved from the countryside and taken up residence together in a townhouse in Albermarle Street upon receiving their separate inheritances.

Lenore strode up to their door with more confidence than she felt, dog and small traveling case in hand, and applied the knocker. Lord Carmichael's carriage remained standing before the house—waiting to take her on to a fancy hotel if need be. Although Lenore had snuck out through the mews behind Lord Carmichael's home, her journey here had been conducted in a level of luxury she was quite unaccustomed to. People had stared at the carriage as she'd passed them by. She felt like such a fraud to have been sitting in it that she'd drawn down the curtain beside her to hide behind.

The Hillcrest butler appeared and looked her up and down but then he smiled. "Yes?"

"I was hoping to speak with any of the Miss Hillcrests. We are old friends."

"And your name?"

She told him, explaining that she'd found herself in London unexpectedly.

He invited her in, casting a glance at the fine carriage

waiting outside before the house. "The ladies are with a caller at present, Miss Griffin," he apologized profoundly.

Lenore smiled. "I do understand, and I'm happy to wait to speak to them for as long as it takes."

The Hillcrest cousins conducted a business from home to supplement their income by offering instruction to gentlemen in need of help polishing their manners for undertaking a courtship of a proper lady. What they did, they did discreetly, but it was still a tiny bit scandalous that they took money from strange gentlemen. They were probably interviewing a client now. Lenore hoped it was going well.

The butler bowed. "Very good, Miss Griffin. If you could come with me."

Lenore glanced behind her, wondering if it was all right to make the earl's grooms wait, too. They had been told to look after her well by Lord Carmichael himself, but should she send them off and find her own way to the hotel later?

The decision was taken away from her as the butler shut the front door and locked it. She was led to a small room at the back of the house, perhaps it was the morning room, given what was strewn about. Embroidery hoops and books were stacked up on any available surface. "Would you care for tea while you wait, Miss Griffin?"

"No, thank you," she promised. She was eager to be alone with her thoughts. She'd made a monumental decision today. All on her own.

She did not believe she'd made a mistake in accepting Lord Carmichael. It was a generous offer from a good man. Yet there was much she did not know about him other than he was kind and wrote an excellent letter very faithfully each year. And he had given her Hero as a gift one year because, she suspected, she'd been sad to be going so far away. Before that, her knowledge of him was as a child, with an innocent and sometimes confused view of the world coloring her memories. She had liked the boy he'd once been because he'd let her play with his toys when she should have been sweeping the floor instead. He'd had so very many of them, too, but had always been happy to share.

But still, marriage and the "bedding," as he called it, were the great unknowns of her future.

She grew warm with embarrassment just thinking about it.

She fanned herself with the nearest ladies' magazine but something caught her eye in it, and she fell to reading. She was perusing the last page when the cousins suddenly arrived. Sylvia, Aurora, and Eugenia had similar brown hair and green eyes, but their personalities were wildly different.

Sylvia was shy, Aurora bold, and Eugenia decisive. Their ages ranged from five and twenty to seven and twenty. Considered old spinsters just like Lenore when they were two and twenty, the Hillcrest cousins had never expected to marry. When their money had come in, the unexpected inheritances had saved them from the desperate poverty that afflicted many older spinsters. It had been Eugenia's inspired suggestion that they open this business instead of buckling to the pressure to marry anyone who'd have them at their advanced ages.

Lenore had felt that pressure when she was younger, too, but her employment had taken her far from home, and that path, until now.

After greetings were exchanged, she stood back. "I have some news. I'm to be married," she told them immediately, unable to keep it to herself a moment longer.

The Hillcrest cousins shrieked en masse, jumping up to surround her. "My dear, this is everything we ever wanted for you," Aurora declared at the top of her voice. "Finally, a man has seen your potential. Who is it? Please tell me it's not Mr. Green from the village."

"Of course, it wouldn't be Mr. Green. Our friend has better taste in men. Is he rich?" Aurora asked bluntly. "Connected?"

"Is he handsome?" Sylvia asked, blushing.

"Is he good enough for our dear friend?" Eugenia asked.

"He is Price Wagstaff, Lord Carmichael. An earl. He has a fine house and country estate, too."

Aurora's face clouded. "Isn't he…"

"He was the boy my late grandmother worked for," she confirmed.

Eugenia stretched forward, placing a restraining hand on Aurora's. "When did this happen? The proposal, I mean."

"Today." Lenore had already practiced an answer that wouldn't include details of their secret correspondence over the years, which would be considered scandalous under any circumstances. "He came to the point quite quickly."

"I'll say," Aurora grumbled. "We'd not heard a whisper. You should have told us sooner."

She couldn't have told them what she'd never expected. She lowered her eyes, pretending shyness in the hope they'd leave their questions at that.

"The best marriages start with a bang," Sylvia said dreamily. "If he's titled, he must be handsome."

"How does that follow?" Aurora complained to her cousin. "A title does not bestow any improvement upon a man's looks."

Sylvia caught Lenore's eye. "But he is handsome, yes?"

Lenore felt her cheeks heating a little. Lord Carmichael should be very handsome when that terrible beard was scraped off his face and his clothing wasn't rumpled. Neglect didn't suit him. It made him seem old and unloved. "Yes, I think so."

The cousins cheered and hugged her again.

Eugenia Hillcrest clapped her hands together to bring order to their reunion. "This calls for a celebration."

"Oh no, you mustn't go to any fuss on my account," Lenore protested.

"No. No. We celebrate every marriage with a little party, don't we girls?"

Sylvia nodded emphatically. "Whether we arrange them or not. We do want to play a little part in your celebrations," she said. "Not many of our clients think to invite us to their weddings. I think they're embarrassed that they needed us to get them going in the right direction."

Lenore shook her head. "You'll be at my wedding, of course."

The cousins exchanged glances, and then Lenore was smothered in hugs again. "This is marvelous news," Aurora cried. "At last, we'll have a chance to attend a proper society wedding and meet important people when she becomes a countess!"

The Hillcrest women survived on the good word of their customers circulated to other gentlemen facing similar difficulties. She wasn't sure it would be the entree into the upper society that the trio would want, however. "I must warn you it will most likely only be a small gathering for the wedding."

"But they will be new faces to us," Eugenia noted. "Members of the *ton* will certainly be in attendance."

"Which gives us even more reason to celebrate. There's been a rather chronic shortage of eligible men lining up at our door of late. It always happens at this time of year. Nearly everyone flees the capital for the comforts of the country if they have any choice in the matter."

The trio presented a unique learning opportunity for the uncertain gentlemen. If their client could charm one of them, or all three, after instruction, they claimed he should have no problem finding a wife in society. They were practice—for introductions, making calls, dance partners, dinner companions. A little flirting, too, Lenore suspected. All conducted within the privacy of this little house with absolutely no danger that the gentleman might find himself expected to wed any of them.

Lenore was in awe of their scheme. It took courage to stand firm in the face of disapproval from everyone you knew the way they had done.

Eugenia rang for a servant and, in asking for refreshments, shared the news of Lenore's upcoming marriage. The maid twirled away grinning, and promised to be very quick.

"Will you forgive us if we seek new clients among the bachelors at your wedding?" Eugenia asked with an apologetic smile.

"Of course. I have no notion yet if there will be any bachelors at the wedding breakfast, though. If there are any in attendance, I will most definitely introduce you to them and leave the rest to you."

"We would appreciate your help with introductions very much," Sylvia said quietly. "Where are you staying?"

"I hadn't yet found a hotel."

"A hotel? No. You'll stay with us until you marry," Eugenia

insisted. "A hotel is not suitable accommodations for the future Countess of Carmichael. Where's your baggage?

Lenore hated to impose but she'd rather stay with friends than alone. "Still in his lordship's carriage outside."

"I'll have it brought in and taken up to our guest bedroom," Eugenia decided, rushing from the room with Hero at her heels.

"Thank you," Lenore called.

Aurora ushered them into the adjacent dining room. "The table is already set for the arrival of one of our clients tonight, but we should soon have it to rights again after we celebrate your good fortune."

"Who is it today?"

"Lord Jeremy Scarsdale will be joining us at eight. He's the third son, and has the most unfortunate habit of stuttering around women he admires. He's been visiting us for the past month in the hope of curing his habit. It's terribly hard to woo when tongue-tied."

"Indeed," Eugenia said dryly. "Doesn't stop him eating well, though."

Lenore laughed. "He's probably happy to have the three lovely ladies to himself."

"Don't think we haven't considered that might be why men come here, but we quickly find out the truth and send them packing."

"I'm hoping to learn how he's fared in society this past week," Sylvia murmured as she moved to a sideboard where a row of decanters were set out. "The last time he was here, he mentioned he'd be attending a few society engagements. He's a good man and deserves to be happy."

Sylvia poured for them all—a small sherry to toast with— and Lenore grinned when Aurora returned with Hero licking his lips. Aurora had tended to spoil Hero when she wasn't looking. But it was like she had a family with her again at this critical time in her life.

"When will your marriage take place?"

"I'm not sure. Soon though. Lord Carmichael has promised we'll be married by special license."

"A special license? Well, well. A man of decisive temperament. I like that," Aurora declared with a sage nod. "He'll be no slouch then when it comes to other matters, too."

Sylvia blushed. "Hush, Aurora. Don't frighten her."

"Frighten me?"

Eugenia rolled her eyes. "What our dear cousin is hinting at is her undocumented suspicion that a brisk proposal heralds a brisk bedding upon marriage."

Lenore was about to prove Aurora's theory very wrong. Carmichael was happy to wait to consummate their marriage. Having just escaped from a scoundrel's pursuit, Lenore was very glad about that, too.

"What did your employer have to say about giving you up to a marriage? I hope she was not put out that you've caught yourself an earl."

Lenore winced. "I haven't told her. To be honest, my situation there was causing me concern."

"Oh, what happened?"

"She had a suitor who expressed interest in me, too."

The ladies gaped and shook their heads. "Men can be such contrary creatures," Sylvia noted. "I'm glad you managed to escape before any awkwardness of an unwanted proposal."

"There wouldn't have been any proposal," she said, wincing. "He had other plans for me."

There was silence at her statement, and eventually, she had to look up.

Eugenia gulped. "You did escape unharmed, didn't you?"

Lenore nodded quickly. "Lord Carmichael arranged a carriage to bring me London, and I could think of no reason to delay going with such a scoundrel prowling around."

"A lady's reputation must remain entirely without reproach," Eugenia agreed. "She must protect herself from *all* unwanted advances."

"You made the only decision you could, my dear," Eugenia assured her. "Never allow anyone to make you doubt that. The earl made the right choice, too. You will succeed in anything you put your mind to. You'll be mistress of your own home and of him."

Lenore blushed. She imagined she and Carmichael would only become close when she was ready to share a bed with him. But those would be brief encounters, and then they would live separate lives, like many in the *ton* were said to do. "True," she said and took a sip quickly.

"And you'll make new friends now as well."

"But I won't forget the old," she swore to them. "I'll need you all very much in the coming weeks as I become accustomed to my new role."

"Of course, you must have a thousand things to do and not much time to complete it all. Do come, let us repair upstairs, and we can set your mind at ease about marriage and what you might need to purchase. We absolutely must talk about what you'll wear on your wedding day, too. You'll of course order a swathe of new gowns to wear as you start your new life."

Lenore sighed. Advice was exactly what she'd hoped for. She'd been a companion to three older ladies, but never in all her life had she imagined to hold a rank above theirs. She would need more help than a few pretty dresses.

But for today, practicalities would stop her thinking about sharing a bed with her future husband.

How long should she wait before inviting him to join her? What should she expect after he'd taken her innocence? These were questions she'd never dared ask before. There had been no need. But her friends would understand her fears and give her strength to face her wedding day to a near stranger, even if they didn't realize he was.

Hero was suddenly at her side, head lapping at her clenched fingers. She gave him a good rub and smiled down at him. Hero liked Lord Carmichael. There was no mistaking his instincts about men. Lenore wouldn't have agreed to any marriage with Lord Carmichael if her dog had shown the smallest distrust of the earl. She'd made the right decision. Their marriage would be a good one.

Chapter Six

———◆———

Price hooked his finger under his cravat and pulled hard. He seemed unable to pull enough air into his lungs to meet his needs today.

"Is it still too tight, my lord," his valet Norris asked, hurrying to join him at the mirror. "Let me loosen it again."

Norris, a fussy fellow he'd recently employed, loosened the knot again and stood back. "There, perfect."

Even with that third adjustment, Price still felt he was being strangled. Had he made a mistake in hiring this new man? Norris was perfect in every other respect. Polite, discreet, and until today, Price had had no complaints at all.

He sighed deeply and looked at his reflection in the mirrored glass.

It wasn't really the cravat, or the valet, that was the problem.

It was Price himself.

He was to be married today to a woman he could not love. Lenore Griffin. A new woman to stand at his side where the love of his life ought to have been. He felt uneasy now, but at the time he'd settled and signed marriage contracts with her, it had still seemed a sensible solution. He would need a son, and Lenore was kind and smart and appeared healthy and in need of a home. She'd make a suitable spouse and companion for him in the years to come.

Only Price was having cold feet about it all now. Was he rushing into a mistake of his own making? How could he have thought marrying the first woman he could think of was the right thing to do the other day?

"Your waistcoat next, my lord."

He allowed himself to be helped into the garment and stared at himself in the mirror again. He stroked his fingers over the sleeve covering his upper right arm. He felt strange without the band of mourning that he'd worn since his godmother's bloody rampage through society's innocent debutants.

He closed his eyes as the memory of Angela's pale, lifeless face swam before him, and then all the others, too. There was blood on his hands. Angela was gone, and so were the other innocent women. His godmother was responsible but hadn't lived long enough to pay the price for her actions. He couldn't do anything but mourn and rage in private and do his best to put the past behind him.

He opened his eyes again and asked for his coat next. Once dressed, he spent a moment contemplating his appearance one more time. He looked like a stranger even to himself now without the whiskers on his face. He'd removed them to please his future bride only yesterday, and he wasn't quite used to seeing his own face yet. His skin felt as raw as his nerves.

He tried a smile and managed a pale imitation of one.

"You look very well today, my lord. If I may be so bold. Congratulations on the happy occasion."

"Thank you," he intoned, feeling the complete absence of happiness. He was doing his duty to the family and his title. Many men made marriages without knowing their bride well, and he would be no different. Lenore would do for him, and if he ever had regrets, he would keep them to himself rather than lay any blame for disappointment at her feet.

He strode from the room, headed downstairs to await his bride's arrival. He would not pretend to be deliriously happy, but he would not diminish the importance of this day.

This was it. He was embracing the future without Angela.

He'd written to Lenore several times in the past few days, explaining the arrangements he'd made, and received a polite response indicating her agreement with everything he wanted.

She should be here promptly at ten o'clock to speak their vows. Price had arranged witnesses and a vicar, of course, and when Lenore had informed him three of her friends would be attending, too, he'd made adjustments. The wedding breakfast seating plan, the food offered, proved no difficulty for him.

He strolled into the dining room, nodding in approval at how the table had been set for the wedding breakfast. His housekeeper had done an exemplary job preparing the house at short notice for the happy occasion.

Even without Monsieur Laffitte's extraordinary culinary skills in the kitchen, there was nothing lacking that he could see and nothing he would change about today. He hoped the man was happy in the employ of the esteemed Duke of Exeter once more, since he'd been lured back to prepare for His Grace's end-of-year and birthday celebrations. It was probably for the best. He did not imagine he and Lenore would entertain often together at home.

Yet very soon, he'd be a husband with a duty to care for a woman, and later, their children. Any happiness would be hard-won and treasured. There was no turning back now.

A loud knock startled him and heralded the arrival of his first guest. The vicar, Mr. Jackson Fielding, was early and very exuberant as they shook hands. "How are you feeling on this happy occasion?" Fielding asked.

"Very well." He offered the vicar a drink, which he declined in favor of consulting his bible.

Lord Wade and Lady Wade arrived next. Seeing them arm in arm and clearly happy in love made his heart pinch. They had both known his lost love well, Lady Wade more so of the pair. "Welcome," he managed.

Lady Wade drew closer, searching his expression, and her smile was tentative. "We are so happy to be with you today," she promised him in gentle tones.

Price had been avoiding most of his acquaintances since

Angela had died, including Lord and Lady Wade. Since he and Angela had not been married, or publically acknowledged as engaged to marry, few had understood his anguish over her death. He'd learned it was better to hide his pain than explain it to friends and acquaintances over and over. "Miss Griffin has yet to arrive, but I expect her very soon."

If she didn't change her mind.

The thought came out of the blue. Lenore could yet cry off, and that hadn't occurred to Price until this very moment. He glanced at the front door in worry that she might not appear. He really should have sent a carriage to fetch her for the wedding but had been denied the privilege. Lenore had promised his assistance in getting here was not required. He hoped he would not live to regret that decision, or be about to be made a fool of.

Another knock at the door brought Mr. Scarsdale and the Marquess of Wharton together. Wharton had been eager to attend, once Price had confessed the marriage that was about to take place. Price had deliberately neglected to give the pair all of the particulars of his arrangement with Lenore though.

They shook hands and exchanged greetings. "So here we are, about to watch another rogue lose his independence," Wharton joked, and then he brushed his hand across his own shaved jaw. "And freshly shaved, too, thank heaven. I really thought you'd have waited a bit longer than a few weeks from our discussion before deciding to take a bride."

Price stared steadily at Wharton, having endured this same conversation two days earlier. Wharton had a low opinion of rushed marriages despite what he'd said the last time they'd spoken together. He couldn't understand why Price was in such a rush to get it over with. "You should start thinking about marriage, too, before your looks are gone," Price replied dryly.

"Heaven protect me." Wharton laughed, patting his own smooth cheeks. He was a bit of a larrikin. Protective of his looks, too. "My pretty face is all I have to recommend me."

"That and the title." Scarsdale drew closer to Price. "Although for all we know, Wharton will probably find a man selling his wife in the marketplace and make them an offer rather than putting in the effort to woo a proper lady," he murmured.

"*If* I should ever choose to marry, you can rest assured she'll not be another man's wife or a rushed affair," Wharton declared, indignant. "She will be carefully chosen with a beauty to match my own. I couldn't marry another man's wife anyway. A charge of bigamy would negate the marriage and call into question the legality of my son inheriting my title."

There was a commotion behind Wharton, and when Price looked around his friend, he spotted Lenore and three women standing uncertainly in the entrance hall. Hero was being led away by a footman, no doubt headed for the kitchen.

Lenore looked very pretty today.

Price felt his stomach swoop and relief filled him at the sight of her. She had not forgotten her promise to him, and had made an effort in her appearance, too.

She looked quite fetching, really.

He dug a finger under his cravat and pulled at it as his discomfort returned. Lenore's dark hair was neatly styled with a few soft curls trailing down her neck. She wore a summery yellow gown that showed off her shapely figure and a hint of creamy white bosom.

This was his bride, the woman he would live out the rest of his day's side by side with. Looking at her now, knowing his heart belonged to Angela still, he wondered at what kind of life they could have together. Would they fight, or would they just politely ignore each other most of the time?

"Bloody hell," Scarsdale cursed and spun about, putting his back to the doorway.

Price glanced at him in confusion. "What's the matter with you?"

Scarsdale was blushing. "I know them."

"You know Miss Griffin?"

"Not her. The other three. Damn it all." Scarsdale drew in a deep breath, and then turned back around, a false smile fixed in place. "It really is too small a world we live in, isn't it," he complained.

"It can be," Price sympathized, but he'd no time to inquire further about how Scarsdale knew those women. He quickly skirted around his friends to greet his future wife.

He bowed deeply to her. "Welcome, Miss Griffin."

She curtsied. "My lord."

Price reached for her hand and brought it to his lips. He'd not planned to do that, kiss any part of her, but reaching for her hand just seemed to come naturally.

He kissed the air above her gloved fingers and then let them fall. He looked at her, saw her friends watching closely, and knew he was expected to say something profound to mark the occasion. A comment memorable enough to be repeated over the years to their children perhaps, and friends. "You take my breath away."

The women around Lenore beamed, and she quickly made introductions. Their names sounded oddly familiar, but he doubted he'd been introduced to the Hillcrest cousins before today. He bowed to each one politely. "I hope to see you often."

"We hope so, too." One of them looked around, peering into nearby rooms. "Is there a private chamber somewhere we ladies can use before the wedding?"

"Of course. This way. I'll make introductions after the wedding if you like," Price promised, feeling his anxiety return just saying that much.

After the wedding...when there was no escape for either one of them.

His cravat was still too tight as he showed the women to the morning room, where refreshments had been laid out for just such a situation and a large mirror brought down if needed.

He quickly excused himself and closed the door on them, turned, and strode back to his guests—trying not to run.

He found Scarsdale in the entrance hall, peeking into the dining room. "Scarsdale, what are you doing? There's nothing to eat in there yet."

He smiled quickly. "I was actually hoping for the first introduction to the future Lady Carmichael. Can't let Wharton have the honor of charming her first."

Price shivered. "After the wedding. Be a friend and help me shepherd everyone into position for the ceremony."

"Of course. How do you want us arranged?"

Price explained and then returned to his guests. He started on one side of the room, directing guests where he wanted them to stand. Scarsdale did his part. Price had decided to be married before the tall front windows. It was a beautiful day, and the room was light and bright. He wanted no shadows on this day, but the clarity of perfect vision as he spoke his vows to Lenore Griffin.

He would never love her, but he would respect Lenore, be faithful to her for all of his life. He would do his best to never let her down.

The vicar took his place between the windows. He patted the top of the bible and smiled at Price. "All we need now is the bride to appear."

Price dug his finger under his cravat one more time and turned toward the door, ready to have Lenore fetched. But then he saw her, standing in the doorway, surrounded by her three friends…and his breath caught.

They'd added a coronet of flowers and veil over Lenore's hair while they'd been apart, and the effect was breathtaking.

Two of the Hillcrest cousins led the way into the room while the third steered Lenore forward by the hand, standing in the place of a loved one for Lenore's sake.

The leading two ladies peeled off to take a position on the right side of the room. The other, Eugenia, he finally remembered, handed Lenore Griffin to him with a secretive smile. She moved to stand with her cousins, leaving Lenore in his care. He felt Lenore's hand tremble in his, and he squeezed her fingers tightly, hoping to show her that he understood. He was nervous too. Marriage was a huge step for both of them.

She offered him a tentative smile in return, and then turned her attention exclusively to the vicar.

But the vicar's words passed over Price in a blur.

He couldn't look away from Lenore Griffin, a near stranger who would be part of his life forever at any moment. Yet he felt connected to the vicar's words through the woman he held so lightly. It didn't feel wrong at all, just strange.

He and Lenore gave their consent in clear, strong voices. Price's hand was steady as he slid a simple gold band onto her finger, and then the vicar concluded their vows.

"...pledged their troth either to other and have declared the same by giving and receiving of a ring, and by joining of hands; I pronounce that they be man and wife together, in the name of the Father, and of the Son, and of the Holy Ghost. Amen," the vicar finished before bestowing a serene smile upon them both.

He was married. A husband. His life inexplicably bound to Lenore's.

"Amen," he said softly, catching Lenore's eye as she uttered the same word.

There was loud applause behind them, and Price looked over his shoulder briefly and grinned, thankful for the distraction. He and Lenore had made a brave choice, but she had given him responsibility over her life, and he would never let her regret it. He would protect her from anyone or anything that meant her harm.

He returned to studying his bride's face. Learning her. It was then he noticed a tiny tear sliding down her pale cheek from glassy-bright eyes. Many women cried at weddings. Was Lenore happy or sad? He couldn't tell what she was thinking, but he hated to see that tear.

He lifted his hand and swept his thumb gently across her cheek to wipe it away. She startled and stared at him. Her blue eyes were huge with emotion, but then she chuckled softly, and any sadness she might have felt seemed an aberration of his own mind.

"Thank you for marrying me," he whispered, keeping his hand in place against her cheek.

Standing this close to her, he noticed several things. His bride was beautiful in her own way. Long lashes and straight dark brows highlighted her expressive blue eyes. And the scent of Lenore, a soft perfume that teased his senses, reminding him of the country and home, was intoxicating and caused him to lean into her before he realized what he was doing.

He straightened quickly, lest she believe he meant to kiss her there and then before their guests. He would not. His bride had asked for time before they became intimate, and he intended to grant her that boon for as long as she needed. Kisses were for later.

The cheek under his fingers warmed with a blush, and her long lashes fluttered and lowered over her eyes demurely. "Thank you, too."

He let his hand drop slowly and exhaled. They'd be all right in the end, he supposed. Marriage was an adjustment they both had to make.

He thanked the vicar, Lenore did too, and they turned to face their guests at last.

"Take my arm, Lady Carmichael," he murmured, offering her his escort and his arm with a flourish. Her hand slid around his arm and tightened, comfortably rather than clinging, he found. He smiled. "My friends are very keen to meet you."

She lifted her gaze to his, smiling. "I'm looking forward to meeting them, too."

He led her toward Lord Wharton first as the highest-ranking gentleman in the room and performed the necessary introductions. Wharton was charming and kind and flattered Lenore outrageously while teasing Price.

Lenore was soon standing with her hand pressed to her side as she laughed at everything Wharton teased Price about.

"I can see now why he took his time introducing us to you," Wharton grumbled. "I do love a lady who enjoys lively banter. One of us might have tried to steal you away from him if we'd met in different circumstances. We still might, if he neglects you."

Lenore's grip on him tightened ever so slightly. "I don't believe I'd allow that to happen."

"Ah, a woman who knows her own mind," Wharton said, then barked out a laugh. "I'd be very persuasive."

Scarsdale shoved Wharton aside. "Pay him no mind, Lady Carmichael. Wharton here has no luck with the ladies and likes to exaggerate his appeal. His only appeal is his title and his choice of acquaintances. I am Lord Carmichael's true best friend." Scarsdale bowed excessively. "It is an absolute pleasure to meet the lady that has rescued my poor friend's heart at last."

Price gave the tiniest shake of his head and moved Lenore to meet with Lord and Lady Wade. Price didn't plan to tell his wife about Angela Berry being the one true love of his life but that was what Scarsdale had alluded to. That was a secret love he planned to take to the grave, and never let Lenore know she hadn't been his first choice for marriage.

They enjoyed the wedding breakfast in good company, sitting side by side, and Lenore seemed amply entertained by the conversation around the table. His friends spilled stories from Price's past until he was blushing, though he told Lenore all the stories were wild exaggerations. He stored up their antics for future use, however, planning to embarrass them when they finally tied the knot with similar tales of missteps.

One by one, their friends bid them goodbye until only they were left standing in the entrance hall. The silence was quite deafening after so much laughter and companionship. More than a few had suggested he should be eager to be alone with his bride.

Price stuck a finger under his cravat and tugged hard again.

Lenore sighed. "I should let the housekeeper know that the dining room can be cleared and returned to order now."

He nodded. "I'll speak with Humphries and have the drawing room tidied as well."

"Yes," Lenore said softly.

"Yes, indeed. Much to do," Price said without looking at Lenore.

"Well then, I'll go this way," she suggested, taking a step toward the dining room.

"And I'll go this way," he agreed, taking a similar step toward the drawing room.

"Lord Carmichael?"

"Yes?" He snapped his eyes to Lenore's.

"That was an extraordinary feast. I don't think I could eat another bite today."

He grinned. "The wedding breakfast was good, wasn't it?"

"Very good," she agreed.

They stood facing each other across the entrance hall for a moment. They were married, husband and wife. One day they'd be lovers, too. His cravat tightened, and he longed to be rid of it. "Well, if you're not hungry, I will bid you good night now, my lady," he said.

"I really couldn't eat another bite. Good night, my lord," she murmured before rushing toward the dining room and disappearing.

Price did the same, going in the opposite direction as fast as he possibly could without running. He ripped off his cravat the minute he got the doors closed…and found the nearest bottle to drink from, too.

Chapter Seven

———◆———

"London in Autumn is a quieter time than during the spring. A great many of my closest friends are absent from the capital," Lenore's new husband informed her as they traveled through London's fashionable districts three weeks after their marriage. "You'll meet many new faces next year."

Lenore glanced out the window at the dreary rain that had begun to fall as soon as they'd climbed into the carriage. According to her husband, there were a lot of things she would do next year. "I had assumed that to be the case."

"They'll all come teaming back in the New Year and we'll be inundated with invitations."

"I'm sure that's true."

Lenore's husband seemed to be popular, so she wasn't surprised that *he* expected an abundance of invitations. One had only to walk with him upon the street to see how many acknowledged him as they passed by. Lenore had received her fair share of curious glances, too—some friendly, some not quite so. People preferred to speak only with her husband for now. It was a tad rude of them but those moments were only brief lows in her new life.

Today, their time together as husband and wife would be as brief. Lenore had been on her way to call upon her friends in

Albemarle Street, and her husband had been venturing out at the same moment. Both needed the town carriage. Carmichael had decided they would travel together, and then he would go on alone without her.

He gripped his upper right arm as he spoke to her, a frequent habit of his she'd noticed. It might be nothing more than a habit, but she sometimes wondered if he had an injury he wouldn't admit to under his hand.

"Will you be staying with the Misses Hillcrests all day?" he asked.

She gave him her full attention. Did he ask that question because he hoped to spend time with her? "That was my intention, but if you need me, I'm sure they won't mind if I leave early."

"No, don't change your plans for me. I was just curious if the carriage should be sent back to you immediately or not," Lord Carmichael explained, and Lenore was disappointed. "I will likely be out for dinner tonight and will not need it again, I imagine."

Carmichael had taken his every evening meal out of the house since their marriage had begun. Lenore felt a pinch of disquiet about that. Her husband must have an appointment book full of invitations he'd accepted before their marriage, and he'd informed Lenore that she couldn't be included. She knew of no event that included her in the future, either, but she would like to attend a dinner with her husband one day, if only to go somewhere with him.

"Of course."

He was silent for a few minutes but then frowned. "Were you staying with the Hillcrests for dinner, too?"

Lenore turned her gaze away from her handsome husband. "I had not decided."

She had no invitation to dine with them, but dining with them was what usually happened. They'd talk, and the dinner hour would miraculously arrive, and having no other plans herself, Lenore would be pressed to stay and accept graciously. However, she did not want to assume a welcome with the Hillcrest women always.

To be honest, her days were busy but also starting to feel a little directionless. She probably would stay with them for dinner if invited, as there was only her dog to consider tonight. Her husband had a full life away from home, and her, and until today, had never changed his plans to remain in her company.

They turned into Albemarle Street, and she picked up her dog's leash in readiness to get out. Sometimes Hero sprang out first instead of staying by her side, and she couldn't bear to lose him under the wheels of the carriage.

They finally drew to a halt, and a groom jumped down quickly, put down the step, and snapped open the door for her. Carmichael climbed out, looked up at the cloudy sky, and then thrust his hand back through the door. "The rain has stopped."

Lenore gave Carmichael the dog leash. She urged Hero to jump out onto the pavement, and she then climbed out herself unassisted.

She looked up at her friends' house. A groom had already run up to the door to present her card, even though she was expected at this hour. Their kindly butler's face appeared, wreathed in smiles at seeing her arrival. She was always welcome here, and it was a lovely feeling to be wanted. She glanced up at the clouds, still thick overhead. "I fear it will rain again soon, though."

She ought to get inside out of the weather and learn about last night's mysterious new client of the Hillcrest Academy. But she cast a glance at her husband when she realized he remained at her side instead of departing. He was watching her, leash still in hand.

"I do beg your pardon." She held out her hand for the leash. "Thank you, my lord. I do hope you enjoy your day, and your dinner tonight."

Carmichael put Hero's leash in her hand very slowly, but he didn't release it. He studied her, a frown forming on his handsome face. It was a little unsettling to have him look so directly at her for a change, and she dropped her eyes, feeling unaccountably flustered.

He stepped closer and spoke quietly to her. "Next time I offer my hand to you, perhaps you will allow me the privilege of helping *you* out of the carriage, instead of the dog."

She was startled by the rebuke but not for long. She was becoming so used to looking after herself that it had become second nature not to expect anything from him. In this marriage they'd made, it seemed prudent to continue to rely upon only herself until she knew her husband's feelings better.

She met his gaze and smiled sweetly at him. "I'll try to remember for next time."

"Please do," he said with a curt nod. He put his hand firmly over hers.

Lenore's smile faltered as his touch warmed her fingers through. She was suddenly very aware of her husband's qualities. He was very handsome. But it was his nearness that nearly made her swoon. Lenore's heart began to race in response. But then his gaze shuttered and his hand fell away. "I'll see you in the morning."

"Yes," she managed to reply. "Morning."

Morning, the only time she could guarantee they'd talk, was also the only time she could count on seeing him for longer than five minutes. He was always running off somewhere without her, never saying where he went even the next day. Did he forget he was a married man when she was not standing right before him? She didn't want to know if he did. "Come, Hero."

She made her way up the front steps of her friends' home, feeling a little low. Marriage was turning out to be something of a disappointment. Not that she had expected great things from their arrangement, but she'd hoped her husband might try to get to know her better before the day came when they shared her bed.

Being together seemed the last thing on his mind…but it was always on hers of late.

The Hillcrest butler took her hat and greeted Hero, who seemed to like the old man very much. From the corner of her eye, she noticed her husband's carriage pulling away. He did not wave or even look back at her as he went on his way.

"The ladies are waiting for you in the drawing room," the butler informed her.

"Thank you," Lenore said as she shortened the leash, wrapping it firmly around one hand. Sometimes Hero forgot his manners, especially if there were cakes left on a low table.

Thankfully today, refreshments had not yet been laid out. She gave him a little more latitude to move but kept him close as she greeted her friends until the excitement of being here again wore off. "Good morning."

"Good morning to you, too," Aurora exclaimed in her usually bold way. "Good morning, Hero," she said as she scrubbed the dog's head fondly.

Kisses were exchanged, the dog fussed over some more, and Lenore ended up seated beside Sylvia.

"We were not sure you would come today," Sylvia confessed.

"I said I would," Lenore reminded her.

"We thought, hoped, you might be off somewhere exciting with your handsome husband."

She made herself laugh. She'd come here nearly every day after her wedding day. Weeks had passed as her husband had gone his own way, and she hers. "Not today."

"Well, perhaps tomorrow," Sylvia murmured, one brow raised. "We have a client coming today, so it is good that you are here to help me."

"Oh?" Lenore looked around. She'd never been involved with the Hillcrest clients before. Usually they came in the evenings, or if, at other times, Lenore would move into another room with one of the cousins to ensure the gentleman's privacy was maintained.

"Aurora and Eugenia must go out together today, and we really didn't want to disappoint the new client."

She brightened. A bit of excitement would be part of her day, after all. "What do you expect of me?"

"Nothing but your presence as a chaperone. We make a promise to our clients that they'll never be put in the position where they might be expected to marry one of us. Our reputations, too, would suffer for that if it was known we'd met with a man quite alone."

At least someone needed her. She nodded, keeping a smile on her face. "I'm happy to help in any way I can."

Aurora and Eugenia rose, kissed their cousin's cheek, and bid them goodbye.

Sylvia stared at the door after they were gone, biting her bottom lip. She seemed nervous.

Lenore placed her hand on Sylvia's, breaking her reverie. "Are you worried about this client?"

"Oh, no. Not really. It is just a different set of circumstances that brought him to us. He's a widow who must marry again."

"I see." She frowned, not seeing the problem. "I thought your clients were the nervous type and inexperienced with women."

"All men are nervous when it comes to marriage." Sylvia shrugged. "This particular client's first marriage was a love match, and his wife died suddenly. Heartbreaking, really. He's being pressured to find a wife soon by his family, but he feels just thinking about it betrays her, let alone actually beginning to court someone."

Lenore nodded. "It must be a difficult situation to be in."

"Indeed. Lord Sullivan is quite troubled, and more than a little lost, to be honest. He does not think cupid will strike twice and bring him another woman to love."

A knock sounded on the drawing room door, and the butler entered, followed by a footman, and Lenore had no time to ask any further questions. "Lord Sullivan has arrived, Miss Hillcrest. Shall I have Hero taken out for a walk while the earl is here?"

Lenore considered her dog's occasional strong reaction to strange men might not be in the best interests of the Hillcrest Academy and nodded quickly. "That might be wise. Thank you," she murmured as the footman took Hero by the leash and promised him an exciting outing.

"Please show Lord Sullivan in now and bring tea to us in twenty minutes," Sylvia said with a bright smile of welcome on her face, standing. It was not her usual smile, it was bolder, and Lenore realized that her friend had donned a different persona since moving to the capital. She was no longer a timid, shy spinster but a woman with business on her mind.

A tall man with thick dark brown hair and an engaging smile quickly appeared. Though he threw an alarmed glance Lenore's way, he bowed to Sylvia. "Miss Hillcrest."

His voice, deep and confident, filled the room.

Lenore could only gape. How could this fellow need anyone's help? He was handsome and had a title. He seemed unlikely to have any difficulty finding himself a bride, in Lenore's opinion. Women should be lining up around the square for his consideration.

Sylvia nodded. "Lord Sullivan. Welcome."

"Thank you for seeing me again and at such notice. I hope you are well."

"Indeed, I am. The Hillcrest Academy is always willing to offer gentlemen support and guidance. May I introduce my friend to you?"

"Of course."

"This is Lenore, Lady Carmichael."

His brows knit together as he held Lenore's gaze. "Carmichael, you say?"

"Yes, a pleasure to meet you." She curtsied to him but noticed his eyes were full of questions.

"I've only recently married," she told him, and his expression cleared.

"I've only just returned to Town myself, so I hadn't heard the news," he said. "Congratulations."

"Thank you," she murmured, feeling awkward now. She still felt an imposter each time someone used her new title.

"Do sit, my lord," Sylvia said as she beamed him a sincere smile. "Lady Carmichael will be our chaperone today, as my cousins discovered they had a prior engagement elsewhere they could not get out of."

Sullivan's shoulders seemed to droop. "I'm sorry to hear they won't be joining us," he said, but didn't really sound at all disappointed. Perhaps he wasn't as confident as he first appeared after all.

Sylvia raised one hand to the hovering butler. "Mills, would you have tea brought in at once."

"Yes, Miss Hillcrest."

Lord Sullivan cast Lenore another glance, and Sylvia noticed it.

"You can be assured of Lady Carmichael's complete discretion. We've been friends for many years, and she understands the nature of our work with our clients."

"Indeed," Lenore promised, quickly making the gesture to lock her lips and throw away an imaginary key.

Lord Sullivan laughed. "Very kind of you."

Lenore beamed. She'd answer him if her lips weren't meant to be sealed. She sat in silence as Sylvia began to question him about his life. They talked about family pressure to make a match for a while, pausing only for the arrival of the requested tea tray. Then Sylvia steered the conversation around to a specific women he'd met recently, and his feelings about her.

Lenore was deeply impressed with Sylvia's ability to put her client at ease. She turned the conversations this way and that in a way that did not seem to pry, but clearly drew out Lord Sullivan's opinions on women over the next half hour.

Lenore was surprised how masterfully Sylvia handled herself, and the delicate subject of making the right match for the right reason. In company, in the country years ago, Sylvia had been the last to voice an opinion, but around Lord Sullivan, she seemed entirely comfortable with so intimate a conversation.

"You ought not to compare the women you meet to your late wife so much," she suggested. "She was unique. Every woman is. What you need to keep foremost in your mind is whether or not they appeal to you now—both physically and intellectually. Could you stand to be stranded with them in a place not your own? Or would you want to strangle them after the first ten minutes of conversation."

Lord Sullivan laughed softly. "You have a unique way of putting things, don't you? Who would you recommend for me then?"

"Lord Sullivan, this is not a matchmaking agency. You will have to find your own bride in society in your own time. My job is merely to support your decision to do so and help you become reconciled to being happy again. I offer advice and an ear to unburden your fears upon. From what I have learned today, you obviously need no tutoring on courtship rituals. You are a gentleman, experienced in women and marriage. You need but to trust that when you do find someone you think might suit, that it is not a betrayal of your first wife."

He nodded slowly.

"It might seem obvious to say so, but you have nothing to fear from women. The lady's you meet in the future will likely come from the right families, possess enormous dowries, and your whole family might approve the match. But *you* are the one who has to live with them. Share your life with them." Sylvia leaned forward a little. "Make babies with them."

Lord Sullivan's smile fell away.

Sylvia offered him a plate of cakes, and Lord Sullivan took a piece and ate slowly in silence. A look of grim determination came over his face, and Lenore could swear Sylvia's words had made him upset. Lenore felt she'd missed something of the conversation, but didn't dare interrupt.

Eventually, he nodded. "I understand."

"Do you feel you have met anyone who fits my description on the sort of woman you might consider already?"

"Perhaps, but the last point you made presents a difficulty," he said, and he turned his face away.

Lenore couldn't see his expression, but she certainly heard him sniff. Was he about to cry?

Sylvia nodded. "You must keep looking until you find the one who makes that future not so frightening for you. There is no reason the tragedy you suffered will happen twice. Keep an open mind, and don't immediately dismiss any woman you meet after barely two seconds of conversation. It is a big step, but I'm confident there's someone for you out there. You just have to be more patient than your family seems to be about the matter."

He nodded. "Thank you, Miss Hillcrest. You've helped me tremendously, and I appreciate your time today very much."

Sylvia tilted her head to the side. "That sounds like we won't be seeing you again."

"Not for a while, I don't imagine. I'm to spend a few months in the country. First, of course, I must visit with my family, who will no doubt bring up the subject of my remarriage five minutes after they get me alone. It's been a pleasure coming here and talking with you today before I run that gauntlet. Give my best to your sisters. I am quite sorry I won't be able to talk to them again before I leave Town."

"I'm sure they'll feel the same."

Lord Sullivan turned to Lenore. "Until we meet again, Lady Carmichael. Perhaps at Exeter's little party, we'll have a chance to talk."

Lenore had not heard of this party Lord Sullivan spoke of, but she nodded. "Until we meet again."

Sylvia walked him to the door and returned a few minutes later, wearing an unhappy expression.

"What's wrong?"

Sylvia sighed. "He's leaving Town sooner than we anticipated."

"Is that a problem?"

"A loss of a new client always presents a difficulty. I mean, we always lose the gentlemen when they marry. As the season winds down and more gentlemen leave for the countryside, the need for our services dwindle. We'd barely begun with Lord Sullivan."

"Ah, well, perhaps you could view it as a holiday."

"Yes, that is exactly what we must do, I suppose." Sylvia shook aside whatever worry she might have had. "How exciting to hear you'll be attending the Duke of Exeter's winter gathering this year, too! They say it will be the party of the century."

Lenore froze in place. Should she lie about going away to the country? Lenore had not the faintest idea if they were even invited, or if her husband had accepted the invitation. Perhaps her husband just hadn't told her yet. Or was he going alone to that, too?

She quickly decided to change the subject rather than face that possibility. "What about becoming a father upsets Lord Sullivan."

"His first wife died after giving birth, and the child died, too."

"Oh," she whispered. "That *is* a reason to hesitate."

"But he cannot forever, of course," Sylvia sighed. "Even you know your husband needs an heir soon."

Lenore felt a blush building on her cheeks and quickly changed the subject yet again. She broached the idea of a visit to a bookseller with Sylvia and her cousins for the next day. Her husband's library, while boasting numerous tomes she might read, included nothing suited to a lady's tastes. Now she had money of her own, and no one to account to for the spending of it, she intended to purchase a few novels to read since she had only herself to entertain at night.

Chapter Eight

Price rubbed his temples. "There's not much to tell, really."

He was in danger of suffering a megrim after the day he'd had. His fellow lords had been loud quarrelsome, so much so that he'd almost walked out before Wharton had finished speaking. However, he could not desert a friend. Not when Wharton was counting on Price's influence to sway the fence sitters in the House of Lords to his cause.

"Oh come on," Wharton chided, punching him on the upper arm. "There should be a great deal to tell. You've been married long enough to voice an opinion. Was it a great sacrifice to wed?"

"No. We have settled into matrimony very easily."

"What does your wife think of your politics? Do you usually agree or disagree?"

Price rolled his shoulders and sighed. "Honestly, I never speak to my wife of politics. I leave my opinions in parliament."

Wharton, a passionate speaker in the house, bristled. "I certainly will do no such thing. Nothing will change without me."

Price shook his head. Only Wharton would make that claim out loud. He wasn't entirely wrong. A great many things did change because of Wharton's advocacy. But it was just the teensiest bit arrogant of him. "Are you not sick of it all yet?"

"Of course not." He grinned. "If I don't speak, whom else would you have to listen too?"

"You might have a point." Price saw an opening to change the subject. "Speaking of wives, are you still considering matrimony for yourself?"

"Hell, no. I brought up the subject in a bid to slow your demise. A pretty woman is always a good distraction, and you, my friend…well, I feared you were headed for an early death the way you were drinking."

"I did not stop drinking when I married," he asserted.

"But you now do not attack a bottle as if it could save your soul. It is now possible to have a decent conversation with you at the end of the evening again."

Price shrugged, looking out at the street Wharton's carriage traveled. "Perhaps I had nothing to say before."

"You had a great deal to say but were wise enough to hold your tongue. You have a great future in politics if you want it," Wharton suggested. "So tell me about your wife. What is Lady Carmichael really like? I've hardly lain eyes on her to find out for myself."

Price hardly had, either. They spent most of their days apart and their nights alone. The current session of parliament, and politicking later in support of Wharton's current cause, was consuming all of Price's free time at the moment. It was the marriage he'd promised they'd have. Each a life of their own.

He made sure not to disturb Lenore when he came home in the early hours of the morning. Often she had retired to her room long before midnight anyway, so if he was early returning, he went to his study and read—if he was sober. He often slept there, too, when he was too drunk to manage the stairs quietly.

They saw each other for breakfast, and that was about it as far as their marriage went. Lenore seemed perfectly happy with that arrangement and, judging by the modest bills he'd received to pay on her behalf, was having a fine time spoiling herself with a few little things. She never suggested she was dissatisfied with their arrangement. She had not broached the subject of sharing her bed yet, either. Until she hinted she might be ready for a real marriage, he would keep a distance.

He was only going home to change into something suitable to wear to Tattersall's today and then would be gone again. He had an idea to buy his wife her own carriage, instead of her sharing his all the time. A pair of matched grays were said to be available at the horse market today for the right price. Once he had the horses, he'd order a carriage to match and employ additional grooms to take her anywhere she wanted to go in style.

"I think I will come in and pay my respects to your wife today," Wharton announced suddenly.

Price glanced at his friend in surprise. "Will you now?"

"Hmm, if I cannot get answers from you about Lady Carmichael, I shall get them from the lady herself. Surely by now, she's something to say about the sort of husband you are."

"I'm sure she has no complaints." Price promised. Hadn't he been the most accommodating of husbands so far? "If she is home, you may certainly talk to her if she wishes to speak to you."

"I'm sure she will," Wharton announced with all the assurance of a marquess certain of his desirability and place in the world. "Where does she go without you?"

Price wasn't always sure of that until the bills arrived, but he knew where she spent many of her days. "The Hillcrest Academy."

"Hillcrest Academy? What's that?"

Price shook his head. "Don't you remember? Her friends run it."

Wharton shook his head. "I don't recall you telling me."

"You do know about it, though. I'm sure you were there when Scarsdale mentioned the place, and what they do for gentlemen."

Wharton laughed. "Well, then there you are. I never listen to Scarsdale."

"And you met the three cousins who run the academy at the wedding."

"Which wedding?"

Price sighed. Wharton had been in a difficult mood all day. Pretending indifference or ignorance of subjects he didn't want to really talk about. "Mine."

Wharton looked at him steadily. "I remember several young women at your wedding. Hillcrest is run by spinsters, or so I recall Scarsdale babbling about now."

So Wharton did know about the academy, after all. "Yes, that is them, I assure you."

Wharton snorted. "What advice could women of their age offer a worldly gentleman that's not considered improper?"

"I've no personal experience with them, but they are well known, and many a friend of mine has had good things to say about the discreet service they offer to gentlemen."

Wharton's eyes lit up. "Service? Now that's more like it."

"Guidance. Advice. Dancing practice. Only that."

Wharton's excitement dimmed. "If it had been the other, I might have paid them a call."

"I'm sure you wouldn't get past the front door." Price laughed at his friend's outraged expression. "You have to want a wife to get into such a place."

"Well, that's certainly not me," Wharton declared, crossing his arms over his chest and smiling smugly. "I'm a long way off tripping over the parson's noose, no matter how pretty the lady might be."

Price glanced out the window and saw his home growing nearer. "Here we are." But would Lenore even be home at this hour? He hadn't a clue of her schedule but hated to disappoint a friend if she wasn't around. "Are you certain of coming in?"

"Absolutely," Wharton promised. "I'm hoping to discover what a well-satisfied wife looks like."

Price gritted his teeth. He hadn't let on that he'd given up his husbandly rights for the time being. Not that he was chafing at the bit to bed Lenore. But if it became known that his marriage remained unconsummated, he would never hear the end of it. His friends would tease him mercilessly—at least until the deed was done.

There were parts of marriage Price felt needed to remain private for the sake of harmony with his wife.

He strode up the front steps with Wharton hard on his heels and stepped through the front door as it was opened by his butler. "Is my wife home, Humphries?"

"Yes, my lord."

He removed his hat and gloves and passed them over. "Would you let my wife know I have returned, and that Lord Wharton is with me? If she has time to spare, she might like to join us in the library for a few minutes."

"Very good, my lord," Humphries murmured, taking Wharton's hat and gloves, too, before he left them.

"So polite a request," Wharton whispered.

Price heard singing…and smiled. He wasn't aware of Lenore's accomplishments in music. He'd have to add that to a small list of discoveries about the woman he'd married.

"Marriage requires it, you know. Come this way," he offered. A pair of brandies should do the trick to settle any tension in him before the auction at Tattersall's began. If the horses were sound, he'd pay well to have them, but he wouldn't spend more than he should.

Wharton threw himself into a chair and sprawled as if he owned the place. "You know, I'm quite surprised you're still going to Bradshaw's with us, given your changed circumstances."

"The company of friends and the supply of liquor there is excellent," he confessed.

"Yes, I suppose, but—

A woman's scream rang through the house.

Price looked about the library wildly, his heart racing in fear of seeing a murderess, his godmother, lurking in the shadows, but then something breakable shattered beyond the room breaking him out of the terrible memory.

Price bolted from the library, angling toward the sound of Lenore's barking dog. Lenore was in trouble, and he had to get to her in time.

He flung open door after door until he came upon Humphries and the housekeeper, frozen in place across from the collapsed figure of his wife. He noticed no one else in the room.

They gave way to him immediately—and he couldn't catch his breath when he saw his wife.

Lenore was on her knees, wailing, her hands raised to her face. The writing table had been toppled over in some sort of struggle, and the dog was franticly darting around his mistress like some savage creature.

Price rushed to Lenore's side but she resisted when he tried to lift her up. "How badly are you hurt?"

"I can look after myself."

"The hell you can. Send for a physician. Quickly Humphries."

"I don't need anything. It's my fault," Lenore answered, but did not lift her face to his. "Stay back."

Hero started barking anew.

"Hero, shut up," he bellowed. The dog had the sense to obey and sank down onto the rug beside his mistress. "Let me take care of you. Where does it hurt?"

"There's no pain."

"Show me." Lenore flinched but then she straightened her shoulders. "It was an accident. It was my fault, my lord." She sighed and started to rise unaided. "There's no good way to explain this and not show you what happened."

Price moved toward Lenore again, but she shied away from his outstretched hand. Lenore's dog instantly growled menacingly, and then snapped his teeth inches from Price's fingers as they fell.

"Don't you dare bite me," he snarled at the dog. Hero growled one more time but then moved back, watching him intently. "If you're not hurt what in the hell is going on?"

"Hero and I started dancing," she admitted, her face turned

from him still.

His heart was pounding so loudly still he was sure he'd misheard her. "Did you say dancing?"

"Yes. We often do. Hero likes to hear me sing, and will stand on his back legs and be my partner to dance with. Something distracted him today, the front door closing, I think, and he leaped away. We both bumped the writing table, and everything flew off and somehow landed on me. And then he did, too."

She then turned slowly, and he stilled when he got a look at her face. He took a step back, and exhaled loudly. She was not hurt after all. "Thank God."

But there were black paw prints all over Lenore's gown, chest, and her face, too. Wherever the gown didn't cover, black paw prints did.

Her eyes were full of misery before she dropped her gaze.

He pointed toward her cheek. "Is that ink?"

She nodded quickly. Her cheek bore the stain of a perfect dog print. He intended only to trace around it, but she reared back a few steps.

"Don't touch me!" she cried.

Price ignored her request and followed, catching her under the chin and lifting her face to his closer inspection. Lenore had possessed beautiful clear skin that morning, but her beauty was decidedly marred now. He carefully cradled her face between his fingertips, and then slide his fingers back a little into her soft hair. She was lovely, this wife of his. Even when she was upset. The pain in her soft blue eyes drew him closer still.

"I don't want you to get any on you, too," she whispered.

"I'm being very careful," he promised softly, quite aware that he had a sudden urge to hold her tight in his arms despite the risk of ruining his clothing.

"There's nothing on the furniture," Mrs. Baker announced. "The rug has plenty of paw prints all over it though, and getting more by the minute," she said with a deep sigh.

"There's more on *her*," Wharton added unhelpfully.

"Greetings, Lady Carmichael."

"What's he doing here," Lenore whispered, ducking behind Price quickly to hide herself.

"Visiting *you*," he whispered back. "Or trying to. Just say hello and get it over with."

"Good afternoon, Lord Wharton," she called, but used his body as a shield still. "I'm afraid you've come to visit at the worst possible time."

"I see that," Wharton agreed. "It's never this exciting at *my* home."

Price looked around, and then he lunged for Lenore's dog, hoisting the beast up against his chest quickly—paws out so he could avoid getting ink on himself. He pushed the animal at the butler, juggling the wriggling beast and jumped back out of range immediately. "Take him to be cleaned, and do not let his feet touch anything as you go. He's to be bathed and clipped, too, to remove as much of the ink as possible. He's not to set one foot inside until I'm satisfied he will not ruin anything else."

Price returned to Lenore and moved to stand between her and Lord Wharton again. "Now, as for you..." He inspected her from top to bottom. The pretty cream muslin gown was undoubtedly meant for the rag pile now, but it was her face that caused him the most concern. The dog had painted her pretty features in ink.

"Perhaps I should head home to let you make husband and wife decisions," Wharton suggested, interrupting.

Price waved his friend away. "Yes, please do go on your way."

"Oh, please don't leave on my account," Lenore begged, even though she was still trying to hide behind Price's wider frame. "I'll go and clean myself up as best I can. You must stay and talk to Carmichael."

Price agreed that she should go upstairs immediately to change and try to do something about her face. The sooner the better, too, because he suspected that ink stain was not going to be removed easily or quickly. Anyone who saw Lenore would think her an outright savage. That was not the first impression anyone should have of a lady, least of all for his countess.

"I think it wise to retire and change and try to remove this blemish." He traced the ink on her cheek softly again, filled with a yearning to comfort her the way he had on their wedding day.

"I'll look after your lady, my lord," the housekeeper promised. "It will be gone by bedtime tonight, I'm sure."

"Thank you," he said, and then lightly grasped Lenore's wrist. He lifted her hand and saw ink there, too. "Be careful not to touch anything you care about."

She pulled her hand back quickly. "I hadn't planned to. Excuse me. Lord Wharton," she said, and then walked away, chin held high but her steps rushed.

He watched her go, thinking he should try to do something to help. She was his wife, after all. He shook himself, and then took Wharton to the library.

"You could have gone upstairs with her," Wharton remarked. "Helped her take her bath. Stoked her skin to cleanse the ink away yourself with gentle husbandly hands."

"I think scrubbing might be the order of the day, rather than tenderness. The ink might need to be worn off." He sighed, hoping that was not true. "Hopefully Mrs. Baker has some clever remedy up her sleeve that will help my wife look more like herself by tomorrow."

"Most housekeepers do have something useful lying around, but I'm not sure in this instance it will be that easy," Wharton laughed. "You might have to bear the sight of that for a while."

"I hope not." But for her sake, not his. He hated to see her so miserable. Price finished his drink and poured seconds for both of them.

After a sip, Wharton glanced his way. "I don't disapprove of the sudden decision you made to marry anymore, you know? You made a good enough choice in my opinion. Tattoo aside, you have someone to come home to. It must be nice, but it's not for me."

"Why do you say that?"

"There's no one I care about the way you do."

"You misunderstand," Price murmured, turning away.

"Oh, come now. You can stop pretending to be indifferent to her. I've never seen anyone move so fast as when Lady Carmichael screamed just now."

"I thought…" he started, but then shook his head. He'd thought the worst. "I made a mistake thinking matters were dire when they were not."

"You overreacted but for a good cause." Wharton grinned at him. "Have you never made her scream really loudly yet to know the difference in sounds? You ought to try harder later tonight when you join her in bed," he teased.

Price drained his glass. "Never mind."

"You really did rush to save her," Wharton said, and nodded. "Made me feel inadequate. I'm glad you have someone to care about again, though. Not all marriages start so well as yours has."

Price let that remark go without comment. He cared about Lenore. Any decent gentleman would. He liked her. That was the only reason he had sprinted through the house to reach her, and yelled at her dog, too. It hadn't seemed foolish at the time but he was starting to feel it now. He should not let his fears get the better of him. There was no one alive who could hurt Lenore. "Another drink?"

"Nothing for me, thanks. I think I should be on my way to Tattersall's."

"I'm coming with you," he reminded Wharton.

"No, you're not," Wharton smirked. "At a time like this, a husband is needed at home—if only to reassure his wife that she's lovely with or without paw prints."

"I don't think—"

"*All* women care about how they look. I'd wager your wife is no different from my mistress. She'd be panicked, thinking I couldn't love her still with that mark—*marks*—upon her skin. If it troubles her too much, promise to blow out the candles and meet her only in the dark for a while."

Wharton had a one-track mind when it came to women, but Price's marriage was not like that. He nodded, though, and agreed he should stay at home for the time being. Lenore had seemed unconcerned about her appearance. He'd thought before she was perhaps less excitable than many women in society, unconcerned about looking in mirrors. But now? He wasn't sure.

When he'd been courting Angela, she was always worried about dust and dirt and messing up her hair whenever he'd met her in the park on a windy day. Angela would probably have fainted to have ink on her skin. Lenore had not revealed the same vanity yet, but then again, he didn't know her well.

Wharton stood. "I'll be at White's for dinner then Bradshaw's later as usual, if you have leave to join me?"

"I'll meet you at Bradshaw's."

"I'll take a look at the horses for you, too."

"Thank you."

When Wharton was gone, Price dithered a minute, and then took the stairs up to his wife's chambers two at a time. He tapped on her bedchamber door lightly.

He heard the rush of feet inside and called out, "How's it going in there?"

There was a splash, and Price turned away from the door, putting his back to the wall quickly as he realized his wife might be in her bath. If the door opened, he didn't want to invade her privacy by seeing what she wasn't ready to share with him. He hadn't set foot in that room since the day before they had married. He should have waited a bit longer before coming up to make his enquiries. Damn Wharton for putting ideas about Lenore needing him in his head.

The door opened a crack. "Carmichael?"

"I'm here. Has any of it come off?"

"Not really," she said in the quietest, most horrified tone he'd ever heard from anyone. "We've tried everything, but its still there."

He felt compelled to see his wife again for his own peace of mind. He moved to view Lenore's face, and yes, nothing much had changed except that her cheek was now red around the ink, most likely from scrubbing. He gulped, sympathizing. "It's not so bad."

Lenore pulled her robe tighter about her body and sniffed. "You always were a terrible liar, my lord. I really am ugly now."

"Nonsense," he said quickly. The mark did not make her *more* attractive, though. He let his gaze drop down her body to her bare feet peeking out from under the hem. His breath caught as he realized Lenore might not actually be wearing very much beneath her robe. He swallowed hard. "You're just the same as ever."

She sniffed. "Another lie to make me feel I'm not hideous."

"Shh," he whispered and caught her eye. Nearly naked or not, his wife did need his support. He opened his arms, and she came out and stumbled toward him. Price pulled her into his embrace and held her close. "Your grandmother would disapprove if she heard you speak like that about yourself."

"She would, too." She was breathing quickly and gripped his coat tightly in his hands. "Thank you for disagreeing with me," she whispered. "But I can't let anyone see me again."

"Of course not. Not for a while." He spread his fingers wide over her back and discovered she wasn't completely naked beneath. Stays, perhaps? "I'll have the knocker taken from the door. Rest assured, Wharton will say nothing about the accident to cause you embarrassment later."

He swept his hands over her back in soothing strokes. Lenore sighed and burrowed closer against his chest. He placed one hand on the back of her head and felt a shiver pass through her body. "It's all right, my dear. At least this happened now and not at the height of the season." Price looked down at his wife, still clinging to him. It was the first time he'd held her, and he didn't find it uncomfortable at all. "It will fade in a few weeks."

She took a deep breath. "I'll scrub my skin raw to be rid of it before then."

"Don't hurt yourself." He gulped. "I couldn't bear for you to be injured?"

She pushed away from him, and he felt strangely lost without the warmth of her body against his chest. She kept her eyes downcast, hand rising to cover her ink-stained cheek.

"Does it hurt after all that scrubbing?"

"Yes, a little."

Price caught her hand, noticed the ink there, too, and pulled it away from her face. He put a finger under her chin and lifted her gaze to his. He smiled despite the horrible ink stain. "Why don't you spend the day upstairs in your room? Get some reading done. Washing will fade the mark a little more each day until its gone."

He put his fingertips on the puffy redness, gently dabbing carefully to see where it hurt most. "I recommend some ice wrapped in a cloth and holding it against your cheek. Ice will help with the swelling the scrubbing has caused, and numb the pain, too." She winced only a little in one spot, and he moved his hand away. "I'll ask Mrs. Baker to send some up, shall I?"

Lenore shook her head. "I can do that."

He inclined his head. "As you wish. Can I do anything for you before I go out?"

Her lashes fluttered, and her face lowered. "No."

"You are sure?"

"Yes. I'll be fine on my own."

He hesitated, but what use could he be now, really? Lenore and the housekeeper had tried everything to remove the mark. "Well, then, I'll be off. Wharton is expecting me to catch up with him."

There were still those horses that he wanted to buy as a gift for his wife. Perhaps that would cheer her up.

"Enjoy your day," she whispered as he turned to go.

He took a few steps away, but then spun back toward his wife and dragged her into his arms again. He held her tight against him. "It really isn't that bad," he promised quickly.

He stroked his hand down Lenore's slender back and turned his lips to her brow. He kissed her there, hoping that by doing so, she would feel a little better about herself.

Her breath hitched, and then she wriggled away. "Liar. I'd

rather the truth than a fairy tale."

"Just trying to be a good husband," he promised. "No more dancing with the dog for a while."

"I'll wait for the right partner next time," she promised, and then darted back into her room, closing the door firmly.

He grinned as he walked away. He could not make the mark vanish overnight, but he could help the time pass more quickly. When the stain was gone, he'd take her dancing somewhere—without the dog present to cause another calamity. However, today, he had another idea of how to make his wife feel better about herself.

He quickly changed his clothes and then ordered his carriage brought round, glancing at his pocket watch to check the time. There was just enough time to make one call, and then go on to the market to meet with Wharton before the auction started.

Chapter Nine

"I simply couldn't believe it when Lord Carmichael told us what had happened to you," Sylvia cried as she studied Lenore's tattooed face carefully. "This is even worse than he made out."

Lenore had almost refused to see Sylvia until she'd heard her husband had gone to request one of the Hillcrest women call on her today to cheer her up after the mishap.

"He said it wasn't so bad," Lenore replied, defending her altered appearance. As the hours had passed since Hero had stamped her face in his paw prints, she'd become resigned to what had happened and her carelessness. *She* had left the ink bottle open. *She* had started singing and had encouraged her dog to start jumping about the room. Lenore had no one to blame but herself for this disaster. Hopefully her husband would not stay angry with her dog for too much longer.

She pressed her fingers over her cheek, aware of the tenderness. In time, yes, the mark would fade away, and all she could do was be patient and hide herself from the world.

The ice her husband had suggested she apply to her cheek had reduced the swelling a little, but it remained very sore, prickly from scrubbing with harsh concoctions. She had to leave it alone for the rest of the day or she might scar her skin.

"I brought everything I can think of to help remove it." Sylvia placed a wicker basket on the bed beside her and showed her the contents.

Lenore was disappointed with what she saw there. "We tried all of that and more. I'll just have to hide until it's gone."

Stay in.

Avoid society.

Probably see even less of her husband if that were even possible.

Sylvia bit her lip. "But that's terrible."

"The alternative is being laughed at. I'm embarrassed enough as it is."

Sylvia's eyes brightened. "What if we tried covering it?"

"With what? I can't wear a hood over my head night and day. That would be just as noticeable."

Sylvia chuckled softly. "I wasn't suggesting any such thing. You could cover it with cosmetics like actresses paint their faces with. We could send out a servant to get some of what they use and try it out. I'm sure with a little practice and careful application, it could work well enough so you could go out with your husband at night with your chin held high."

She thought of her husband and felt a little disappointed in him for going on with his day. But of course, he'd made plans that he wouldn't break even to stay at home and cheer her up himself. It had seemed hopeful when he'd held her, kissed her brow, but still he'd left her. His plans never seemed to be less important than her needs.

But that was their arrangement. To live separate lives.

"I'm sure we'll manage something." She sighed and got up to pace, wondering where he'd gone to today. Somewhere gentlemen went, most likely. Somewhere she wasn't wanted.

Sylvia caught up her hand, stopping her in her tracks. "Are you ready to talk about it now?"

"Talk about what?"

Sylvia squeezed her fingers. "Come now, Lenore, dear friend. It's obvious something was on your mind the other day when you stayed to chaperone me, and I can hazard a guess it's to do with your absent husband. You can trust me to button my lips, too."

Lenore could use a friend who knew how to keep a secret, and Sylvia was someone she trusted. Sylvia was in the business of being above gossip and helping people with marriage. Lenore's was a horrible, polite disaster, and she'd no idea how to change it into something better. When Price had held her today, she'd felt hopeful.

But awkward.

Shy.

She didn't know how to encourage him.

She'd been married for weeks now, and only when she was not in her best looks had he paid her the slightest bit of attention. She'd appreciated the gesture for what it was, sympathy, but she had no belief anything had changed between them. It had been a hollow gesture, without intent behind it. She didn't believe she'd see any more of him in the coming days than she already had.

Sylvia pulled her to sit down on the edge of the bed. "I never see you together."

"No."

"You haven't announced any dinners or gone to parties with him so far that I know. But he is always out, and you come and see us nearly every day. Not that we don't want your company. Far from it." Sylvia sighed. "But today, he called, told us what had befallen you, and then rushed off, saying he was in a hurry. I had hoped he'd return home to you, but he's not here, is he?"

"He had plans."

"Plans that never involve you?" Sylvia suggested.

Lenore nodded, unwilling to pretend anymore.

"And I suspect you haven't the faintest idea what he does with his time, either. Tell me, do you suspect Carmichael has a mistress?"

Lenore gaped, shocked at that question. "I never even thought of that."

"It's always the wife who is the last to know." Sylvia shrugged. "How well do you really know your husband? The aristocracy live by a different code of honor."

"I thought I knew him well enough to be married to him." She took a deep breath. She needed to talk to someone who wouldn't judge her for the rushed decisions she'd made in marrying Lord Carmichael without knowing him. If he did have a mistress, she didn't know what she could do about that. She'd be humiliated, cast off before their marriage was even consummated. It would mean she'd misjudged Lord Carmichael's character very badly, too. "Sylvia, I haven't told anyone the truth. I promised not to discuss this, but now…"

"You have my word and my discretion, always. I wont tell anyone, not even my cousins."

She took another deep breath before she dared to speak. "Lord Carmichael wrote to me. I know it was wrong to answer him, but we've been writing to each other every year at Christmas. He was drunk when he wrote this last time and it was very hard to read. I thought he was offering me employment as a companion for his wife. Lady Kelly's current beau had revealed himself to be a scoundrel, and I rushed to abandon my position for what I thought was a better one."

"Go on. I'm sure there's more," Sylvia murmured.

"He didn't actually remember writing that letter until I arrived. Or that he'd offered marriage. It could have been avoided if I'd not misunderstood or stupidly shown the housekeeper and butler the letter. But since I'd been under his roof overnight, he was adamant. He pressed for a quick marriage between us. He said it was to save my reputation, because the housekeeper and butler might talk. They apparently understood his handwriting better than I did, and conspired to keep me there. I think Carmichael felt obligated to make the offer. You could say our marriage was arranged. By *him*."

Sylvia stared at her. "And now? How are things between you?"

"I know little about him still. I asked for time to get to know him, but he's never around to talk to. He never even told me he was spending Christmas at the Duke of Exeter's estate this year. I fear he will go and leave me behind." She swallowed. "My husband and I barely speak to each other, except at breakfast. You're right, he doesn't tell me anything he's doing or what he's done. It's awful. We're as much strangers as we were on the day we married." Her lip trembled, and to her horror, a tear slipped down her cheek. She brushed it away, angrily. "I don't have the faintest idea how to be his wife."

"Many marriages feel uncomfortable in the beginning but given enough time…"

"What if he does have a mistress? I fear he's already forgotten he's my husband," she blurted out. "I think I might have made a horrible mistake when I agreed to it. I might have nice clothes and servants and a more comfortable bed, but I've never felt more lonely or out of place. And I've only myself to blame."

Sylvia gently folded Lenore into her arms and held her. "Oh my dear, you could have told any one of us and been reassured. We would never judge you for making such a marriage. They happen every day, and often become good ones, too. It helps everyone to talk about the challenges they face."

Lenore nibbled on her bottom lip a moment. "Have you ever heard of a marriage like mine becoming more?"

"Sometimes, but I won't lie to you. Not always."

She nodded. She had married Carmichael, knowing love might never find her, and yet she must have wished for it deep down.

Sylvia patted her hand. "That's not to say love couldn't happen for you both. You're lovely, and one day Carmichael will realize what he has found in you. Has he come to your bed yet?"

Lenore was startled to be asked that question outright, but couldn't ignore it. Sylvia might be unmarried, but she obviously knew a great deal about what went on in a marriage. Perhaps she could offer advice on that subject, too.

She shook her head slowly and didn't dare look up. Given the marriage remained unconsummated, it could be annulled…but then everyone would believe the fault lie with her.

"Has he discussed it?"

"Not since before we married. I told him I needed time to adjust, but now I wonder if Carmichael is glad."

Sylvia made a dismissive sound. "If you hardly spend any time with him, its impossible to know if that's true or not. Don't go imagining the worst about him without cause. If he does have a mistress hidden away somewhere, you must put your foot down about it and make him give her up. He chose you to be his wife. Never forget that."

Lenore shook her head, shocked. "I cannot ask him if he has a mistress."

"He'd only deny it if you did, I suppose." Sylvia stood. "We need a plan."

"A plan for what?"

"You chose to marry Carmichael, too, expecting to be a wife, and by God, you shall have him. You were the one who asked for time before consummating the marriage, is that correct?"

"Yes, but now I—"

Sylvia shushed her. "The solution is simple: You, my dear friend, must be bolder than you know how to be right now. It's time to stop sitting at home, waiting for him to notice you exist. You've been too diffident with the earl. It's time to carve out your own life, show him what he's missing. He cannot go on as he pleases and ignore he's a married man. You must take charge of your own marriage, and your future, too. You decided he'd be your husband, and he chose you for a wife, and so that is what you must be to each other."

"How?"

"You will invite the earl into your bed. Seduce your own husband, and if there is another woman, he will give her up so he can keep coming back. We'll need to be discreet in our planning, but we have time, thanks to that unfortunate ink on your cheek." Sylvia grinned.

Lenore returned her smile skeptically. "How can I possibly seduce my own husband? I'm a virgin, and so are you. I should know more than *you* do by this point in my life. I've never even seen him without his coat on."

She kept to herself that she'd seen his bare legs the day he'd proposed though.

Sylvia leaned close. "My business dealings with men in

search of a wife have opened my eyes to what men want. What they want is a proper lady in public, and you are already that, but they want a wildly exciting bed partner in the privacy of the boudoir. They want to feel they are the most handsome, desirable, skilled lover a woman has ever met. By the time we're done, he'll be mad for you. Unable to think of another woman."

"Do you really think that's what he wants?"

"He's a man," Sylvia said with a laugh. "He may not know it yet, but he'll come around, I'm sure. I've learned they think of intimacy anywhere and anytime. Day or night. It amazes me now that they get any work done at all."

Lenore hadn't thought her husband was like most men. Perhaps he was simply hiding that side of himself behind his polite smile. Lenore had been doing that, too, in a way, without knowing what she was missing out on. She had been the one to put a halt on him sharing her bed, after all.

Lenore's stomach fluttered with nerves, but she did want a real marriage, babies too, just as Carmichael had promised. She thought she might do anything at all to win her husband's affections if they could be hers. She wouldn't allow any other woman to stand in her way. The mistress had to go, even if he loved her. "I'll do it."

Sylvia clapped her hands together quietly and cheered. "When will your husband be home?"

"I honestly don't know." She bit her lip. "Not for dinner, certainly."

"Good. We have a lot to accomplish before you see him again," Sylvia warned. "We're going to reinvent Lady Carmichael to be exactly the sort of woman he craves more than anything in the world. It's time to make Lord Carmichael chase after his wife."

Chapter Ten

Price stumbled from his room, late to take breakfast with his wife, but hoping to catch her still. He'd an invitation to offer if she hadn't already made plans for the day. Unfortunately, he'd overslept, and his new valet had foolishly let him.

His head was pounding in his skull. He'd definitely consumed too much drink last night while he was out with friends again. He'd been celebrating Wharton winning the most stubborn lord in parliament over to his cause.

Lenore was usually in the dining room reading the paper at this hour, but today the room was bare of her, and the table cleared as if breakfast hadn't yet been served. He turned around, pulled out his pocket watch, and checked the time again. Five minutes had passed since the last time he'd looked. He was definitely late and wondered where Lenore might be.

Price headed to the library, only to see those doors shut. He knocked and stepped inside. Finding the room cold and empty of his wife, Price returned to the hall and headed toward the back of the house. The morning room door was ajar, and he finally caught sight of Lenore there.

Or at least part of her.

She was on the ground, on her knees, nicely rounded bottom facing him.

He blinked, instantly and shockingly aroused as that lovely bottom wiggled from side to side hypnotically as she reached under the settee.

Dear God, he couldn't look away from the tempting sight.

He could have Lenore on her knees just like that one day. His cock wedged deep and driving into her over and over again as they made love.

But he couldn't think of that; he'd promised to give Lenore the time she needed.

He started to sweat as her wiggling continued, Lenore unaware of him at the door, and he yanked at his cravat for air as his cock gave an eager twitch in his trousers. He could not seduce her, not until she showed signs she wanted to be.

"Hero, I swear you do this on purpose every single time," she complained. "Bad dog!"

She sat back on her heels, huffing, while Price silently struggled to regain control of his body before his wife noticed him standing there at full attention. He could not meet her with his trousers tented like this. He clasped his hands in front of his groin and imagined something awful.

He thought of his godmother, and his budding erection withered and died. Thank God.

Lenore brushed her hair back from her face and put her hands on her hips. "I'll have to call in a footman for help with this one. You know how I hate doing that."

In control at last, Price stepped into the room and cleared his throat. "Perhaps I could be of service."

Lenore yelped, spinning around and falling on her lovely rounded bottom. "Oh, you scared me, my lord! When I didn't see you at breakfast, I assumed I would not see you until tomorrow."

Should he apologize? If he did, he might also feel obligated to give an accounting of where he had been last night. He would prefer not to. She probably would not like the idea he'd spent the night at a place like Madam Bradshaw's. He touched none of the women there, of course, but he'd certainly been invited to partake. And it was not as if he and Lenore had a standing appointment to see each other over a plate of eggs each day. But it had become a habit. Time well spent, but he'd never sensed her interest in him, so he took himself away.

He strolled closer and offered his hand to help her up. "What seems to be the problem?"

The mark on her face had almost completely gone now. Just a lingering trace was discernable when he drew closer to her.

She slapped her palm across his, and he quickly put her on her feet. They swayed close together only a moment before she pulled away and turned to scowl at her dog, putting her hands on her enticing hips again. The scent of Lenore, a delicate fragrance of lavender and honey, washed over him, and his body warmed anew. He kept a firm grip on his reaction this time, though, knowing the moment was still not right to explore passion with his bride.

Lenore clucked her tongue. "Hero has tossed his favorite toy into a hard-to-reach place. Normally I can snare them, but today it's too far under."

Price chuckled as the dog sensed her disapproval and flattened himself in supplication, tail still wagging back and forth as he stared at his mistress with mournful eyes.

Despite her disapproving tone, it was obvious Lenore was still very fond of her animal. They were always together. She took him everywhere she went. Visiting friends or shopping on Bond Street, everyone who saw them mentioned his wife and dog were happy together.

"Let me see what I can do," he murmured. Price approached the chaise and looked around it for handholds. It was large, well-cushioned, and deep enough for two to sleep upon. Sturdy, and most likely too heavy for Lenore to shift on her own, and she really should not try. He picked up one end easily, moved it out from the wall, and dropped it down with a thump.

Price wriggled behind the piece and bent low. After searching around one-handed, he tossed out a length of knotted rope and a small leather ball, too, that was hidden by the bottom edge of the window drapes.

"So that's where it went!" Lenore cried, rushing to snatch up the ball and denying her dog the opportunity to play with it, lest he lose it again.

Price wriggled back out. "Was that everything he's lost?"

"Yes, thank you," she said, but her focus was already on her dog and a game of tug of war.

Price felt decidedly overlooked as the game continued as if he wasn't still standing there. Eventually, he cleared his throat.

She spared him a fleeting glance. "Was there something else, my lord?"

"It's Price," he snapped.

"I'm sorry?" She dropped the rope and Hero snatched it up and ran away. "Oh, Hero come back," she called, glancing out to the hall after her dog.

"My name is Price."

She turned back to him and blinked. "Do you want me to call you by your first name now?"

"You did when we were younger."

"I did a lot of things then that I don't do now." Her chin lifted. "All right, Price, it is. Was there something else?"

"No." He shook his head in frustration, noticing she had not granted him permission to use her given name in return. "Yes. We have been invited to attend a luncheon at a friend's house today. It was a last-minute decision to have a gathering. Last night, actually."

Her fingers rose to her cheek.

"That has faded enough that no one will notice."

She swallowed. "At what time should I be ready?"

Price checked the time on his pocket watch. "We need to leave in the next twenty minutes, or we'll be late."

Her eyes rounded. "But, it is only ten?"

"There's a long drive ahead of us."

"I see." She looked after her dog, and then at herself, and her shoulders sagged. "I was about to take him for a walk. You go, and give your host my sincere apologies."

That did not suit Price. He had honestly thought Lenore might be eager to see some of London with him by now. He also had a present for her that he was keen to show off today, too. "What if I take Hero outside while you change into something more appropriate?"

"I couldn't ask you to do that."

"You didn't ask. I offered. Bring a cloak, too. There's bound to be a cool breeze coming off the Thames in the afternoon."

She hesitated a moment, then gathered up her skirts one-handed and fled at a run. The dog returned, but Price was able to call Hero back. Apparently, the word "walk" was enough of an incentive for the little beast to stay with him.

He gathered up the rope and walked the dog out into the square. Hero bounded off a little way but returned in short order. Price threw the rope, and Hero always brought it back. Price threw until his arm began to tire, and the dog was more than happy to fall to the earth, satisfied and panting.

"Good dog," he praised.

He turned to look at his home and caught Lenore watching them out of an upper window. He raised his hand, pleased to see her watching him. Lenore offered him a brief, almost embarrassed wave back, and promptly disappeared behind the curtains again.

He sighed. "We're a long way off being comfortable with each other," he confessed to the dog. What he wouldn't give to know what she thought of him right now. It seemed forever since their marriage, and that decision they'd made to wait to consummate the marriage niggled at him. But he had to be patient with her. "I'm hoping today's gift will make up for me never being at home."

Hero barked. Price crouched down and gave the dog a good rub then they played tug of war with a stick. After a while, Hero ran a few steps toward the town house, and then barked at him.

"Quite right. We'd better go back to our lady and be on our way soon after."

He was looking forward to spending the day with Lenore. He longed for the end of this parliamentary session so he had time take Lenore away from London for a honeymoon trip perhaps.

He strolled back to the house, making sure Hero was close as they crossed the roadway. The dog bounded up the steps, and Price let himself inside.

He heard the commotion at once. The high-pitched voice of another woman. The shrill tone he recognized all too well, unfortunately.

Lady Berry, Angela's mother, was in his home.

With Lenore.

He followed the sound of her angry voice and found her and Lenore in the drawing room, with Lady Berry looking daggers at his wife.

"Lady Berry," he barked.

Hero barked, too, and rushed across to his mistress, ready to defend her. Hackles up. The dog growled, and Lenore bent down to shush him, exposing her deep cleavage to all in the room.

He nearly groaned as lust hit him hard.

"I see it didn't take you long to turn your attention elsewhere," Lady Berry sneered, and then turned back to Lenore. "Scandalous. Brazen."

"She's beautiful," Price declared, but then caught hold of Lady Berry's arm and dragged her away from Lenore. "We will talk in my study, madam."

Lady Berry attempted to shake off his grip, even if he was having none of it. "I should have known your words were as cold as your heart must be."

He wrestled her from the room before she spewed out the hate she customarily lashed Price with in front of Lenore.

Lady Berry blamed him for Angela's death. Price agreed with Lady Berry to a point. Angela had snuck away from her chaperones to rendezvous with him on the night she'd been murdered. If he'd known about his godmother's intent, he'd never have risked Angela's reputation or her life. It was *his* fault that Angela had been all alone the night she'd died. She had been waiting for him.

But Lenore had nothing to do with any of it.

He assisted Lady Berry down the hall as politely as possible, and once they were in the privacy of his study, and the door firmly shut, he released her. He would try again to comfort the distraught woman. "I did not know you had returned to London."

"As soon as I read your *happy* news in *The Times*, I had to come to see for myself the sort of woman you'd take as a wife after all you've said to about your supposed undying devotion," she hissed. "I wonder if you profess to love her, too, the way you deceived my innocent daughter."

"I deceive no one." Price sighed. "I had a duty to marry. To have a son."

She tipped her head in the direction Lenore had been. "So, you married a...what? A nobody? A woman so insignificant that her name and connections cannot be found in Debrett's?"

"Do not speak of Lady Carmichael in that fashion," he told her in a biting tone. "She is a good woman."

Lady Berry's eyes narrowed. "She's a dried-up spinster. Was she the only woman you could get with your reputation in tatters now? No proper family would have you in their midst now I suppose. You disgust me!"

She had expressed that opinion before, and yet still sought him out. Lady Berry had decided to rail at him, and only him, since the killer had been his late godmother and he'd been involved with her daughter.

"For Angela's sake, I'll forgive your words today, but never again. I'm a victim of my godmother's murderous rage, too. She stole my happiness, murdered the woman I loved, and killed others. Many women died, or have you forgotten their families' pain is as great as your own?"

Price advanced on the woman. Lady Berry might have the distinction of almost being his mother-in-law once, but his patience only went so far. "If you *ever* try to speak to my wife again, try to malign her to others the way you just did, I'll see to it your name is wiped from society's memory. Don't think I haven't the influence."

The lady had the decency to dip her gaze, but he was confident she hadn't finished picking at his conscience. She was bitter and lost without her daughter. She'd had high hopes for Angela's future, which was why their relationship had been conducted in secrecy at first. Lady Berry had wanted her daughter to marry higher than him. Anyone but him, really. A duke or a marquess, perhaps. She'd never believed Price's interest in her precious daughter to be sincere.

"You can put a ring on her finger and dress her up in pretty gowns, but she'll never belong in our society. You'll see," Lady Berry warned. "You'll get what you deserve—a life of unhappiness and misery await you."

She stood there a moment, and then turned on her heel to march out.

Price pinched the bridge of his nose, and then followed behind to make sure Lady Berry was truly gone and didn't have a chance to speak to Lenore again.

The door shut behind her with a great crash, and Price immediately went in search of his wife.

Lenore was still in the drawing room but peeking out the front windows at the departing figure of Lady Berry.

Price approached her slowly. "Are you all right?"

She nodded. "Who was that woman?"

"She didn't tell you?"

"Not really. She just sailed into the room and started saying horrible things to me about you."

"What sort of things?"

"She mentioned your godmother. She suggested you must have known what was going on and could have stopped her."

Price took a deep breath. "I didn't know, and I am ashamed of that."

"I know you're not responsible."

If only that were the whole of it. Lenore would hear things when they went out together, and when she went out alone in society soon. Some people knew all of it, that he'd been romantically involved with some of the victims in the past, and particularly with Angela, who he'd planned to do the right thing by and marry her.

He hadn't the stomach to relay the whole story anymore. He didn't want to distress Lenore either. But she should be prepared with some version of it should they reencounter Lady Berry in society. "Lady Berry is the mother of one of my godmother's victims."

Lenore nodded. "I gathered as much. Angela?"

"Yes, Lady Berry blames me for her daughter's death. Many of the families have asked how I missed the signs of madness in my godmother, but I swear, I saw nothing that gave me cause for alarm."

Lenore rubbed his arm. "We never really know what is in people's hearts and minds, do we?"

The touch was unexpected, and he moved closer to her. "I didn't, and I regret that very much."

His life might have been entirely different. He would have married Angela, not Lenore. Strangely, after so many weeks, he couldn't imagine not being married to Lenore now. "I think—

Lenore's fingers settled over his lips. "Regrets are poison for the soul and spoil the day if dwelled on for too long. What your godmother did is in the past. We don't have to talk about it now."

He looked her over, *really* looked at Lenore for a change. She'd donned a pretty new gown for their outing, and her hair was simply styled, ready to place a bonnet over her head. He liked what he saw very much. He liked his wife, and didn't want to say anything that would possibly upset her and spoil the day.

No, today wasn't the day for regrets but for new adventures and a little politics too. "We do have a party to attend."

"And I am ready," she promised, reaching for a bonnet that had been set down on a table behind her. As she turned, Priced noticed that her paw-printed cheek was absent. He squinted at her face when she turned back, discovering the slightest hint of cosmetics there to hide it.

"Indeed, you are, and I promise you will have a marvelous time." He noticed her cloak spread over a chair and gathered it up. "I'll have the carriage brought round immediately."

She followed him to the door, talking with her pet the

whole way there. He knew she wasn't paying attention to him but waited until the carriage had pulled up before whispering her name.

"Yes?" Her eyes lit up when they fell on the carriage.

He grinned, enjoying her surprise. "What do you think? Will it do?"

The new carriage—black-lacquered sides, and bright green trimmings—shone in the daylight. The grooms, newly employed and wearing freshly tailored livery, snapped to attention once the carriage door opened. Lenore's carriage pleased him very well. It was created to fit a family instead of just a pair traveling through Town.

"It's beautiful," she whispered. "Is this yours?"

"No. It's yours, Lenore. And Hero's too, of course. Climb in and tell me what you think."

Hero sprang inside, jumping up on the new seats and sniffing the olive velvet upholstery. Lenore climbed in more slowly, allowing Price to help her this time.

When she was seated, he joined her, and the door snapped shut.

She fingered the green fringed window drapes and looked around at everything with wide eyes. "You shouldn't have done this for me."

He reached past her and opened a compartment on the wall of the carriage. Inside was a crystal bowl and a corked bottle. "The carpenter thought me mad not to have wanted wine glasses in here, but I thought you might prefer me to be practical instead. The bottle is water instead of wine. The bowl is for Hero to drink from."

"That's so thoughtful," she said, smiling even wider now.

He settled their cloaks on the opposite seat beside Hero and sat back, comfortable, and very pleased with his new purchase. He was glad he'd been able to surprise her. "Now, you don't need to share my carriage anymore," he told her.

"Thank you." Lenore nodded slowly, and then turned her face to the view out the window. She sighed softly. "Yes. It is a lovely carriage for Hero and me to travel about in."

Chapter Eleven

All things considered, Lenore was happy to have her own carriage, and she waltzed out the front door as often as she pleased. But as she was driven through Mayfair in her expensive carriage with just her dog for company, she longed to have her husband by her side more than ever.

She was at the end of her patience with him. Yes, she could use her carriage when she liked, and Hero quite loved sitting in it beside her. But the arrival of a second carriage meant there was no need for Price to travel with her anywhere now, unless they were going to the same place.

Which they never did.

Today, she was going shopping yet again, meeting Sylvia Hillcrest at a discreet place of business to ensure the consummation of her marriage had the best chance of success. She had decided now was the right time. She wanted it done before her husband could leave her behind or send her to the country while he attended some house party.

Lenore had become very close to Sylvia of late and they spent much time together planning and discussing how she'd phrase her request to her husband. They practiced and discarded Lenore delivering subtle hints and had decided a blunt, direct invitation would be easiest for her to deliver. It wasn't going to be at all romantic. It wasn't meant to be.

Aurora and Eugenia Hillcrest remained in ignorance about Lenore's unhappiness with her husband. That pair were pursuing new business opportunities outside of the *ton* and she was glad for their distraction. Sylvia was the only woman she really trusted to be honest about her marriage to, and she had been an excellent listener—cautioning Lenore not to imagine refusal but agreement.

Lenore hoped her friend was right. She was to deliver her request to her husband soon, before she lost her nerve.

Carmichael had been, as usual, nowhere to be found in the house after they had breakfasted together that morning. They were ships passing in the night still—polite strangers who shared a home and his name. The one party he'd taken her too had unfortunately come to an abrupt halt due to rain. They had been having fun together, she thought. But he had taken her home to change into dry clothes and abruptly taken himself off again for an urgent meeting with another lord.

At least he'd told her where he was going and why, for once.

Their butler, Humphries, became uncomfortable every time Lenore asked about her husband's whereabouts, so she had stopped asking. She had promised to be a good wife to Lord Carmichael, and she meant to be—and that included allowing him to live his own life while she did hers.

But she believed it was past time for her to take the next step in their marriage, which was why she was traveling along Bond Street today in a slightly nervous state.

The carriage drew to a stop in a narrow lane. Nearby was a shop reputed to be the only one a lady could ever need to pull off a seduction. Lenore did not want to draw attention to herself lest it get back to her husband. She could not see Sylvia, but Lenore alighted with her dog, dismissed the carriage for one hour, and entered the little shop trying to control her nerves.

The little bell on the shop door gave a happy jingle as it closed behind her, and she immediately ordered Hero to be good. Sylvia had not arrived yet but Lenore was not unduly alarmed. She stood looking about the chamber for someone to attend her, gripping Hero's leash tightly.

A small woman rushed out from the rear of the building. Lenore assumed there was a fitting room back there, though she'd never visited this particular establishment before. "I have an appointment."

"La, you must be Lady Carmichael," the small woman proclaimed, beaming widely. "Welcome, welcome to Madam Du Clair's establishment. I am her assistant, Maxine."

"Thank you. I trust Madam can see me today."

"Oi, my lady." The woman drew closer. "Unfortunately, she is running just the teensiest bit late with a fitting if you do not mind a delay of a few moments more."

Lenore had nothing else to do, so she inclined her head graciously. "I will wait."

She moved to a table and chair in the corner and sat with her hands folded in her lap. Hero at her feet. The assistant served her up tea and put a plate of little cakes on the table, too. Lenore was too nervous to eat, so she fed a bit of one to her pet while she waited.

From behind the drape, she heard whispers, then an excited utterance of her title.

Lenore looked up at the far room door just as it cracked open wider. A woman, only one eye to be seen, peered out at her and blinked.

Lenore drew in a sharp breath but then merely picked up her cup, ignoring the woman spying on her. The door shut quietly, and silence reined within the establishment again. Just as Lenore was starting to feel she'd waited long enough, the fitting room door opened, and one of her husband's friend's wives emerged.

Lenore inclined her head. "Lady Wade," she murmured, striving for calm. She had hoped to complete today's purchase without meeting anyone acquainted with her or her husband.

"Lady Carmichael. What a pleasure to see you again, and here, too," the redhead promised, with a grin. "I trust you are well."

"Indeed, I am."

The lady nodded. "I was saying to Carmichael the other night that it has been much too long since we last sat down to dinner together."

Lenore's smile felt frozen in place, and she recognized the emotion surging through her as jealousy. This beautiful woman had seen her husband one night when Lenore wasn't with him. She fought not to reveal her upset. "Is that right?"

Lenore was more than a little annoyed—but not with Lady Wade. She felt abandoned and uneasy that her husband had been having conversations with other ladies about her and had not told her about them. Of course, he could not avoid his friends, but Lenore would have felt better to be told about such meetings so she was not unprepared the way she was today.

"I shall have everything ready for you next week," the modiste announced, emerging from the workroom, but she stopped and looked between them curiously. "I gather you are already acquainted, my dears?"

"Indeed we are." Lady Wade smiled affectionately. "Could any lady of the *ton* be happily married without patronizing your wicked little shop?"

"I should hope not, Lady Wade. I fear your poor husband would feel neglected without my creations to tempt him." Lady Wade was steered away to the door. "Adieu. You must not keep him waiting."

"Until next time, Lady Carmichael," Lady Wade sang as she was shown out, throwing a last regretful look in Lenore's direction that she had to go.

Madam turned and smiled. "A thousand apologies for the delay, Lady Carmichael. If you would come this way, it shall be my pleasure to serve you," she claimed.

Lenore stood, her mood soured by that unexpected meeting. "I am expecting my friend, Miss Hillcrest, to meet me here shortly but she is late. I hope that is not a problem."

"The more, the merrier, my lady," she crooned, ignoring Lenore's clipped tone. "Everyone is welcome in my little shop. Here, a lady is ensured complete discretion and a level of personal service not found anywhere else in London."

Lenore found the woman's confidence that anyone held their tongue premature. What sort of woman was Lady Wade, really? Would she tattle on Lenore to her husband and spoil her plans to seduce him?

She rose and tugged on Hero's leash. Hero followed her obediently into the workroom and, once released, found himself an out-of-the-way spot to lie down in.

Madam frowned as she put spectacles on her nose. "I usually do not admit pets in my workroom, my lady."

That was going to be a problem. "I go nowhere without my Hero," she explained.

The woman clucked her tongue, considering. Hero was freshly bathed and his coat was glossy black. He would soil nothing. Touch or lick nothing.

Eventually, Madam nodded. "As long as he behaves, he may stay."

"I assure you he is very well trained. He will not be a bother, and I made sure he was exercised before coming here. He will most likely sleep through the appointment."

"Good, for we want no distractions." The woman looked her up and down. "How may I help you today?"

What Lenore wanted to buy would be considered scandalous, or could have been if she was still an unmarried woman. However, she *was* married, and would not be made embarrassed by her request. "I require a negligee. Something suitable for the boudoir or bed. Do you offer them?"

The front doorbell jingled again, and Madam froze, listening in. The voices outside continued on a few minutes, so low Lenore couldn't understand at first. But then she finally heard her friend's tones, and flew to the doorway to poke her head out.

"Oh, there you are!" Sylvia exclaimed, rushing over. "I was afraid I'd come too late and missed you entirely when I saw a carriage leaving."

"You're just in time." She returned to the workroom, drawing Sylvia with her, and moved to the center of the room. "I apologize for the interruption. My friend is here to lend her opinion."

"Oi." The modiste nodded, sizing up Sylvia, too. She smiled and then faced Lenore. "Something in satin?"

"Please."

The modiste brought out a length of thin knotted ribbon and took all of Lenore's measurements first. She turned away when she'd measured all of her and snatched up bolts of fabric to hold against Lenore's body in all different colors, but then discarded each and every one.

Hero slept, his feet twitching occasionally.

Sylvia sat in a deep armchair, eyes alight with keen interest as she oversaw proceedings. Their eyes met, and Sylvia's danced with excitement. "How is your husband today?"

Lenore shrugged. "The same."

"Tomorrow morning, he will be different," Sylvia promised.

"Tonight?" Lenore experienced a small pang of anxiety, but nodded. It gave her less time to reconsider. "Tonight it is."

"Not satin, after all, I think," Madam murmured to herself, and then found a roll of very dark navy fabric. Lenore frowned when she realized the material was sheer netting, the sort worn over the top of a satin gown. Ladies often dressed that way when they were in mourning. If she wore two layers to bed, Lenore felt she might as well be dressed in an ordinary nightgown dyed dark. This was not a time to be sad. "I don't think—"

"This is just the thing to tempt your husband," Madam promised. "Please let me show you."

Madam Du Clair rummaged in a nearby cupboard and brought out a neatly folded garment in the same dark navy. It was clearly an order meant for someone else.

She held it against Lenore and smiled. "Your husband will fall at your feet when you wear this and nothing else."

Lenore blinked several times. "Nothing else underneath?"

Sylvia began to chortle and clapped her hands together, sitting forward. "I told you this was *the* place for wives to shop. I love it!"

Lenore bit her lip, uncertain whether such provocative and scandalous attire was truly necessary. "But do you think he will?"

"Oi," Madam beamed. "What could be more erotic and seductive than the skin so very nearly revealed? Many of my customers buy similar garments to this…and then return for replacements because they inflamed their husbands entirely too much."

Lenore was not convinced she wanted Carmichael to lose his manners over a daring negligee, or *her*, either. She had not been intimate with her husband, so she had no idea how he might behave in the bedchamber.

But Lenore did feel she needed an edge when it came to pleasing him. She was no young beauty. Some considered Lenore downright plain. That was why Lenore thought a negligee might prove helpful for Carmichael to get in the mood to bed her. Something daring like Madam suggested now might just be in order...or it might be too much altogether.

Sensing her doubts remained, Madam smiled. "At least let me show you how you will look in this before you say no," the modiste suggested.

"The gown clearly belongs to another."

"No, I have made this and put it aside for urgent orders from my customers. This one has no home to go to."

Lenore considered, and then nodded slowly, glancing at her friend and seeing her nod enthusiastically, too.

The modiste helped Lenore undress down to only her stockings, and then slipped the garment around her. It fell to her ankles and to her wrists, but the sleeves were full and would reveal her arms when she lifted them to embrace her husband.

Lenore blanched at just how little the creation hid from view though.

Sylvia came closer and started taking pins out of her hair. "For the full effect," she murmured. "A little color on your lips and a welcoming smile. No jewelry but a sweet-smelling lotion on your skin, and you'll be irresistible."

While Sylvia fluffed out her hair down her back, Lenore caught the net in her fingers.

It was softer than she'd first imagined it would be, trimmed with lace and little embroidered adornments all over. A satin sash for the waist was the only means to hold the garment together and accentuate her waist. It concealed nothing. Her nipples, dark splotches under the net, and her curls lower seemed much too obvious.

As she looked at herself in the mirror, she couldn't imagine Carmichael becoming aroused by the sight of her in this. She still looked like herself. "No. I can't."

"But wait, my lady." Madam's hands were suddenly in Lenore's hair, too. Madam drew some strands forward over her breasts but kept a middle section down her back. But the daring plunge to her navel remained. "Like this, or perhaps all across one shoulder."

When Lenore looked again, she jerked up her chin in surprise. She turned to view herself from all angles. She looked different, indeed. Almost a temptress.

"He won't be able to keep his polite hands from you," Sylvia promised with a wicked laugh.

A slow smile spread over Lenore's lips as she imagined standing before him this way. She looked more appealing now with her hair closer around her face. Younger. Prettier. More enticing, she hoped. She could hide both breasts if she was too nervous, and reveal them later depending on Carmichael's reaction. She revealed a little more of her cleavage and some leg also. Her pale skin shone in stark contrast to the barely there negligee.

Sylvia chuckled. "My friend the siren. Perhaps without the stockings for him, and point your toes a little."

She turned her foot then blushed furiously. She liked it very much on her, and her confidence grew the longer she stared. She was not herself, and that was what she needed to be. She was a wife intent on seducing a reluctant husband. She was a woman meant to be bedded the moment he saw her.

"Oi," she murmured without hesitation now. "I want this."

This would do for consummating their marriage. If Carmichael proved partial to the costume, she would wear it again for him until she was big with child, and perhaps buy something else just as scandalous to tempt him to try for a second child when she judged the time was right.

Lenore didn't want or need her husband to fall in love with her. Lust was enough, and only needed at night between them. Their marriage wasn't about being physically close to each other outside of the bedchamber. During the day, they'd still go their separate ways, she was sure.

Madam helped her out of the garment and held out a robe. "What else can I help you with today?"

"That was all—"

"Actually, my friend is in desperate need for an entirely new wardrobe," Sylvia declared, cutting into the conversation as she jumped to her feet. She drew close, and Madam stepped back as Sylvia began to whisper. "Don't worry about the cost of new gowns. You will need them when the season begins, and I am sure Carmichael can afford to spoil you after all you're doing for him. We need to show you off to your advantage, and make that husband of yours shower you with some attention. Some lower-cut gowns in sheer fabrics are just the thing to drive him out of his mind."

Lenore wavered but then nodded again. She had not been extravagant so far. Especially knowing the size of the bills run up by her last employer, Lady Kelly. They had been greater than hers could ever be. Lenore did have to look the part now and prepare for next season. The cost of additional gowns was a reasonable decision.

There were a few of her newest gowns she had become dissatisfied with after talking with Sylvia, anyway. They had been perfectly befitting of a lady her age. But they were not exceptionally pretty.

When the carriage returned to collect her, Lenore sent it away for another hour as she poured over the modiste's recommendations and redesigned her entire wardrobe around the impractical ambition of feeling herself a countess at last.

Chapter Twelve

———◆———

Price slipped the mourning band around his upper arm, buttoning it into place, and then held his arms to his valet for his coat. As the garment slid over him, Price cast a glance at the connecting door to his wife's bedchamber. He would like to speak with Lenore before breakfast. Figure out how and where they would spend the winter months. He had an invitation to the Duke of Exeter's house party yet to answer, but she might want to go home to Edenmere Park instead first. "Has Lady Carmichael gone downstairs already, Norris?"

It still felt strange to ask that question and mean Lenore Griffin, the shy granddaughter of one of his former servants. He hardly felt married at all, even after so many weeks together, but there was no escaping the fact that he was a husband and he had to consider her wishes.

"Yes, my lord, though I believe she's gone out with her dog."

Price shrugged his shoulders, settling the coat into place and tugging down his shirtsleeves. Every time he thought to do something with Lenore lately, his wife was absent from the house. He was starting to find it annoying. "Walking in the square before breakfast?"

If she was in the square, perhaps he could catch up to her and get their plans settled before he went out himself.

"No, my lord. She took her breakfast on a tray in her room then went out in the carriage."

Price hid his disappointment as best he could. She'd gone out before breakfast yesterday, too, without telling him she wouldn't be joining him then, either. If she'd taken the carriage, then she was going farther afield and might not be back for a little while. He was not going to make any decisions without her, so the decision about Exeter's party would need to wait for another time.

Besides, he was more than happy to keep the duke waiting on his answer since he'd stolen back his remarkable chef, Monsieur Laffitte.

And if Lenore was still not back by the time he finished dressing, he had no reason to linger at home. Wharton had been complaining that he never visited him often enough at home. Perhaps he'd go there now and drag Wharton out of his bed for breakfast.

But should he ask where Lenore had gone? Did husbands do that when they didn't love their wives? Perhaps they didn't. However, Price was becoming curious about his wife and what she did with her time when he wasn't with her. "Did you hear where my wife was bound for?"

"Bond Street. Gone shopping, I heard, my lord."

"Good." He didn't see anything wrong with his wife having her own busy life and interests outside their home. But it was starting to concern him that, after weeks of marriage, he really didn't know what her favorite things might be. Lenore was a sensible, practical woman and had the right to buy herself anything she wanted, but one day he might just want to give her a small gift. He should know her favorite color and favorite flower, if he'd paid proper court to her.

The rush to marry had been entirely his doing.

Now she was out in the carriage he'd purchased for her, and that was all he'd hoped for when he'd decided she needed one of her own instead of sharing his. Still, he missed the comforting routine of starting each new day talking to her over breakfast foods.

He gave his cravat one last-minute adjustment, and he was ready to face another day.

So far, this marriage he'd arranged for himself was turning out to be quite uneventful. Sometimes it seemed he was still a bachelor, and that didn't seem right. Lenore didn't ask him where he went or when they might speak to each other again. She made no demands on his time. She seemed determined to be a silent spouse and let him find amusement elsewhere, while she did, too.

He glanced at her door again. Shouldn't a wife want to spend time with her husband and say so?

"Mr. Humphries asked me to mention that there are a great many letters for you, my lord," Norris remarked. "He put them with the rest downstairs in your study."

"I'll look at them later."

Norris winced. "If I might be so bold, my lord, the butler also said I should mention that your desk is getting a bit full."

Price sighed. "Yes, I am aware of that."

"You could engage a secretary to tidy up for you, my lord," Norris suggested.

Price stared at the man, jaw clenching. Hiring a secretary was an idea the butler, a man who'd been with him since he'd come of age, had brought up before. Unfortunately, Price didn't trust easily anymore. Certainly not when it came to his business affairs. He would muddle through on his own, though perhaps he should not leave the matter of answering his correspondence to languish entirely. He *had* been out a lot of late. There were likely things that needed his attention.

He made himself shed his irritation with the new valet. Humphries had thrown Norris into the fire to do his bidding rather than risk dismissal himself. "Perhaps when you are finished tidying up here, you could tell Mr. Humphries to look to his duties instead of fussing like an old woman over mine."

A hot flush of color stole up the man's cheeks. "Sorry, my lord. I was just trying to do what I was told."

"Humphries should know better than to send my valet to do his reminding. You can go, Norris," he ordered.

The valet hurried to finish and fled.

Price headed downstairs a few moments later, filled a plate from the sideboard in the breakfast room and then detoured into this study to eat alone. The latest crop of letters should at least be seen, if not read through.

The first dozen were unimportant. Invitations and announcements from acquaintances, but he dealt with each just to be rid of them. However, as he neared the bottom of the pile, one letter caught his attention. He noticed the address was the same as Lenore's last employer. He grimaced and opened it.

Lady Kelly begged his pardon, but she was in a panic and appealed to him for advice. Lenore had apparently abandoned her employment, and no one knew where she'd gone. Since Price had written one of Lenore's letters of reference, she believed Price might want to know about her disappearance, should his letter of reference be used again.

The lady suggested some ill or other had befallen Lenore to make her run away from a much-admired place of employment and position.

Price read the letter a second time, and then caught a hint of suspicion and disapproval of Lenore in the wording. Lady Kelly did not accuse but she suggested, very subtly, that Lenore had changed since he'd written his letter of recommendation.

What exactly had been going on there before Lenore had joined him in London?

Price's lips twisted, as did his gut. It seemed not to have occurred to Lady Kelly that her companion might have run off to get respectably married.

It was wrong of Lenore not to have given her notice, though he knew why she'd fled in such a hurry. At the very least, they should have written to Lady Kelly to give her the good news of her marriage and improved situation. Price would not allow his wife's character to be maligned out of ignorance. Lady Kelly should be set straight before she caused embarrassment for them all.

He sat behind the desk and pulled out a sheet of paper. He wrote and politely informed Lady Kelly not to be concerned, and briefly explained that Lenore was now Lady Carmichael, his wife, and that the new countess would write her a letter when it was convenient to her.

By the time he was ready to sign it, he heard the front door open and voices ring out in the entry hall. Recognizing his wife speaking to a servant, and Hero's bark, Price hurried out to meet her.

Lenore was just removing her bonnet from her dark hair when he saw her. His steps slowed as she smiled at Humphries and declared she'd had a wonderful morning.

Wonderful—without him. What exactly had she been doing to smile so contentedly now? "Good morning, Lady Carmichael."

Her smile slipped as she heard him but then quickly returned before she curtsied deeply in his direction, as if she was in his employ. That would not do, and he moved to catch up her hand in his.

Hero licked his free hand and jumped about as he usually did, full of excitement.

Price studied Lenore in the light. She seemed quite flustered. "Are you all right?"

"Yes, my lord. It's just a surprise to see you home at this hour," Lenore said, her cheeks slowly becoming flushed with bright color as she pulled her hand out of his grip. She hadn't expected him…or was it that she'd hoped not to see him?

"I was attending to some correspondence," he said, watching her closely, wanting to hold her tiny hand again. "Might I have a moment of your time, Lady Carmichael?"

"Of course." She nodded quickly but first handed a package to the footman. "Could you have my maid put that in my bedchamber, on my writing desk, sir. Tell Molly she must not unwrap that package under any circumstances."

"Of course, my lady."

She looked at Price expectantly when the footman was gone. "You wanted to speak to me?"

"Yes. But it would be better if we had this talk in the privacy of my study."

"How intriguing," she murmured. "I am at your complete disposal, of course."

He gestured her ahead of him, and she preceded him to the back of the townhouse. Price's gaze drifted over her, down her back, and up again to the simply arranged bun at the back of her head. Lenore's appeal had definitely increased since they'd married. Or perhaps he'd been blind and stupid about her attractiveness before.

Once inside his study, Lenore looked around curiously. "Very cozy."

Had she not set foot in this room? When he thought about it, he wasn't sure if Lenore spent very much time downstairs other than in the morning or dining room. He'd certainly not heard of her having callers, but then again, he'd often been out for the latter half of the days since they'd married. He wasn't at all sure of her schedule. "I'm glad you approve."

"So, what is this about, my lord? You seem very serious."

"I had a letter about you today. I have written an answer, but perhaps you should read it first in case I've said something wrong," he suggested, and at her frown, he explained. "Your last employer is beside herself with worry over your whereabouts."

Her brows rose as she read Lady Kelly's letter, and then she picked up his response.

She quickly read his letter and handed it back. "You realize the moment we tell Lady Kelly anything is the end of our peaceful coexistence."

"I don't follow," he said.

"Lady Kelly is the sort of woman who will come to London, appearing full of concern but really just wishing to poke her nose into your affairs. She will expect a full explanation and to stay the night, most likely."

"We cannot have her suggesting to others that you ran off to avoid some imaginary scandal."

"Well, that's certainly true. There might well have been a scandal if I'd stayed."

The hair at the back of his neck stood up. "Explain that, madam."

"I was not happy in Lady Kelly's employ." She sighed. "I found Lady Kelly to be difficult right from the start, demanding as much of the nobility can be. She expects absolute obedience and propriety, and then allows scoundrels into her home. I never told her the exact reason for my going, which, at the time, I thought was to take up a position as a companion. In all honesty, I would rather not see her again until I know he is gone from her life."

"What exactly happened?"

Lenore shrugged, and she did not meet his gaze. "Her suitor suggested that I would become his mistress when he married my employer."

Alarmed, Price moved to stand directly in front of her. "Did he impose upon you?"

Lenore stepped back. "He did not touch me, but he's not the first male friend of one of my employers who sought me out behind their backs. This particular fellow had lingered harmlessly long enough for me to let down my guard a little and think him honorable. He even offered me a gift of a gold necklace as inducement, which I refused. Your offer of employment couldn't have been more perfectly timed, which is why I left Lady Kelly's employ as quickly as I did. I suppose she has blackened my name to all who knew me there."

Price clenched his fist. "If either one dares to show their faces here, I will—"

Lenore chuckled, glancing down at his hands. "You'll be a good husband and drive the pair off with your fists? Violence solves nothing."

"I will draw his cork if necessary," he promised sincerely. "Lady Kelly should have protected you."

"*She* should have been protected, too. I feel badly now that I may have left her and the other female servants at the mercy of such a scoundrel." Lenore suddenly perched on the edge of his desk, one leg beginning to swing back and forth. She looked at him sheepishly. "I should be ashamed to admit that it might be fun to witness you planting the man a facer, however, I can be of no interest to scoundrels, now I am married."

How little she knew about the world still. There were men who thought married women fair game and a challenge. He was surprised she hadn't encountered them already. "Scoundrels are everywhere and would definitely be interested in you."

"Doubtful, but I now possess a veritable army of footmen and my own grooms to beat back such men, should the need arise."

"You also have me. Your husband will defend you from all impertinences from now on."

She laughed and patted his arm. "The footmen and grooms will be more than enough of a deterrent, I think."

He did not like that she preferred the servants' protection to his. She was his wife and responsibility. "Lenore, you will leave the matter of…what is his name?"

"Lord Thorne," she supplied helpfully, smiling.

"Lord Thorne to me. I'll teach him to mind his manners around my countess and deal honestly with your former employer, too. No one deserves to be so ill-used."

She stared at him a moment then shook her head. "You were always a kind boy. I'm glad to learn that hasn't changed."

"I was a brat," he declared. "You were always the better behaved out of both of us. Your grandmother was stern but was a better influence than my father. She always made you stay by her side when you were impertinent, whereas I…"

"Was shut up alone in the nursery for weeks at a time. You only misbehaved to get your father's attention," she said very quietly. "You felt the sting of the strap and isolation rather than his love."

He nodded slowly. "I suppose we get the life we deserve in one way or another. I discovered too slowly that I'd never win his approval and learned to please only myself by striking out alone," he said, looking again at Lenore. "Not many people would realize our struggles for independence were similar."

Lenore laughed softly. "We have been poles apart all our lives, my lord. You were born with a silver spoon in your mouth and my first memory was polishing that silver until my fingers hurt." She shrugged and looked down at the letter he'd written again. "Your letter is succinct and to the point. I have nothing to add. Lady Kelly will be excited enough by hearing from an earl to have the horses flogged to reach London as soon as possible. She's sure to want to interrogate us both so she can tell her friends all the juicy details. I hope she doesn't make you wish you'd never written to me."

"I could not do that," he promised. He smiled softly. "I have always wanted you to be happy wherever you found yourself. Now I get to make sure you always are. And Hero, too."

She laughed. "Was there anything else?"

"No, not really."

Lenore quickly jumped off the desk. "I'll make sure the house is ready for Lady Kelly's imminent arrival, then. Do you mind that I will offer Lady Kelly a room for a few days if she presses me to do so?"

"Not at all. This is your home as much as mine now, and you may entertain anyone you please here." He caught up her hand to prevent her going, though. "What will you tell her about us?"

"That you asked me to marry you," Lenore said with a heavy sigh. "She might want to know how the proposal came about. The where and when, but I can twist a simple story before she arrives and embellish only if pressed for more particulars. I'll not reveal the truth, even though she probably wouldn't be surprised. I'm not the sort of woman an earl should have married."

He frowned, disliking how she talked about herself. "That is simply not true."

"It's nothing *less* than the truth. A companion isn't that far removed from a housemaid. My prospects were never great." She smiled quickly, almost painfully. "But I am the Countess Carmichael, and I won't allow her to ride roughshod over me just because she made me help tie her into her corset each morning for the last year."

"Do companions help their employers dress? I thought a lady's maid would have that responsibility."

"Usually, yes, if Lady Kelly had kept one." She scowled. "But now, while I still have your attention, there is one other matter I'd like to discuss with you."

"Oh?" he said, brightening a little at her sudden interest in talking to him.

She clenched her hands at her waist. "I should like to consummate our marriage tonight. Is that enough notice for you?"

Price gulped, taken so entirely by surprise by the turn of conversation that he took a step back. "Tonight?"

She shrugged and looked down. "Yes. Unless you were engaged elsewhere tonight, then perhaps tomorrow night instead." She looked up at him expectantly, as if she were afraid of the subject and his response. "Do you have plans that cannot be put off?"

His mind went blank for a whole moment as the possibilities for the evening improved. If she was ready now, he'd have to... His mind reeled. "Ah, no. No, I don't have anything particular on my schedule for this evening," he managed to choke out.

She smiled quickly. Nervously. "Very good then. Tonight after nine would suit me, but before eleven if you please. It only takes a few moments, doesn't it?"

Price dug his finger into his cravat and tugged hard, fighting a blush. "Yes, it does."

"Good, until tonight then." Lenore smiled again and then fled, calling out for the housekeeper as she went.

Price waited a moment for the ground beneath his feet to become steady again, and then he shut his study door so no one could see his blushes.

Chapter Thirteen

⸺ ◆ ⸺

Lenore peeked out her bedchamber window, observing her husband's carriage pull up before the house with a calmness she hadn't expected to feel tonight. She was ready to make this a real marriage. Sylvia had given her enough information that Lenore felt well prepared to be bedded by her husband. And afterward, when he'd returned to his own bed, she knew how to take care of her body.

The grand clock downstairs rang out the late hour, and she took a deep breath and turned from the window. It was ten in the evening, and there was plenty of time for their rendezvous to happen. But she was aware that he had disappeared straight after their talk, and Lenore had had to pass the afternoon and most of the evening with Hero as her only company.

She was nervous. Was he nervous? She hoped he wasn't *too* nervous. She hoped her husband was experienced enough to teach her how to love him well.

Lenore had become accustomed to the quiet most nights, but it had weighed on her a little more than usual as she'd prepared herself for bed. Lenore had asked the maid to wash her hair earlier but had dismissed the girl as soon as it was dry, asking for her solitary meal to be served in her bedchamber. Once the tray had been removed, she asked for Hero to be kept downstairs for the night.

Lenore had brushed her hair until it shone and smoothed sweet-smelling lotion over her skin. She felt new, clean and fresh, and all her senses were awake.

After everything was done, and she was as prepared as she could ever be, she had started to consider again what sort of lover her husband would turn out to be. Sylvia had explained that gentlemen's habits when it came to desire varied considerably, not that Sylvia knew from personal experience. It was just information her friend had stumbled upon in her line of work and quietly shared with Lenore.

How men behaved in public was apparently no indication of their private intimate natures, Sylvia had said. Some men could be cruel. Others, as gentle as lambs.

Men could be shy, too, or bold, just like women. Lenore only hoped Price knew what he was doing, because she hardly did.

Carmichael stepped out of the carriage, head to toe in his usual impeccable dark garb. He crossed to the front door, but he did not glance up to her window on the way there. Why would Lord Carmichael expect his wife to be watching for him? It was not as if he had revealed any affection for her so far. He was only doing his duty, and so was she to a point.

But she did feel affection for him. Carmichael had once been a funny boy, and had been an amusing and faithful correspondent in recent years. His yearly letters at Christmas had made her smile so often. She still thought of Edenmere Park as her home. And now she was married to him, it would always belong to her.

But sometimes, when they met each other within the house, Carmichael looked at her with such surprise. As if he had forgotten Lenore was his wife. She was not about to let him forget she existed tonight.

The front door shut loudly, and Lenore jumped at the sound. She blew out a frustrated breath, annoyed with herself for overreacting. What was there to be nervous about besides a little discomfort as he took her maidenhead? She would never have given it to anyone at all if she had not married Carmichael. She trusted him to be as gentle with her as it was possible to be at such a time.

As the minutes ticked by and he did not knock on her door, Lenore tried not to imagine what she would do if he did not come to her bedchamber. It was difficult not to be worried when she could hear no movement beyond her room. Their exchange earlier in his study had been more uncomfortable than Lenore had expected, and it occurred to her later that he'd not been expecting her invitation at all.

She was ready to be bedded, but what if he didn't want to tonight…or any night? What if he'd changed his mind about coming to her bed? What if he took one look at her and fled?

She put her hand over her face as a thousand doubts filled her. What if, what if, what if?

Lenore moved to the mirror and looked at herself. The negligee she had purchased today was utterly indecent, and she covered up a bit more of her breast, though it didn't help very much. How long should she wait for him? Half an hour. An hour? All night?

She would not wait for him all night.

Lenore pinched out the candle beside the mirror, shrouding the room in more flattering shadows just in case he liked her better in the dark. Perhaps she ought to let him know she was ready and waiting for him.

Lenore turned—and nearly screamed.

Carmichael was standing just inside her door, and she hadn't heard him come in. He hadn't knocked on the connecting door. She was sure she would have heard that.

He put out one hand. "I didn't mean to startle you."

She blew out a breath. "You move very quietly."

"Sorry," he said, then bit his lip. His eyes were upon her, and Lenore turned more, relaxing her shoulders, showing him her figure the way she had practiced before her mirror.

His eyes widened, and he started fumbling for the door latch directly behind him.

"Don't go," she begged, stepping toward him, and then she heard the lock turn.

"I wasn't leaving," he promised. "I just needed to be sure the door had shut properly behind me. I wouldn't want my

valet to see you. No one but me should ever see you like this."
His voice sounded a little strange, thick and deep, and he
straightened before he crossed the room to stand directly
before her. His eyes held hers for a moment too long, and she
grew uncomfortable. But then his attention dropped to look
down at her body.

A whimper of sound escaped him, and his breathing
became ragged and fast.

Lenore's nipples hardened under his scrutiny, and she
suddenly found she was having trouble breathing, too.

His hand rose and settled lightly on her arm. "I apologize
for being late."

"Were you?"

"Unforgivably." His lips quirked, and then his eyes rose to
catch hers again. "I was half afraid you'd be in bed already."

"Lying in bed waiting for you might be what some mothers
advise their daughters on their wedding night, but it seems a
silly thing to do when I had invited you," she managed to
squeak out, fighting a blush. She shook her head, astonished
with herself. She was no wallflower. She was looking forward
to getting it over with.

He walked his fingertips along her arm. "I'm glad you were
not in bed. I'm glad I got to see you like this."

He leaned forward slowly, but he didn't kiss her lips.
Instead, he angled away at the last moment and brushed his
mouth across her cheek. His kiss was light as air, but she
quivered everywhere just the same. He dropped soft pecks
across her skin until she could feel his breath warm against her
throat. He kissed her there more purposely, until she shivered.

Lenore felt a tug at her waist as her husband undid the
satin sash holding her garment together.

It dropped to the floor, and the garment gaped.

Price's breathing roughed as he moved her hair behind her
shoulder, taking some of the gown with it. He'd deliberately
exposed her breast and shoulder just to look at her.

Lenore nearly swooned.

His fingers returned to her waist, and then suddenly she

was swept off her feet as he picked her up.

Instinctively, Lenore lifted her arms around his neck and held on to him. Price wrapped her up tight in his arms, and a groan left his lips. She felt him shake.

The bed was not far away, and she was grateful when he carried her there and set her down without dropping her.

He did not join her immediately but stood beside the bed, looking down at her through hooded eyes. When Lenore looked at herself, she quickly tried to cover up. One whole leg was exposed up to her hip and her quim was clearly visible.

Price stayed her hands. "Do that, and I'll only unwrap you again."

She considered what to do, and then left her gown gaping. "Very well."

A slight smile played over his lips, and his fingers trailed along the top of her exposed thigh and back down again. But then he eased the comforter away from beneath her and helped her move higher up the bed. In the process, he covered her limbs again.

Lenore sighed with relief at being decently covered. "Should you blow out the candles?"

"No." He smiled as he tucked a pillow under her head. "I've always been partial to unwrapping gifts in the light."

He sat down beside her on the mattress again and placed his hand flat on her stomach.

Lenore sucked in her belly, pulling away from his warm palm.

He smiled. "I'm not about to tickle you."

"I'd get you back if you tried," she shot back without thinking.

That made him laugh. It wasn't a sound she'd heard since they'd married. It made her feel warm all over and clever.

Lenore shifted her leg closer to him, bumping his thigh.

He laughed again and shook his head. "We'll get back to that."

But he did run just the tips of his fingers back and forth along her leg again before he stood abruptly.

His touch was thrilling, but she wanted more than that brief touch from him.

He turned away slightly and began to undo the buttons holding his robe closed. Lenore wet her lips, her breath stuck in her throat, but her heart was beating very fast as he unveiled himself oh so slowly.

She shivered when she got a good look at him naked, but this time her quim clenched as well. He was beautiful. Manly. Like a painting she'd seen once in a former employer's home.

Price had a dusting of hair on his chest that trailed downward. His limbs were long, muscular, and pale. The skinny legs she'd once teased him about were perfectly proportioned for the rest of him. His member was curved slightly to one side. It moved, twitched suddenly, and she looked up.

Her husband regarded her silently, his breathing loud in the quiet room. He was, to a fault, utterly breathtaking in every respect, and she was glad it would be him she gave her innocence to.

He moved toward the bed and set one knee upon the mattress. Lenore moved slightly to give him room to settle beside her. He looked so serious in the shadowed light that she reached out to brush her fingers across his chest to reassure him it was all right.

He settled on his side next to her, resting his head on one hand and placing his hand flat on her stomach again. Slowly, he moved his fingers beneath the edges of the sheer fabric covering her and slid them back and forth.

Lenore closed her eyes and let him touch her—tease her. She knew being aroused by him would make the bedding more comfortable for her in the end.

When his fingers found the curly thatch of hair between her legs, she let out a startled whimper and bit her lip. His touch felt better than she'd expected it could. When his fingers lowered more, she turned her face into his shoulder to hide the blush burning up her cheeks.

He parted her folds gently, sliding through more wetness than should ever be ladylike for an inexperienced miss to have.

She pressed her face harder against his hot shoulder and shuddered and shuddered. He played with her for a while, and Lenore squirmed and sought more of his intimate caresses. Harder. There. Again. Yes...

When he moved on top of her at last, she widened her legs instinctively to accommodate his hips the way she was supposed to do.

Carmichael buried his face in the crook of her neck as he wriggled and arranged their bodies until she felt the tip of him at the apex of her thighs. He was warm, solid...and her husband.

She threaded her fingers into his hair at the nape and opened her legs a little more, eager, just as he pushed forward hard.

Lenore hissed, caught by surprise, and dug her nails into his scalp. In that instance, what they were doing went from really feeling quite all right, to strange as he started moving against her, inside her.

The strangeness didn't last long.

Lenore clung to her husband, quickly swept up in sensations entirely foreign to her but utterly compelling. Her entire world centered within her husband's hot embrace. His skin slipped against hers, and the desperate sound of his breath against her ear made her shiver.

They'd made this a real marriage at last.

There was no escape for either one of them, no chance of annulment anymore.

Just as she was starting to feel wonderful, nearing the bliss that Sylvia had whispered she might feel, he suddenly stiffened and shouted out. His grip tightened on her head, pulling her into him hard.

Then he lay atop her, heavy and warm, protectively cradling her close for only a moment before he lifted up and away to fall on his back beside her, gasping.

Lenore lay still, satisfied that she was his wife even if her body felt empty now. Lonely without his touch. She had certainly enjoyed what they'd been doing up to a point, but she guessed that was over now. She wouldn't mind if her husband kept touching her that way but didn't know how to ask for more.

He sat up suddenly and swung his legs over the side of the bed. Lenore stared at the back of his head and at his hunched shoulders. She instinctively knew something was wrong by the way he sat there so long and so quietly. Was he displeased with her?

He turned slightly but did not meet her gaze. "Lenore?"

She gulped, suddenly worried. "Yes."

"Do you want me to stay with you tonight?"

She almost gasped at the question. Did she have that choice? Would he stay and make love to her again if she asked him to?

But if he thought to ask, give her a choice, she suspected that he didn't want to stay. The only way to know was to ask him. "Do you want to?"

"I shouldn't impose." He stood up immediately, circled the bed, and snatched his robe from the floor. She could not see him very clearly because the candles were almost out now, but she could see enough to know he could hardly look in her direction. "If you need me during the night, just call out."

Just like that, he was leaving? That was it? She gulped back her disappointment and smiled. This was the bargain they'd made, after all. "I will. Good night, husband."

He nodded. "Wife."

And then he was gone, the connecting door shutting quietly behind him. Lenore listened to her husband moving around in the next chamber with a heart that grew heavier with each minute that passed. Could Price really expect her to go to sleep after that experience? She wanted to talk to him so badly, but not if he didn't want to just as much. What happened next between them? Would she always be the one who initiated lovemaking or would he?

She drew her legs together and pulled the blankets high, remembering how he'd felt inside her. The touch of his hands on her body. The feelings he brought to life. She felt incomplete without him touching her now.

She ran her hand across her stomach, and then lower down.

Her fingers made her body quiver, but nothing compared to her reaction to Price. The need she felt before was just there, waiting to be rekindled again by him. She peeked at the door connecting her room to his. Could she call her husband back to continue making her feel the way he had? She should have asked him to stay instead of letting him go.

She lay there, staring at the ceiling until her candles spluttered and died, wracked with indecision and regret and listening for the sound of her husband returning to her of his own accord. She wanted to call out but she felt foolish. Her husband could be asleep by now, and she didn't want to wake him when he spent so little time at home.

But then she heard a door close in the hall outside and sat up. Footsteps crept past her doorway, their sound becoming fainter by the minute as whoever it was went down the main staircase.

Lenore scrambled out of bed when she heard the front door open beneath her room—and ran to the window just in time to see her husband climb into a waiting carriage and drive away from their home.

He'd bedded her and then left her straight after!

Lenore sagged. He hadn't meant his offer to come back if she needed him. And he must have known he was going out again if he'd kept his carriage waiting for his return.

Lenore turned from the window and let the drape fall closed, deeply hurt by his abandonment. She had not expected him to be enraptured by bedding her, but she never imagined he'd leave straight after he had done the deed.

Deep down, Lenore discovered she had expected more from him.

She put her fingers over her lips, unwilling to cry over him. Lord Carmichael hadn't really wanted her. He couldn't even kiss her. He'd only bedded her because she'd made him feel duty-bound with her coarse invitation and her provocative manner of dress.

He had run away, obviously repelled, leaving Lenore behind with a breaking heart.

She dragged herself to the washbasin, cleaned herself in the dark, and changed into a proper nightgown to sleep in. The negligee she'd bought to please her husband, she hid among her oldest dresses. She'd throw it away the first chance she got tomorrow morning.

Lenore climbed back into bed and pulled the covers over her head.

Feeling a little sore now, and dejected, she hugged the blankets tightly around her. For the first time since her marriage, she paused long enough to wonder what type of place it was that her husband escaped to every evening. Did he go to a mistress after all? Or was anywhere else better than here, with her?

Chapter Fourteen

Price delayed as long as he could the next morning, but he couldn't avoid Lenore forever.

They had shared a bed last night. He'd made love to her.

Despite his unspoken concern that it was too soon in their marriage, he thought bedding her had gone well—at least from his perspective. He'd harbored the tiniest doubt that he might have been capable of performing last night. She wasn't the woman he'd loved and wanted in his bed for so long.

But whatever doubts he'd entertained before opening that connecting bedchamber door had disappeared the moment he'd seen Lenore standing in next to nothing beside her bed.

After that, well, Price had found it hard to hold back, and it was unlike him to be at the mercy of his desires. He hadn't wanted to reveal how her unexpected appearance had inflamed him. It was her first time, and as she'd put it once, they didn't really know each other. He hadn't wanted to frighten her with the depths of lust she'd made him feel last night upon seeing her nearly naked. He'd forced himself to leave her bed, her room, after the deed was done, though it had cost him to not explain his reasons for going.

How could he consider himself a gentleman if he told her he'd wanted nothing more than to take her a second time last night?

Immediately.

However many doubts he might have had about himself, Lenore had seemed well prepared for intimacy between husband and wife. Someone must have told her what a wedding night would entail, because he hadn't had to explain one thing about what he'd done to her. She'd been a virgin, and tight, but not unprepared for the ways of passion between men and women. If he could have held out longer, she could have experienced bliss, too.

Price had but one regret about the previous night. He'd failed to pleasure his wife properly during the bedding. He wondered if she realized it yet. No doubt she would eventually, and think him a selfish cad.

He would not be next time.

But this morning could be awkward. He squared his shoulders and marched himself to the breakfast room doorway, prepared for awkwardness between them, but resolved to confront it head-on. He was ready now for the impact of having a desirable wife to bed. The next time he went to her, he'd keep his wits about him far better.

Lenore was seated at the table already, but there were no servants in the room right then. Only her dog was with her today, the beast staring with devoted bliss at his mistress the way all dogs did. His wife was dressed in a blue gown and held a slice of buttered bread in one hand, the paper in the other. Her delicate pink lips parted, and then she stuck the bread in her mouth so she could use both hands to turn the pages.

And then she went back to munching and reading.

Charmed to catch her in an unguarded moment, Price leaned against the doorway, studying his wife unobserved. This morning, she looked no different than when she'd first arrived in his home. Was that the same dress, too? He wasn't sure but it didn't matter. The temptress of last night might be gone now, but he knew she was still there, carefully hidden behind a tight bun and a prim, unfashionable morning gown.

Even now, his treacherous body reacted to her. Just being so close seemed to make his cock twitch and swell a little, eager for further bed sport if the time was right. But it *wasn't* the right time. Lenore would need a few days to recover before he went to her bed again.

The dog barked suddenly, and she sighed. "I don't bite, Carmichael."

"I might," he warned, and then cursed his traitorous tongue for revealing too much when her shoulders stiffened. "I'm starving."

"There's plenty," she told him without turning.

Hero ran to him, and Price gave him a hearty good morning rub as he always did. Then he strolled into the room, attempting to quell his desire, put it back in their proper place, and be his usual self once more around her. The morning room was no place to make love to a wife the night after her first time. Perhaps the third or fourth time. He didn't know how bold his wife might be outside of a bedchamber but he vowed to find out one day.

Her face was creased in a frown as he moved around the room to view her better. She looked a bit tired around the eyes but her customary smile was in place for him. "Did you sleep well last night?"

"Like the dead," she promised, folding the paper neatly and sliding it toward the head of the table, where a second place setting was laid out for him. She looked down at her fingers. "Did you sleep?"

"I don't sleep as much as I used to," he warned, hoping his comings and goings last night hadn't disturbed her.

"I'm sorry to hear that."

"I'm growing used to searching for the stars when I'm in London, when the air is clean enough to see them, that is," he replied, smiling. "You can get a lot of thinking done at night when it is quiet."

"Yes, you can," she agreed.

Sleep only came when he was deep in his cups. Last night he'd not indulged in spirits at all, and as always happened, restlessness had plagued him the minute he'd left Lenore's bed. He'd gotten up again and left the house to chase away the blue devils that haunted his night hours.

It was the first time in a long time he'd not gone to Madam Bradshaw's to get through the night, though. He'd just had his men drive him around, and when they'd complained the hour was growing late, he'd ordered them inside his coach and driven the team himself while they slept. He'd found the sound of the horse's hooves on the cobblestones soothing.

Price glanced over the sideboard and noticed everything he wanted to eat was in plentiful supply. This morning, because he'd not been drinking, he felt decidedly seedy. A hearty breakfast would certainly help and a few drinks later would fix him, but not yet. Not until after he and Lenore had talked today. After ensuring she was happy about last night, he'd retreat to his study and take away his restless urges with whatever drink fell to hand.

He looked at the table's place settings and hesitated. The breakfast arrangements had certainly become more elaborate since he'd married. The second-best dinnerware was on the table, along with a few foods he'd not eaten at breakfast for a long time. They were probably Lenore's choices, and he was glad she was altering his prior arrangements to make this their home. But there were things that had not changed, unfortunately. Price had always sat at the head of the table. It had worked well for a bachelor who always ate alone.

But he was a married man now, and in this marriage, he found he wanted to be nearer his wife for conversation. He didn't want to raise his voice to ask her a question. Occasionally, he might even find the urge to touch her hand— or elsewhere—unstoppable. If they were closer, it would make their marriage more like a good friendship and a pleasure for both of them.

He decided to sit in a spot directly beside Lenore—and moved everything laid out for him to the new location. Satisfied with the change, he loaded a plate himself then sat down to eat at last, feeling ravenous.

After a while, he realized he could have heard a pin drop in the morning room. He glanced sideways and couldn't help but notice Lenore wasn't eating. She seemed uneasy as she watched him wolf down his breakfast. She looked away just as quickly, and he set down his knife and fork beside his plate. "I do apologize."

"For what?"

"For ignoring you."

Her cheeks began to redden, and he sat back in his chair to look at her. He wasn't the only uncomfortable one sitting down to breakfast this morning, was he? Was she angry with him because he'd left her unsatisfied? Price had thought Lenore unaware of his failure when he'd left her last night. Had he been wrong about her expectations?

"Would you care for tea, my lord?"

He noticed she referred to him as "my lord" again, and had stopped using his given name.

She was definitely unhappy about last night, and he didn't know what to say that could fix it. Any course of action to satisfy his wife would have to wait until tonight and the privacy of her bedchamber.

She looked at him, one brow rising as she waited for his answer about tea. "No, thank you, Lenore." He smiled, studying his wife's blushing face, and was reminded of last night all over again. He could feel his own face heating up now. "Humphries will bring the coffeepot directly."

He dug into his food again before it grew cold, pushing aside his worries about Lenore for the time being. If he had hurt her too much last night, he was certain she would have said something or tried to push him off. He distinctly remembered her arms wrapped around him, pulling him closer instead of away.

He shifted in his seat and glanced at her again. There was that blush on her cheeks still, letting him know she was aware of him as much as he was of her. He would bring up the matter of last night with her when he could be certain a servant wasn't about to waltz through the door.

Sure enough, a minute later, a footman arrived carrying a tray. He settled both coffeepot and cup at Price's elbow and went away.

He heard a sniff and looked at Lenore, half afraid that his wife was weeping.

However, Lenore was leaning forward a little in her chair, nose twitching as she stared at the coffeepot recently set down by his plate.

He leaned toward her. "I take it you'd like some?"

"I've never had coffee." She sat back. "The women I worked for would never allow it in their households. They said it would straighten my hair."

He grinned. Lenore had lovely hair, long and thick, and with curls that had flowed out across her pillow in gentle waves as he'd made love to her. He would not allow her hair to be changed, or anything else about her, really. He longed to take her hair down right now but that would mean he'd also want to make love to her again. He couldn't do that, so he pushed the inclination ruthlessly from his mind. "Superstitious nonsense."

"Yes, there is a lot of that in the world."

Price laughed softly. "When I see friends tossing salt over their shoulders it usually makes me laugh. Not a good idea when it's the Prince Regent, though."

Lenore nodded absently as she continued to stare at his cup and sniff the air—enhanced with the scent of his freshly brewed coffee.

"Would you like to sip my coffee, Lenore? A taste?"

"I was considering asking for another cup to be brought in by a servant. I shouldn't impose on your pleasure." A sad smile curved her lips. "But I guess if you don't mind sharing what you have just this once, I could be persuaded to try a sip."

This marriage would be easier if they were more comfortable around each other and shared a great many things. Breakfast, amusements, and their beds. "Be my guest."

He filled his cup, added sugar, and stirred it well. Then he slid the cup along the table toward Lenore. "It can be very hot. Blow a little before sipping, or you might burn your tongue."

She pouted her pink lips and blew across the dark surface before taking a tentative sip, and then flicking out her tongue to taste her own lips.

Price shifted in his chair again as his body responded to the innocent gesture as if she'd blown across his skin instead. He couldn't tear his eyes from her mouth. The sight of her pink tongue was immediately provocative. He stared at her, wanted to taste her lips, too. They had not kissed last night, and he regretted denying himself that pleasure. He'd deliberately avoided her mouth because it had felt too personal and intimate. Still, the taste of her skin, the softness of her body under him, had been almost too much anyway. But he'd considered kissing her near the end. When he had got back out of her bed to leave, but he'd felt too awkward to try as he said good night.

He could kiss her now.

He leaned toward her just as she took another sip, and then she grimaced before putting the cup back down. "I wasn't missing anything, apparently."

Lenore pressed a napkin to her lips.

Price swayed back without kissing her. "It is an acquired taste," he murmured. At least he would never have to share his morning coffee with Lenore. Some husbands did, he'd heard, though soon purchased a larger coffeepot.

When Lenore attempted to pass the cup back, Price reached to take it from her. Their fingers brushed. That worrisome desire rose within him again, making him tremble. A need to take up her hand, pull her close and perhaps make her deliriously happy this morning grew within him. Was Lenore adventurous enough to make love here? He wasn't sure what Lenore required to be happily married, but he wanted to find out.

He fumbled the cup, spilling the contents over the tabletop. The hot coffee ran everywhere, and they both reared back to avoid getting any on their clothes.

Price swore an oath, annoyed with himself for his clumsiness. "What the hell is wrong with me?"

"It's only coffee," she murmured calmly. Lenore turned away, walked around him to the mantel, and pulled the bell for a servant to come clean his mess.

She returned and stopped at his side. "Don't worry about this. The servants will have the table sorted in no time at all and the table reset."

Price felt profoundly foolish for his clumsiness and outburst, and then she touched his hand, and everything became worse. His cheeks heated and his cock swelled, too, beyond his power to control himself.

He wanted Lenore—to hold her, kiss her, make love to her right now and never stop.

But his wife had been an innocent last night. She deserved better from him than ravishment.

Knowing she might see his arousal, and expecting embarrassment, Price snatched up the paper and put it across his groin. He turned away from her and walked to the window, pretending he was going to read the day's headlines while standing up as the servants went about their work cleaning up after him.

He knew he was being rude but he had not the words to explain how out of character he felt around her. She confounded him. He'd never expected to react to a woman like this in his life. Not even Angela had stirred such unprovoked desire in him the few times they'd managed to be alone.

Lenore spoke to a servant, her voice confident, calm, as she conveyed her instructions for the table to be cleaned and reset.

He wished he felt the same but he couldn't pretend to be unaffected by his wife. This marriage he'd arranged was supposed to have had a simple purpose—the getting of an heir and then pleasant, uncomplicated companionship for the rest of their lives. It helped that he found her attractive, but that was where the line had been drawn in his mind.

The intense desire Lenore stirred in him was utterly unexpected and confusing. He was not in love with Lenore, but he seemed to crave her now.

He shook his head, disgusted with himself. He'd promised to be a good husband, not a wild beast in the bedchamber with only one thought in his head. He only needed to join her in bed to give her a child, as promised. Besides that, he was supposed to live his own life, and she would, too.

Could their marriage be more than he'd arranged? Would she even want things to be different between them?

He slowly turned to face Lenore.

She was watching the servants at work, and not him. They were stacking plates onto a tray under her watchful eye. She nodded as they worked, casting quick glances in her direction and smiling at her encouragement. He'd never noticed them so happy when cleaning up his messes before. Lenore certainly knew a thing or two about how households should be run properly, and how to get the best out of the servants in her employ.

Maybe that was why he'd written to her in the first place. He certainly trusted her to do things the right way and understand the importance of the family legacy.

He suddenly couldn't wait to take her home to Edenmere Park. To see her stroll through those halls as its new mistress. Watch her with the housekeeper and cook as they managed the grand old house. When the day was over, they could stroll out onto the lawns together, breaking the rules his father had once set to keep them apart. As the only two children living in the house, he'd always been drawn to seek her out.

Price had married someone he didn't expect to love, but desired beyond anything he'd ever felt before. He was supposed to be in mourning for Angela, and the other poor women his godmother had murdered. He'd promised to love Angela forever on the night she'd died...but looking at Lenore, being married to her, brought those intentions into conflict.

He hadn't intended to give himself permission to be truly happy until a full year had passed, and yet...

Perhaps he was unsettled because he'd gone a long time without pleasure, first in waiting for Angela to accept his suit, and then because Lenore had asked for time. Either way, his wife was turning out to be quite the surprise to his starved senses.

She looked up suddenly, and he became lost in her eyes for a moment. Lenore dropped her gaze first. Her lips pressed tight together for a moment as she stared at the floor between them where Hero lay.

Lenore wasn't happy with him right now, and that was entirely his doing.

He had to get himself under control before the next time they were together. He had to find a way to explain himself and not embarrass her too much. If only the damn servants would hurry up and go away again, he might explain himself now over breakfast.

If they were alone, he could cross the room and pull her into his arms and make the mistakes he'd made last night a distant memory for both of them.

Lenore suddenly turned on her heel and headed for the open doorway. "I'll find out what's keeping the servant who went for a fresh coffee cup for you," she called over her shoulder.

And then she left without looking back at Price, and although he remained until after the servants had come and gone, Lenore did not return to finish breakfast with him.

Chapter Fifteen

Lenore did not see Carmichael for days after that awkward first breakfast after they'd made love. He kept to himself, and she didn't even have to try to avoid him. She'd no idea what he did with his days and nights, and she didn't care. Lenore was not curious about him anymore. He'd made his feelings clear. He didn't want to be with her beyond exchanging pleasantries over breakfast.

Lenore did check with the butler sometimes that her husband had actually been seen by a member of the staff. The answer was always yes, and she considered herself a good enough wife and to have done her duty.

Carmichael never returned to her bedchamber of his own accord, even though she'd not locked her door against him. Lenore still prepared herself each night, knowing it would take more than one night to make a child, and she wanted one, more than she'd believed possible.

Even without her husband around, her days were busy. She had enjoyed the challenge of making Lord Carmichael's home hers, but she was now running out of things to order to be dusted or rearranged. With free time on her hands, she was starting to ponder what her life should become now that she would always be Lady Carmichael.

She'd not had a lady's education but the time spent at the

Hillcrest Academy was slowly filling the gaps in her knowledge, as were the numerous books littering her night table. She devoured anything and everything to ensure she'd never embarrass herself when she met another lady in society.

Without her husband's involvement in her life, invitations to meet women of similar status had not eventuated. Nothing much had changed in her life except for her address and the quality of her garments.

Having her own carriage was quite a boon, though. She was able to go to places she'd only read about in the newssheets. She visited Albemarle Street often, ventured out on shopping expeditions with the Hillcrest cousins, and Hero, too.

As the days passed and conversations were shared with friends, she picked up a few things about the murders that she hadn't realized. Her husband had been involved with the capture of the culprit—his godmother, Lady Scott. It had been an ugly business indeed, more than she'd read about in the papers months later. Carmichael was rumored to have slain the woman in defense of a friend. He'd been injured, too, though he'd never mentioned that.

Lenore remembered seeing no scar upon him the one and only night he'd come to her bed. However, at the time, she'd had other things on her mind than looking for imperfections.

She still thought of their night together when alone, too, but it was with a trace of regret now for what might have been.

Aside from her husband's continued absence, her days were uncomplicated. Settled in a way she'd never expected to be in her life. She had made some new acquaintances through the Hillcrest Academy but they were not of the *ton*, not from the same circles her husband moved in. Unfortunately, most were male clients, but some were women, newly married like her and eager to make valuable connections.

She was expecting her first caller later today for luncheon.

Hero had been bathed again and Lenore dressed with particular care for her new station in life, choosing to wear one of Madam Du Clair's more modest creations. When the pretty new gowns she'd ordered from Madam had arrived, Lenore had put most away in wait for next season. What was the point of dressing seductively if her husband could hardly stand to be near her?

Today, she was wearing a simple cream muslin day gown embroidered with tiny blue stars all over. There wasn't a ribbon or awful flounce to be seen anywhere about her.

She primped her hair in the mirror, added a pair of tiny pearl earbobs she'd bought for herself, and smiled. She was ready to face whatever came her way today.

Despite the loneliness she sometimes felt, this marriage suited her very well. There was nothing better than choosing your own destiny or your wardrobe.

She dismissed her maid and departed her chambers, casting a brief glance at her husband's closed bedchamber door as she went by. She'd never ventured inside that room. That was her husband's private domain. That and his study, she felt, were off-limits to her.

The rest of the house was hers, and she simply adored adding personal touches to each room. Soon she would depart for their country estate, Edenmere Park, with or without her husband. She was going to take herself home and lay flowers on her grandmother's grave.

Carmichael hadn't mentioned when he would leave London, but Lenore felt she shouldn't have to wait for him to decide. Like many *tonnish* wives must, she considered her own feelings in the matter of her amusements. Perhaps she'd spend all of the winter in the countryside. Maybe she could even persuade the Hillcrest women to join her for a month or two. Sylvia mentioned her worries about their finances for the coming winter from time to time, though she'd refused Lenore's offer of charity or otherwise making an investment in their enterprise.

She let her fingers trail down the recently polished oak banister railing as she descended to the lower floor, enjoying the lingering odor of beeswax. The black and white entrance tiles gleamed brightly this morning, and the butler appeared as soon as her first steps on the tile sounded through the house with her dog leashed at his side.

"Good morning, my lady,"

"Good morning, Humphries," she said with a serene smile. Lenore and Humphries and Mrs. Baker got along very well. They knew her origins were humble, had known her grandmother by reputation, too, though they sometimes gently rebuked her when she forgot she was supposed to be the lady of the house and not the maid.

Hero panted enthusiastically. She held out her hand to the dog, and he came closer to lick her bare fingers. "Morning, my dear Hero," she said with a soft laugh as his tail began to wag quite fast. "Have you been a good boy?" She glanced up at the butler quickly. "I trust he was no trouble?"

"None at all, my lady. Lord Carmichael took him out for his run himself earlier, and he's been in the kitchen ever since."

"Well, that explains why he didn't return to me," she said wryly, putting her hands on her hips. She wasn't commenting on her husband but on her hound's absence. The dog had quickly realized where his best chance for a full stomach was, and had spread his attention about to all under this roof. "The prospect of food has ever been Hero's weakness."

The butler nodded as if he knew it already. "Cook has been warned not to spoil him and let him become fat."

"And he would if he could." She gave her dog a vigorous rub, wondering if she had time to take him outside again. However, she wanted to be sure everything was well in hand for her luncheon and took the leash from the man. "I appreciate your help with him. My last employer's cook had to keep being reminded not to overfeed him all the table scraps, and the footmen were no help at all."

"I shall keep a firm grip on the situation," Humphries promised with a grin. "I have placed today's letters to you on the drawing room writing table."

Lenore lit up with excitement. She'd always loved receiving mail. "Thank you," she murmured before she hurried to that room, taking Hero with her. Once in the room, she shut the door for privacy and let Hero off the leash. He immediately leaped onto a chair to watch her with his usual devotion.

There were a pair of letters, one of them from the lady meant to be joining her for luncheon today. Lenore ripped it open first. The lady apologized but had to cry off. Her mother-in-law had arrived unexpectedly and intended to stay for a few days. She did not want to impose by bringing the lady with her, too. Lenore was disappointed but completely understood. She penned a quick response and set it aside.

The second letter was from Lady Kelly. Carmichael must have sent his own man to deliver his message to have a response so quickly returned. Lenore wasn't entirely sure she wanted to read it, but she pried off the seal and flattened the pages on the desk.

Lady Kelly proposed a meeting later that day in Green Park, where they could talk in private away from her husband. She had come up to London immediately on receiving his letter, determined to make sense of Lenore's actions and the unexpected marriage.

Lenore didn't like the idea of having to explain herself to the woman, or of meeting her in private, either.

But as she read Lady Kelly's letter again, she thought perhaps she could meet with her here instead. Set the record straight, and ensure the woman aired no grievances in a public park. Lenore had left her employment without warning, and that had been rude. However, given the alternative had been staying and having Lord Thorne make trouble for her, attempt to seduce her, she would still have run away to somewhere else.

Lady Kelly should know the truth from her own lips and decide whether to act on her warning or not in the future.

At a knock on the door, Lenore quickly put her correspondence in a drawer. "Come in," she called.

Humphries hurried to her side. "Forgive the intrusion, but Lord Carmichael has callers and is nowhere to be found. They've asked if they might speak with you, instead."

"Who are they?"

"It is Lord and Lady Wade."

Lenore frowned. The pair had attended her wedding, but

she'd not known of them calling on her husband since then. He had spoken with Lady Wade at some dinner somewhere recently, though.

"I see," Lenore murmured, but she was uncertain if she should talk to them. She'd rather not hear from Lady Wade that she had spoken to her husband again, but it seemed uncivil to avoid them for that reason. "Do show them in."

Humphries was quick about it and brought the smiling pair into the drawing room to meet her.

Lord Wade bowed deeply. "I do hope you will forgive our impertinence for dropping by without waiting for an invitation. I've called before to visit your husband and found he's never been at home."

She winced inwardly. So her husband wasn't spending time with the Wades when he wasn't here. "Yes, he is a very busy man."

The husband and wife exchanged a glance. "I suppose he must be," Lady Wade murmured with a nervous smile.

"Please, let us not stand on ceremony." She gestured them toward chairs. "Would you care for tea?"

"That would be lovely, thank you," Lady Wade said quickly.

Lenore requested it and then cast her eye over her unexpected guests. They were people of means, obviously. Lady Wade, a beauty, and Lord Wade, well…he appeared intelligent and inquisitive as he looked about the drawing room. She cleared her throat. "I haven't had a chance to meet many of my husband's friends yet."

"Yes, so we've noticed," Lord Wade murmured. "I've actually been trying to catch him for some weeks now to discuss that very thing."

"Have you?"

"Merely the concern of a friend wishing to know he is well, I swear," Lord Wade murmured, eyes again flickering about the room then shifting to study her carefully.

His inspection made her uncomfortable. "I will let my husband know you wish to speak with him as soon as I see him."

Though she did not mention it might not be that day.

Lord Wade sighed. "It goes against the grain to dissemble, and so I will not. I must admit that our reason for coming here today was to satisfy our curiosity about your sudden marriage."

"Not that we don't think it's not the most wonderful news that Lord Carmichael has married a lovely lady," Lady Wade hastened to explain. "He is such a dear man, and we have worried about his welfare for several months."

"You have no reason to worry about him. I'm no impediment to his happiness, I assure you." She smiled at the couple, wondering how good a friend this pair really was to her husband if he was avoiding them. The wrong word to pretenders could cause the worst sort of gossip. Did they suspect she'd entrapped him? Taken advantage somehow? There was no way to explain how she came to be married to the earl that wouldn't be breaking her promise to him. How this marriage came about was private. How it went on was undoubtedly bound to be remarked upon.

Lenore would prefer to avoid any unpleasantness if his friends disapproved of her. "If you have concerns about my husband, I suggest you discuss the matter directly with him."

"I would if I could find him. Carmichael and I are both members of White's Club, though I have not seen him there for some time," Lord Wade told her.

That startled her. Her husband had gone out every night since her arrival in London, returning sometime in the early hours of the morning. She had assumed he'd probably gone to the club and met with friends. If Carmichael had been avoiding his own club, he must be going somewhere else at night. And he wasn't taking this particular friend with him, either. Perhaps he kept company with Lord Wharton more often now.

"It's not like him to be so elusive." Lady Wade sighed. "I first met Carmichael when I made my come out. He quite dazzled then. He was top of every ladies' list to dance with until…"

Lady Wade fell silent, looking at a loss for words now. So this pair knew about the murders, perhaps the victims, too?

Did they blame Carmichael the same way Lady Berry had? "I have heard, of course, of the tragedy, and know of my husband's long connection to the murderess."

Lady Wade nodded. "I was acquainted with all of Lady Scott's victims, of course. Many came out the same year I did."

"You lost friends?"

"Yes and no. You know how it can be among unmarried ladies sometimes. We're all vying for the same gentleman's attentions half the time and conspiring to make each other appear less worthy. Hoping to be noticed and singled out and married quickly." Lady Wade gazed adoringly at her husband. "That all changes when the right man comes along, of course. They become all we desire, and we forget all those little insecurities that once meant success or failure in society. I'm sure you've noticed your ambitions changed upon marriage."

"Of course." Lenore lifted her chin. She had never been that ambitious about finding herself a husband. Employment and a fair salary had been her goal all her life. Although she hated to pretend she had captured her husband's heart upon marriage, she would from now on. Lenore had his name, his title, and she would protect their reputation and avoid gossip spreading about them.

Lenore had been unprepared when confronted by Lady Berry, but it had been clear the woman though her unworthy of marrying Lord Carmichael. Lady Berry hadn't returned, but Lenore didn't think that was the last she'd seen of her. Perhaps this pair could provide her with information to use during their next encounter. "I wonder, do you know Lady Berry, by any chance?"

"We are acquainted," Lord Wade admitted. "Why do you ask?"

"Lady Berry came here not so long ago, very angry with my husband. I have not seen her since, but I do worry about her health. It must be terrible to lose someone you love, especially a daughter fully grown."

"I did know her daughter," Lady Wade confirmed. "Though not as well as some people I could mention."

Lord Wade took up his wife's hand. "She was well-liked by everyone. She had a very bubbly personality and was much in demand as a dance partner."

"Much like my husband must have been for you, Lady Wade," Lenore noted. "I never had the honor to meet her myself."

Lady Wade glanced at her husband, who shook his head. The lady smiled quickly. "Lord Wade and I have only recently married, just like you and Carmichael."

Lenore smiled. "Congratulations."

"Three months wed."

Lord Wade smiled at his wife fondly. "I faced stiff competition for her hand in marriage. I freely admit I was not her first choice, but hopefully, she'll still be happy when we're old and gray."

Lenore's smile felt frozen in place at the realization she was sitting across from an actual love-matched couple. Dear God. They must think Carmichael could love her, too. Lenore really had nothing in common with this pair.

She felt the acute need to send them away immediately. Carmichael could barely spend much more than five minutes in her company, and anyone watching them too closely might come to see that, she suspected. "Well, it was lovely to have met friends of my husband again. I will pass along your hope to see him soon."

She hoped not to see *them* again too soon.

She stood, and the pair did as well.

Lord Wade frowned. "Before we go, I should like to be blunt."

"I thought you were already," she blurted out, and then winced.

Lord Wade's lips quirked. "Please do not misconstrue our reasons for wishing to speak to you and your husband today. We really are both delighted Carmichael has married. He took the betrayal of his godmother to heart, and the murders…well, I knew he held himself responsible for those long before many realized. For many months, Lord Carmichael has been a ghost, hardly seen but sorely missed. It was painful to witness his grief, but his withdrawal from polite society only makes matters worse. People are talking about him, and not favorably, I fear. However, now he has married you; we both hope the gossips will move on to others. We feel certain he's put the past behind him at last and is making a fresh start."

"I'm sure he is," Lenore murmured, but wondered if that could ever be true. He was a ghost for her as well. At least she wasn't the only one he ignored. "Thank you for your honesty."

Yes, there was a sadness in him that she'd noticed and accepted. What else could she do but ignore the lost look in his eye? He didn't confide in her. Lenore hadn't chased away his feelings of betrayal and grief. He'd made a choice to marry when he'd been deep in his cups, chosen her because…well, she still did not really know why he'd picked her when he could have married just about anyone. He could have married for love. "I'll tell my husband you called as soon as he comes home."

The pair thanked her and turned away.

As she watched Lord and Lady Wade stroll from the room arm in arm, and finally step out of sight, she sighed deeply.

The continued distance between her and Carmichael was a ridiculous situation since it was his idea to marry in the first place. Lenore might have given up employment that would have become untenable, but was this situation, her unhappiness here, a better alternative? She didn't want to be a forgotten wife. She intended to become no shrew, either, that he couldn't talk to or trust with his private regrets.

She deserved to be his equal, and she wanted to be his confidant, too.

She needed him to be her guide in this new life they were making together. Her companion and lover, too, if she was to have her wish for children fulfilled. She was lonely in this big house all by herself.

With her luncheon with a friend now canceled, there was a kitchen full of food that would only spoil before tomorrow.

Lenore returned to her writing desk and pulled out a sheet

of paper. She wrote a brief letter to her husband, politely announcing that his company was required at home for dinner that night.

Let him ignore that, and she'd know where they stood.

Tonight she would confront her husband about his life, his friendships, his comings and goings. She'd figure out where she really could belong in his life, if anywhere, and if he wanted to be part of her life, too. If he did not, she'd stop waiting for him to come back to her bed of his own volition and make a schedule for that facet of their marriage.

She wanted her husband back in her bed tonight, and every night, until she carried the child he'd promised her.

Chapter Sixteen

———◆———

"Another drink?" Lord Wharton asked late in the afternoon.

"No, thanks," Price murmured, nudging his empty glass a little farther out of his reach. They were sitting in Wharton's study, going over an investment opportunity making the rounds. Price had already made his decision not to invest but Wharton was on the fence.

"Suit yourself," his host replied with a shrug before picking up the sheaf of papers he'd just been reading. "So what do you think?"

Price glanced at his copy of the documents. "What do you think?"

Wharton grimaced. "There's just something about the deal that feels a little off to me."

"Then don't invest. I'm not. It's not as if you need the extra income."

"True," Wharton agreed then tossed the paper aside. "I'll look into that mill closer to home."

"You're going home?"

Wharton nodded. "After Christmas."

"After attending Exeter's little gathering?"

Wharton nodded slowly. "Have you told him you're planning to go yet?"

Price shook his head. "I haven't decided if I am or not."

"Nonsense. When Exeter entertains, you always attend, just like I do."

He knew that. "I want to talk to my wife about it. She might have reservations."

"Afraid she'll not be made welcome by our acquaintances?"

He wasn't afraid of that. She'd find her place in society eventually, just like everyone new did. "I haven't talked to her about it yet."

"Dear God, man, why not? If you leave it too long you might find yourself bunked down in the stables."

"He does have more rooms than he knows what to do with."

"What woman wouldn't want to spend the winter in a duke's home? Besides, I'll be there."

Price rolled his eyes. "My wife will hardly be swayed by your presence."

"Don't been so sure. After weeks of being married to you, she might long for a change of scenery in the bedroom."

Price leveled his friend with a cold stare. "Don't."

Wharton chortled. "See, now we're getting to the heart of the matter."

"What heart?"

"The reason you're not at home tonight." Wharton pointed his finger toward Price. "You, my friend, are afraid to go home for some reason."

"I am not."

"I think you are, and it has something to do with your wife?"

"Ridiculous," Price said, reaching for his glass. It was empty, so he had no choice but to set it down again.

"Could you not perform?"

Maybe he could pick up the glass and throw it. "Wharton, you had better watch what you say next?"

"All right, all right." Wharton smirked. "But from what I've heard, most newly married men usually are eager to be with their wives more often than you seem to be."

"I am."

Wharton smirked again. "Is *that* the problem?"

There was a tap on the door and a footman rushed in. "I have an urgent message for Lord Carmichael."

Price flung out his hand, glad that the message might have

saved him from further impertinences. He was doing his best to curb his fantasies about Lenore, to no avail. But he was now plagued by desire instead of haunted by dreams of murders.

He read the letter quickly, it was terse and to the point. He was to come home for dinner. A private dinner. Just he and his wife to attend. "I am afraid I will have to take my leave."

"Nothing wrong, I hope?"

"Nothing, but I do have to go. Send me the papers about the mill if you want my opinion on that, too," Price offered, already heading for the door. His carriage was brought round soon after.

On the way home, he felt impatient. He found being summoned to dinner by his wife vastly unsettling. He should have expected to have to sit down with her again at some point, he supposed, but her demand for him to come home, made via a note she'd had a footman deliver, had caught him by surprise. For a moment, he'd thought something terrible had happened to Lenore, and he would have liked to have more warning than an hour to prepare himself.

He threw himself from the carriage before the steps had been put down and raced up to the front door. He used his own key to let himself in and immediately looked for Lenore. She wasn't to be found in the dining room so he paced the drawing room, waiting for her to come downstairs and join him.

It would be a quick dinner, he assumed. Just pleasantries and the meal, and then he'd probably go out as he usually did.

He did not want to abandon his wife, but he had not yet found peace with his attraction to her. There was also the unsettling discovery that he did not entirely trust himself. Time apart was for her own good, as well as his. Perhaps next year things would be different, no doubt. After the anniversary of Angela's murder had passed, and the others, too, he would set his mourning aside and make a fresh start.

Price finally heard her step in the hall when he had stopped right beside the door she would come through. He spun about and made a quick dash for the nearest chair and threw himself into it. His aim was to appear patient and unconcerned by her arrival—the embodiment of gentlemanly reserve and decorum.

He'd not want to frighten her with what he was really thinking.

Lenore swept into the room, and her eyes immediately fell upon him.

Her look was decidedly unfriendly. He took her in from head to toe, and quaked. Gone was the dull gown of the morning, and in its place was a woman of sensual beauty who drew him close even as he tried not to allow it. Lenore had a lovely figure, and she showed it off now to her advantage. What had happened to the sensible companion he'd married? She'd vanished to be replaced by a woman of style and elegance. A woman certain of herself.

She styled her hair differently now, too. Soft, unformed curls framed her face, giving her a lustrous quality he wanted to hold on to and never let slip through his fingers. Price's lustful thoughts roared back to life as he remembered the night he'd spent in her bed.

His attention was drawn to the lush rise and fall of her breasts above her elegant evening gown, and he tried to loosen his cravat in vain.

He wrenched his eyes upward to look at her face in a desperate bid to control himself.

Lenore's eyes were upon him still, and a slow smile appeared on her face.

Price clenched his fist by his side, but he wanted to dart across the room and sweep her up in his arms again and kiss her.

Take her to bed.

Make love to her all night.

She was not the spinster he'd wed but the siren he'd bedded by candlelight.

He gulped hard, fighting his need.

His wife looked…

…very well indeed.

She drew closer. "Carmichael, how glad I am that you could join me tonight."

"I was thrilled to receive your note," he promised, though he was still uncertain it was a good idea.

"I hope I have not upset your plans for the evening."

"Not at all."

"Good." She rubbed her hands together. "I had invited company for luncheon, but they could not join me at the last minute. The housekeeper had gone to a lot of trouble on my behalf, and I didn't want to be wasteful. It seemed a shame not to share at least one evening meal with you."

He heard the rebuke about his absence and jumped to his feet. "Shall we go in to dine together?"

He held out his arm to take her. Her touch was not light upon his arm, and the scent of her perfume curled around his senses, causing him no end of trouble. He hoped she did not look down before they reached the dining table.

But Lenore shook her head and turned him from the door, back into the room, with a pressure he found impossible to resist. "Let's talk first. Would you be so kind as to pour me a sherry, husband?"

Tasks. Price could perform those without needing his brain that was engaged in a battle with his libido. He also would have his back to her for several much-needed minutes.

He managed the feat of pouring and turned. Lenore had sat down on the love seat. There was room beside Lenore to sit with her, and when she patted the space, it was clear he was expected to join her. He wet his lips. "Where is Hero tonight?"

"Probably in the kitchen, making eyes at the cook again and whatever food is nearest to hand."

He nodded. He'd heard the dog had the kitchen staff wrapped around his tiny paw.

On legs that were not so steady, he managed to cross the room to deliver the drink to his wife.

Lenore patted the space beside her again. "Please sit here next to me."

"I... Yes," he said, and then gulped hard. "Of course."

He sat and crossed his leg over the other, which helped conceal the thickening inside his trousers that had never really gone away. He placed his arms so they too afforded cover for his tented trousers.

Lenore sighed.

Finally, he looked at her again. There was an expression on her face that he didn't recognize. "How are you?"

"Quite well." She tipped her head and studied his face. "*You* don't look well, though, husband."

"I'm fine," he promised.

She wet her lips. "When was the last time you slept a whole night through?"

"Not for months," he admitted. Sleep was the enemy, providing new ways to torture his conscience. He'd begun to fear it.

Lenore settled her hand on his sleeve. "Would you like a potion to help you sleep? I know a good one," she promised. Her fingers tightened on his arm. "Perhaps if you stayed at home tonight, I could be a wife to you."

Embarrassment heated his cheeks, and he knew they'd look red to Lenore. He turned to her a little, not wishing to refuse the kind suggestion outright. Potions were less effective than spirits. "I'll think about it."

"Good." She slid her hand up to his shoulder and across his upper back. He stilled. "Let me know after dinner, and I will mix it myself and put it beside your bed for you."

"Thank you," he managed to say, but a trickle of sweat slid down his spine as she put her other hand over his thigh. He stared at her tiny fingers and the golden ring upon one. She could be wearing the family jewels tonight, the rose-cut diamonds should have been hers long before now. But he'd forgotten to give them to her when they'd married. There were other jewels, too, but the diamonds had always been worn by the Countess of Carmichael. He'd not been a good husband by any stretch of the imagination to have forgotten that important fact. "What was it you wanted to talk about?"

She smiled. "I wanted to tell you that I met with Lord and Lady Wade today."

"Ah," he murmured. "The most unique match of last season."

"Yes, they mentioned they were recently married. How is that unique, though?"

"There were rumors that Wade was in desperate straights, and Portia, his now-wife, was an heiress engaged to another man."

"So he…"

"Ruined her? No, I don't think so. She was set to marry a duke, actually. She cried off, a week from the wedding. There was a bit of a scandal and a lot of criticism for her family. And then a week later, it was announced that she'd accepted Lord Wade's proposal, and they were married shortly after. There was a bit of nastiness circulating over the situation, what she'd done, the timing. You know how women come in for the most censure after they cry off. She had turned down a chance to be a duchess, and not many thought she should have. Although the duke himself was not well-liked in certain circles, Lord Wade was hardly considered a catch. I like him, though. He knows how to find out things and keep them secret, too. I can't blame the woman, really, for choosing such a man if he makes her happy."

"They were snubbed," she murmured. "People can be cruel."

"Wade, though, comes from an old family title and has wealthy friends in high positions of society, so it's all blown over now."

She nodded slowly. "They're fond of each other."

"I know he was always fond of her, but with just a viscount's title and lack of funds, he couldn't hope to compete with the Duke of Montrose in the beginning."

"So they surprised everyone and married because they liked each other? It's undeniable that they do."

He chuckled, feeling more at ease beside his wife. "Portia had something of a reputation for appreciating beauty in gentlemen and, well, you've seen her husband. No one was more surprised than I that they'd make a match."

"So they are *good* friends of yours? When they were here, they expressed concern about your absence from society. I wasn't sure what to say to them."

Price scratched his head. "I suppose they are friends, but not close ones, even though I invited them to our wedding. Wade has stuck his nose into my business before. Portia is a good friend of Lady Sorenson, my godfather's daughter. I think you might be acquainted with Anna. She came to visit Edenmere, too, when she was younger."

"I was never introduced to visitors unless they needed something fetched when everyone else was busy," she whispered, withdrawing her hands from him suddenly. "To be honest, I've always been surprised that you wrote to me after I took up employment."

"We were friends." He smiled, thinking how nice it was talking to Lenore. "You were utterly fearless to try anything I challenged you to do."

"Less so now."

"I don't know about that. You married me, after all." He leaned close to her. "The time I spent with you, when my father and your grandmother were not looking, are some of my best memories of home," he promised as he picked up her hand. "It's why you stuck in my memory."

"And here I thought you chose me for my scintillating conversation," she said with just a touch of sarcasm.

Price looked at her in surprise because it didn't suit her at all. He didn't want her to change. "I chose you because we always got along, despite the difference in our stations in life. Shall we go into dinner now?"

"Not yet. There's a question I need to ask you," Lenore said softly. "One that cannot wait."

"All right. What is it?"

She gripped his hand tightly. "Was it so horrible, making love to me? Does it sicken you to be near me? I can feel you pull away from my touch every time we're close."

"No!" he replied, horrified she'd think so.

"But you left me! Left the house that night even though you said you'd come back if I needed you. What else was I supposed to imagine?"

"I enjoyed…touching you."

She shook her head. "I don't believe you. I know I'm not truly beautiful or young, but surely, if you closed your eyes, you could…"

"Could what?"

"Pretend that I was anyone else but me."

Price rubbed a hand over his mouth, deeply ashamed of himself. In trying to control himself, he'd made Lenore doubt her appeal. "I would never do that to you. I swear you've done nothing wrong. It's me. All me."

Her lips settled into a mulish line, as if she didn't believe him.

He gripped her hand firmly. "I wasn't ready for how you made me feel that night. I'm still not."

"Then how do we fix this?" she begged of him. "I want a child, Price, and I need you to be my husband for that."

He lowered his eyes, but her fingers slipped under his chin, and she turned his face to hers.

"Am I not your wife? Is it not my duty to give you an heir? That was the deal we struck when you proposed. Or do you want me to seek the attention of other men, as other women have done, to spare your sensibilities?"

He grabbed her shoulders. "Invite anyone else into your bed and my seconds will call on them."

Her eyes widened a little in surprise at his threat. But then they narrowed in annoyance. "I won't be ignored anymore."

"I'm not ignoring you." He wet his lips. "I'm trying to *resist* you. There's a difference."

"Not from my perspective," she argued, but then her lips quirked. "I have never felt more invisible since I became your wife."

"You're not invisible to me," he started, and his hand rose to caress her cheek but he quickly pulled it away. "I see you. I am aware of you in a way that's unsettling."

A frown line appeared between her brows. "Wait. Did you say I was hard to resist?"

"Yes," he said. The frustration of his inner conflict was overwhelming at times. Just sitting here beside her taxed his resolve to take things slowly.

But as her smile grew wider, he realized he was in trouble. She liked that he was waging a battle—and that he was losing. "You are lovely and sweet, but inexperienced. I don't want to frighten you before we truly know each other."

"I already know you, Price. You're my husband, and your affections belong only to me."

He groaned at the realization that resisting his wife was beyond his strength after hearing her declaration. "As you wish, my lady."

Lenore shrieked as he swung her onto his lap and finally kissed her the way he should have the night they'd made love—with no plan to ever stop.

Chapter Seventeen

Lenore clutched her husband's wide shoulders, surprised and thrilled with her success. She was safe in his strong arms once more with no intention of letting him go tonight. Even if it was an unconventional place for him to be kissing her, and they risked being found by the servants, she wouldn't change a thing. Her bones seemed to melt on the spot to feel him so close, and yet so far. The sensations he had stirred in her before came rushing back, making her feel so warm and wanted and very desirable.

She returned his kisses eagerly, determined to be bold and leave him in no doubt of her interest in being his wife. When his tongue darted into her mouth, she mimicked him, rejoicing when he moaned. How strange that he'd thought resisting her was something he should have done. Tonight, she'd make it obvious that wasn't the case.

Price suddenly pulled back, his eyes full of questions. "Dinner?"

"I'm not hungry."

"I am. For you." He grinned, and then his fingers were in her hair. Pins fell and scattered willy-nilly, and she was too excited to care about decorum, or the lack of it. He was holding her lips to his in another devastating kiss, as if he planned never to release her. As if he couldn't get enough of her, the way she felt about him.

He drew back again, breathing harsh and uneven in the quiet room. "I'm sorry I made you think I didn't want you. I do. I can hardly think straight when you're near."

He touched her face softly, letting his fingers brush across her cheek. Lenore shivered, wiggling into his touch. He chuckled softly, and his hands moved down her back, sliding low until he cupped her bum. Price stood, effortlessly taking her with him, and crossed to the door. With one foot, he kicked it closed completely, and Lenore, realizing he meant to ensure their privacy, leaned down to turn the key in the lock so they would not be interrupted.

He walked to a long chaise and eased her down. "I think we'll be more comfortable here."

While she appreciated his consideration of her comfort, Lenore was reasonably sure she'd be comfortable anywhere Price wanted to kiss her. She leaned back and smiled up at him. "Come to me," she whispered.

Price swooped down to join her. But instead of her kissing her mouth, he pressed his lips against her throat, and then she felt the nip of his teeth.

Lenore moaned and shivered again. It felt so good. "So that's what you meant about biting me at breakfast after our first night together."

"You have no idea where else I want to do that, too."

"Show me," she whispered. So much of what he did to her felt new and unexpected that she couldn't wait to find out what would happen next. His hands tormented her body, grasping and sliding along her side as they kissed. It was lovely, but her fresh gown was going to be as rumpled as an old rag soon.

She found the buttons on his waistcoat and undid them slowly. When the garment gaped, she slid her hand inside, across his chest. Price was delightfully warm beneath his linen shirt. She curled her hand around his ribs and pulled him to her a little more firmly.

Price eased to one side and started lifting her gown above her knees. She stared at him, eager and excited that he again touch her sex. She dipped her fingers beneath the band of his trousers, anticipating, yearning for what he would do to her next. "Price," she whispered.

"I'm here," he answered, drawing back to look into her eyes.

She hadn't a question in mind. She'd just felt the need to say the name of her husband out loud once more. She looped her arms around his neck and wriggled until his body rested between her thighs. "I'm glad you came to dinner."

"This is all the feast a married man could yearn for." His lips fused to hers in an all-consuming kiss, and they were making love. Their bodies writhed against each other, even with the barrier of his clothes still an impediment between them.

She knew now what was to come, and when Price lowered one hand between them and fumbled with his trousers, she let her knees fall farther apart.

When he was finished, he caught her legs and wrapped them around his waist. He settled against hers, bracing his weight on his arms beside her shoulders. He toyed with her hair, smiling as he twisted it this way and that between his fingers.

When he dropped it, he wrapped his fingers over her hips and held her still for a moment.

The speed of their breathing merged, aligned, as they stared into each others eyes. Lenore smiled as the weight of what they were about to do again settled between them comfortably.

There were no shadows in this room. She had a clear view of her husband's face as he bent to kiss her lips softly. Lenore grasped the waistband of his trousers and tugged and pushed, sliding them down his hips as far as she could reach.

He chuckled softly and helped push them out of the way. Lenore spread her fingers over the firm globe of his backside and squeezed. Her husband shifted lower, moving out of her reach, and buried his face between her breasts. "These are my favorite."

He moved, kissing around the edge of her gown's bodice.

"All I see of you arouses me, Lenore."

Lenore was aware her nipples had hardened, and she lifted her chest a little, seeking relief from the sensation. A hot breath suddenly caressed one, and then Price's mouth was on her nipple, kissing and licking the hardened point, making her moan.

She looked down to see his eyes were closed as he suckled at her breast. It felt good, wonderful really, and he seemed to be enjoying himself there, too.

She cupped his skull, holding him close, but after a little while she felt discomfort. When she pushed at him, he released her breast with a grin but soon uncovered the other. He lavished attention on her until she was nearly boneless.

But between her legs, her pulse started to thrum.

When she pushed Price away from her breasts a second time, he willingly gave way and came back to her lips again. "Your lips are so kissable," he whispered, before kissing her again.

Lenore couldn't seem to lie still tonight. Kissing was lovely but not enough. Her husband held her body against his hips and the way they moved against each other excited her too much.

When her fingers found hot bare skin, she slid them lightly over his body under his shirt and coat, and then wound her arms loosely around his waist to embrace him. Lovemaking such as this was a pleasure that should last longer than a few minutes.

As her fingers spread over his muscular back, she felt him hot and hard against her inner thigh. A little more adjustment, and bare skin met bare skin at the apex of her thighs.

Price had rested his weight on his elbows. He looked down at Lenore, and she appreciated the small distance between them to catch her breath. She could move, fling herself against his heat or retreat at will in this position.

She slid her hand down his back until her fingers could spread over his firm bottom once more. She squeezed, and Price bent his head and moaned against her ear as his hips pressed against hers. Lenore widened her legs a little more, anticipating what would happen next.

She felt him there, hard at her entrance. With an encouraging wiggle, he filled her in one slow thrust that left them both gasping.

She writhed on him, squeezing his flesh, digging her

fingers into his bottom to hold him deep inside her.

But he rose up on his hands too soon as he withdrew. Price stared down at her, his expression open and unguarded. A smile played over his lips. She reached out one hand to cup his cheek. Price closed his eyes and leaned into her touch as he began to thrust with short jerks of his hips that made her feel incredible and warm.

She loved the way he lit up her senses, helped her feel she was part of him. If only it could last, but she had no delusions. They were man and wife, yes, but they might never be closer than this.

Lenore drew him back down to lie heavy against her, curled her arms about his body, and wrapped her legs about his hips tighter. This and only this mattered between them. What did it matter if he lived his own life as long as he could be drawn back for this?

The change of position brought Price deeper into her body, and she began to tingle, ache where they were joined, like the first time.

She tried not to gasp as his thrust became wilder, harder, and she clawed at his back, feeling desperate for something just out of her reach. She thrust her hips up to meet him, eager to explore more of that sensation.

"Yes," Price whispered against her ear. "You're excited. Don't fight against it. Use me."

She didn't know what he meant, but as they moved together, she began to understand what brought her the greatest pleasure. She loved his hardest thrusts, hated his withdrawal. Lenore eagerly rubbed her body against his any way she could to feel more of what she wanted. She enjoyed making love.

She loved the way Price made her feel like she was the only woman in the world who mattered.

Price suddenly grasped one of her legs, held it wide and high as he bucked wildly against her. He shifted her leg onto his shoulder, and then brought the other one up, too. He reared up on his knees and grinned.

She should have been so embarrassed to have her legs so high in the air, but it only excited her more to see that smile on his face. And then Price touched her between her legs—and her senses exploded wide and far.

She came down to earth slowly, gasping, to find Price had placed his hand over her mouth. He was still inside her, his chest heaving as he watched her from so far above. Lenore smiled a little sheepishly against his palm, and then flexed her hips.

Price shuddered, and then he was slamming into her again and again, only to groan and jerk as he found his satisfaction inside her.

Lenore smiled softly as he collapsed over her, heavy and hot. He hugged her close, as if she was dear to him, and then kissed her cheek softly. It had been good for both of them this time, and that was all she'd ever hoped for when she'd decided to marry him.

A little while later, when her body had cooled, Price was still entangled with her on the chaise as if he didn't plan to move anytime soon. His arm was heavy across her waist, and she was loathe to dislodge him. However, there was the matter of their dinner growing cold. The servants were waiting to serve them, too.

"We should get up," she whispered.

"I *am* hungry," he said.

Lenore sat up immediately and swung her feet onto the floor. "Why didn't you say something?"

His fingers closed around her upper arm. "I've had my first course. We could have the seconds upstairs in your bed, if you like." One of his brows lifted high.

"You want to eat dinner in my bed?"

He sat up slowly and pressed his lips against the back of her neck. "I want *you* to be my main course and dessert."

She looked at him over her shoulder. "How do I explain that to the servants?"

"You don't. I'll tell them I have other plans tonight for our dinner. You run upstairs and hop into bed. I'll be with you as quickly as possible."

It seemed a very scandalous thing to do, but they were married, and she'd not spent enough time with her husband yet. She stood, wobbled a little on weak legs, and hurried to straighten her gown into some sort of order.

Price stood too and buttoned his trousers but left the rest of his clothing undone and untidy. A knowing smile crossed his lips. "There is no way the servants didn't hear us making love."

Lenore blushed.

Price pulled her close to his side suddenly. "That's how it should be between us from now on. No more nights spent apart."

Lenore nearly swooned to hear Price promise her the moon. A future together.

He caught her hand and pulled her toward the closed door. He stepped out and, after a moment, tugged her to join him. She hurried for the staircase and rushed upstairs, hearing only her husband's steps moving away as she headed for her bedchamber.

Inside her room, she undressed quickly and pulled on a robe. She pulled any remaining pins from her hair and brushed it out before her mirror. By the time she was done with her preparations, her husband was stepping into her room—completely naked and holding a large tray.

She sighed, and felt her body quiver again as he set the tray on her writing table. "Reinforcements for later consumption," he promised.

"Later," she whispered.

"Much later." He joined her quickly and urged her toward the bed, removing her robe before pulling back the covers. As Lenore slipped between crisp sheets naked, she marveled at how easy she found it, being alone with her husband. She draped her arms around his shoulders when they came together again, and when he kissed her, she closed her eyes and thought only of making them both as happy as possible the only way she knew how.

Chapter Eighteen

White's Club had been one of Price's favorite haunts in recent years, though he hadn't spent much time here in the last six months. It was a place where gentlemen could meet and discuss politics. Argue, plot, and scheme. Price had felt at home here for as long as he'd been a member. There was always something to do worth hearing about.

He strode inside in the late afternoon, a spring in his step and a smile on his lips. He was self-aware enough to know he'd not wanted to be around other lords for a long time until today. That was no longer the case. He found he was looking forward to the future with hope in his heart once again.

A future with a wife who'd let him make love to her anytime of the day or night for the past five days.

"Look here, it is Carmichael, come to White's at last. We thought you'd gone to the country," Lord Newbottom exclaimed as soon as Price made it inside.

Newbottom and his group were on the verge of leaving the establishment.

He smiled and waved them past, eager to find his closest friends, who expected to meet him here. "No. I haven't left London. Obviously."

"But where have you been, my good fellow?" Newbottom sang out, trying to detain him a few minutes more. "You missed a great party at Lady Henry's last week."

"I was otherwise engaged," he called out, because he had spotted Wharton and Scarsdale just ahead and hurried his steps in the other direction. He clapped both on the shoulder. "Gentlemen."

"My God, he is alive," Scarsdale exclaimed, stopping in his tracks and staring.

Price laughed as they made their way into the dining room and found an empty table. "Why wouldn't I be alive?"

"It's been five days since we've seen you. We were about to mount a search and rescue," Wharton remarked.

"I hardly needed rescue," Price murmured as he gave the hovering footman his order. His time at home had been well spent. "I was with my wife."

Scarsdale choked. "Every moment of every day?"

Close to it. "We had a lot to discuss."

Not that he could remember now exactly what they'd talked about. None of it had been truly important.

His drink arrived and he took a small sip, hiding a smile. He felt good. Rested. He'd been sleeping a lot lately, and drinking far less each day than he'd done in the last half year. He rubbed his hands together. Eager to enjoy the night with friends. "So what have I missed?"

"Nothing important. Wharton's mistress left him at last," Scarsdale murmured quietly.

"It was a mutual leaving, thank you very much."

Price smiled slowly. "Did she demand you give up all other women or expect you to marry her?"

Scarsdale snorted. "Both."

Price pressed a hand over his heart, feigning shock. "She expected you, of all people, to be monoga—"

"Don't even think that word," Wharton warned, raising one finger.

Despite the loss of his long-term mistress, Wharton looked to be in good spirits.

Price knew the benefits of committing to just one woman outweighed any sacrifice. He doubted he'd have the energy to devote to two women, especially if they were anything like his wife in bed. He sipped his drink, intending this glass to last him longer than any other had recently. "There's nothing wrong with a narrower focus."

"I suppose not—for someone like you," Wharton murmured, tossing back a healthy mouthful of his and asking for a refill immediately.

"Like me?"

Wharton looked at him sourly. "Married and besotted."

Price looked away. Was he besotted? Satisfied, certainly. He had to admit he was only here because Lenore had a prior commitment to meet with friends and hadn't invited him to join her. If she had stayed at home, he never would have come to his club at all. It was too early for Bradshaw's, and he'd no plans to go back there ever again.

They hadn't indulged in sex every night and day, though they'd had a lot of it. Thankfully, he no longer felt awkward around Lenore, and having been so well satisfied in her bed, he had found the control he'd thought he'd lacked wasn't even required anymore. Mostly they'd stayed at home together in the same room, talking and reading. Playing with her dog and deciding, together, that they should obtain another animal in the spring.

He could be very happy being married to Lenore, so long as nothing upset the balance.

Wharton nudged Price's foot. "It happens to all married men eventually."

"What does?"

"Smiling without good reason. Introspection instead of conversation." Wharton sat forward, an evil grin on his face. "What you *did* miss of note this week was Scarsdale admitting he's become a client of that Hillcrest Academy you were telling me about."

Price didn't bother to hide his astonishment as he stared at Scarsdale. "Good lord, why are you going there?"

"Mother insisted," Scarsdale answered but sank into his chair, looking highly uncomfortable.

Price laughed. "I can't believe you're still doing what your mother tells you to do?"

"You're probably doing what your wife says these days," Scarsdale shot back a bit defensively.

Price shook his head. "My wife has made no demands whatsoever."

"We haven't seen you in days." Scarsdale's glare intensified. "You stayed at home with her to stay on her good side, and that's my point. If I refuse mother, she threatened to toss me out."

Price laughed, along with Wharton. "Isn't it time to get your own place?"

"Out of the question. If I trusted my mother's so-called friends, perhaps I could leave her unattended. But I don't, and I also don't want to talk about it again tonight."

Price exchanged a glance with Wharton and let the matter drop. Family brought difficulties. Price was lucky he only had Lenore to worry about.

They ate a companionable dinner, joined by others later. There was a rousing good debate on the merits of marriage and mistresses. Price freely admitted he had no strong opinion against mistresses but plenty to say on the value of a wife.

It was good to be among friends again, but he found himself aware of the time and was counting the minutes until he could go home to her.

When they rose to take their leave of White's, Wharton invited him to join them at Madam Bradshaw's for drinks and amusements, as usual.

"Not tonight," he murmured.

"Rushing home to the little woman," Scarsdale teased with a hearty laugh.

"Not rushing, but I am keeping a promise."

"Leg-shackled," Wharton said to Scarsdale as the pair headed out to meet his carriage. "We'll drop him safe and well at his front door. Make sure he doesn't run the whole way."

When Scarsdale laughed along, Price winced, but he did follow them out and make use of his friend's conveyance. His home was only a little out of their way.

"So what lie did you tell the Hillcrest cousins to get through their front door?" he asked Scarsdale. "It must have been a good one, because I know you need no help when it comes to charming the ladies."

"You'd be surprised," Wharton teased.

"I mentioned my stutter," Scarsdale admitted.

Price frowned. "You don't stutter."

"I do," he admitted. "Or I did when I was younger. Every now and then, in certain circumstances, I feel it coming back."

"What sort of circumstances?"

Scarsdale pressed his lips together tight.

Price glanced at Wharton. "Not at White's."

"Not at Bradshaw's," Wharton noted.

"Not anywhere I've been with him."

"Or I," Wharton said as he leaned against the window to look fully at Scarsdale. "You know there's only one place I can think of that I've never been with him."

Price frowned. "Where's that?"

Wharton's grin widened. "In the bedchamber, of course."

Price choked, trying not to laugh out loud. "Neither have I, and never plan to."

Scarsdale scowled.

Wharton slapped his thigh. "Well, isn't he an odd fellow. He actually talks to his lovers."

Price shook his head. "Many men do, I'm sure."

"Talking leads to discussing feelings, or the lack of," Wharton said, smiling, but then a frown crossed his face as his carriage came to an abrupt rough halt. "Devil take it!"

Price righted himself and heard shouting outside. He glanced out the nearest window while Wharton opened the trap door to the groom's perch above him. "What is it, Merrow?"

"Another carriage blocking the road, my lord. We're not the only one, either."

"For heaven's sake, hurry them up."

Scarsdale opened the door and poked his head out. "Can't see anything from here."

Just as Scarsdale was about to shut the door, a woman

called for help and a dog began to bark.

Price recognized those voices. They were his family.

He burst out of the carriage and stumbled a few steps as he looked around wildly for Lenore.

Ahead was chaos. People were coming out of their carriages and the nearby houses to watch the spectacle unfolding on the street.

Wharton strode forward to take charge, pushing his way past anyone who got in his way. Price followed, desperately searching for Lenore in the crowd all around him.

The crowd thinned, and he saw a woman was lying upon the road, unmoving and still. Her back was to him, but her hair was dark like Lenore's…and her body was twisted about at an unnatural angle.

He froze—and then his heart started to beat so fast that his ears rang. A hollow rushing filled him, much like it had on the night he'd found Angela's body.

He placed one foot in front of the other until he was standing a yard away from the still form, but his heart was in his throat.

In the failing light, he could see the woman's clothing was of good quality.

The sounds around him grew dim as he stared.

He couldn't move.

Couldn't believe the woman he loved had been lost again.

"Lord Carmichael. Price!" Lenore's voice soared over the din, and he snapped his head around toward the sound. It took a long frantic moment to find the source.

Lenore stood in the crowd with Hero at her side, waving at him.

She was safe and well.

Unharmed.

He dragged in a life-giving breath then looked down at the body lying on the road. It was not his Lenore, but another woman. A complete stranger.

His heart restarted, almost painfully. He rushed toward his wife and dragged her into his arms to hold her close to him as hard as he could. "I thought I'd lost you, too," he whispered.

Lenore looked up at him and cupped his face. "I was coming home when we had to stop. Like you must have done."

Price kissed her lips, and then turned his head to place a soft kiss on her wrist over her pulse. He couldn't lose Lenore, too. Not now.

He realized he was reacting badly and eased his grip on her to look at the scene again. The woman was much older than Lenore, thin but well dressed. The quality of her clothing was the only detail he'd observed correctly.

Lenore turned in his arms. "They say he *meant* to kill her!"

"Who?"

"That man over there."

A young man was being restrained on the other side of the street. He was resisting but surrounded by men and by women who were shouting at him. He likely wouldn't escape them but he was certainly trying.

The man's jaw was set, and his face showed not a shred of remorse for the victim.

Price suddenly remembered Lady Scott had seemed much the same when she'd been confronted about her crimes. It was a memory that haunted him sometimes, how she'd killed and actually shown pride for what she'd done. She'd seen nothing wrong with her actions, just as this fellow didn't seem to yet.

"Another murderer," Price said as bile rose up his throat. "There's nothing we can do if they have her assailant."

Around Price, the talk rose in volume. Someone said they had seen it all. Someone claimed the pair had argued. Another professed to have witnessed the moment the old woman had been pushed into the path of the oncoming carriage. He noticed the team of horses and carriage stopped just beyond the victim.

The truth would be harder to discern when morning broke tomorrow. He'd spent some time working with the good men of Bow Street. People should not be allowed time to think about what had happened and change their stories. Unfortunately, every retelling of this tragedy would make it a more interesting tale. It was important to collect as many statements as possible so some version of the truth could be decided tonight.

Wharton and his men were wading through the mass of onlookers, pushing some back, sending others back to their homes and moving those with statements to give into a line.

He looked around him again, saw a poorly dressed fellow with his head bowed, cap in hand, talking with someone he recognized from half a year ago. The man was being questioned by a shady fellow from a scandal rag. He was shaking his head, but the man kept pestering him. Believing it to be the coachman who might have been driving, and most likely blameless, he was also the best witness to the victim's final moments and had to be interviewed.

Price reached out to Wharton and tugged his sleeve. "You should find out what the driver has to say before he's persuaded to sensationalize his story," he whispered.

"Where is he?"

"I think that will be him over there, with a fellow from the newspaper."

Wharton sent men to bring the coachman to him immediately.

Another familiar face came into view and Price reached for Wharton's sleeve again to get his attention. "Davis is finally here. You'll find him competent."

A woman started screaming and fighting her way through the crowd to reach the victim.

He paled, remembering the anguish of his godmother's victims families all too well. The young woman fell over the corpse, crying for her mother and begging her to wake up.

Wake up? She never would.

He pulled Lenore back a step with him. "Come."

Wharton frowned at him. "You're not staying?"

"No. I've seen enough death and loss to live without more." He kept one arm around Lenore's waist. "I'd better get her home."

Wharton searched his expression, and then nodded. "All right then. Go. I'll have one of my men inform her coachman."

Price looked for Lenore's carriage and found it blocked by the scene, too. It might take some time for her carriage, or even Wharton's, to be free of the traffic. The night wasn't particularly cold and the sky was clear. "We'll have to walk, I'm afraid."

"All right," Lenore said, and then drew her shawl tighter around here shoulders.

He bid Wharton goodbye and then guided Lenore round the onlookers to the empty pavement beyond. He kept one arm around his wife, holding her close to his side as they began the trek home. "Are you all right, my dear?" he asked of her.

"I am. It's not the first body I've seen, unfortunately."

"Nor I. Death is never pleasant."

"No, it is not." Lenore wiggled for her freedom but reached for his hand and squeezed it tight. "Were you reminded?"

He understood what she meant without asking her to clarify. "Yes."

"Do you want to talk about it?"

"Not tonight." Not ever. The panic he'd felt when he'd believed Lenore had been injured matched what he'd felt over Angela Berry six months ago. He never wanted to worry about Lenore like that again.

They may have started their marriage in the worst way, but already, he didn't think he could live without Lenore in his life.

Price lurched to a stop as he remembered an earlier thought. He hadn't thought he could love anyone as much as he had Angela—but he cared about Lenore a great deal more than he'd thought he might.

The pain of Angela's loss had never been too far away. But now...it didn't hurt so much anymore when he thought about losing her.

Lenore tugged on his hand and his vision clouded. He looked away for a moment, striving to master his emotions. He'd once thought falling for another would mean betraying Angela's memory. Had his love been too brief, too slight, to last forever?

Lenore squeezed his hand again, and at her encouraging smile, his heart soared and he took a step forward. She urged him along toward home and he followed in a state of shock.

His home was *their* home now.

They made love there.

He loved Lenore there.

He loved her.

Price nearly fell over his own feet there and then.

He had done the unthinkable.

He'd fallen in love with Lenore somewhere along the way, when he'd promised himself he never would.

Chapter Nineteen

———◆———

Lenore waved goodbye to her friends from Albemarle Street the next afternoon and climbed into her carriage, headed for home and her husband. Hero had been too energetic today to make shopping on Bond Street an enjoyable experience for her. If not for Aurora's insistence they persevere in their search for the perfect feathers for her hat, Lenore might have given up hours ago.

The grooms seemed to be keen to get underway, cracking the whip over the team and laughing together. Lenore had made a point to learn all the servants' names from the moment of her marriage but had little excuse to use many of them.

She listened now, and learned the servants had a small amusement planned for their evening below stairs. She quickly deduced there was a birthday to celebrate and dancing to be had. For a moment, she felt a little envious. Once Lenore would have been part of that merriment, but those days were behind her now. She was a lady, and expected not to notice what the servants were doing in their own time or feel nostalgic for the simple way her life had once been.

She had no reason to complain about her situation. She was a married woman, a countess, and she still had her own friends. Old friends who treated her only a little differently now that she was a countess. She supposed eventually she'd make friends within the *ton*, but she was in no hurry to become part of the rarified world her husband moved in. Amusement within the *ton* was by invitation and rarely spontaneous. Nothing at all like the fun the servants would have that night.

Lenore folded her hands in her lap and considered again the good she could do now with her new situation. She had bought nothing for herself that day, having already received a surfeit of new possessions upon her marriage and after, when she'd hatched her plan to seduce her husband, but she thoroughly enjoyed shopping for others, too. Aware that the Hillcrest cousins' finances were predicted to decline over the coming winter, Lenore had asked if the ladies would mind if she purchased each of them a gift. The Hillcrest cousins were proud women, and she'd known not to offer too much. She had settled on giving them something entirely practical and entirely useful for an early Christmas gift. Lenore had suggested new winter cloaks for each of them and had not been turned down.

Hero tried to burrow under her hands, and she laughed again. "Well, that is my friends sorted out for Christmas," she told Hero, giving him a vigorous rub. "They'll have those warm cloaks by next week and I won't have to worry so much about them catching a chill when they go out. Am I very bad not to have mentioned the hats, muffs and scarves Madam will secretly add to my order and deliver, too? What do you want for the holiday? A nice juicy bone?"

Hero licked her face.

She laughed and pushed him away, wiping at her cheek. "Oh, you are unstoppable today. How about a walk in the park before we head home?"

As soon as she said *walk*, Hero started barking and bouncing around the carriage like a puppy. She tapped on the roof and asked the coachman to change direction for Green Park instead. She'd only keep the grooms out a little while longer, and then they'd have their party to go to. It would probably go on all night…or she hoped for them that it might.

Green Park should be quiet today, and Hero would bother no

one as he dashed about and expended his abundant energy without getting in anyone's way or knocking over inkpots. If he wore himself out now, he'd be less trouble for the servants later.

She got out with him when they stopped but one of the footmen, Peter, attempted to accompany her onto the grassy lawn. She waved him back. "I hardly need an escort, sir."

"Lord Carmichael expects it, my lady. It wouldn't be proper to let you go walking alone."

Lenore sighed. Since her marriage, she'd found the ever-present servants hard to adjust to. They were not following her out of devotion but out of duty. She understood why they were nice to her. She had been one of them once, and knew they were only doing what they were told so they would not risk their position. However, today, she'd just like to enjoy some time alone with her dog in the outdoors. "We'll just stretch our legs and be back before you now it. Wait here, please, Peter. Do not follow me."

Although the fellow didn't look happy, he had no choice but to follow her orders.

Lenore strode off, with Hero darting around her excitedly and barking.

She tossed a stick she found on the ground and Hero gave chase, bringing it back for a second throw and then a third. She started to meander through the park, enjoying the time alone and letting Hero chase after her and the birds.

When she went home tonight, she hoped to make merry herself with her husband. They'd become very close in recent days, and that could only improve. She felt there was no one in the world who could have understood her better right now than Price. She was often overwhelmed by her new position, but he promised she would become used to this life of ease soon enough. Never in her wildest dreams had she imagined to marry into the nobility. But she was the wife of an earl and counted her blessings daily.

Price was a good man. A wonderful lover, and he was becoming a dear friend. She smiled whenever she thought of him...and of falling asleep in his arms at night. He was still never in her bed when she woke, though. He didn't want to disturb her rest. Lenore didn't mind but sleeping late had never been her way or even possible as a paid companion. Besides, everyone needed privacy. Especially husbands and wives.

It wasn't long before she noticed a pair of women walking toward her and Hero. The sun was slowly sinking behind them, and Lenore was almost upon them before she recognized Lady Kelly walking beside Lady Berry. Lady Kelly hadn't called or responded to her letter. Lenore was quite surprised to see her and with Lady Berry of all people.

Lenore came to a complete halt.

Lady Kelly smiled at her. "Why, Miss Griffin, what a remarkable surprise."

She blinked that Lady Kelly had used her former name, when she had most definitely written to Lenore, and used her title, too. Deliberately leaving off her title in front of Lady Berry was an insult and could not be allowed. "It's Lady Carmichael now, my lady."

"Oh, how forgetful of me." Lady Kelly tittered, looking anything but contrite. The hair on the back of Lenore's neck began to rise when she gestured to the other woman. "I understand you are already acquainted with my old friend, Lady Berry."

"We have not been formally introduced," Lenore said quickly. Her husband had not thought an introduction was required, and Lenore wasn't sure she needed to be friends with this lady. Lady Berry wasn't a happy person and certainly was no friend of her husband's. The last occasion she'd met with Lady Berry had not been pleasant.

Lenore brought Hero close to her side when he made a sound and fixed his leash to his collar. If there was a scene to be made, she wanted to ensure her dog behaved himself.

When she stood again, Lady Berry stared at her in such a way that Lenore began to wish she'd not left her servants behind.

Although unwanted, Lady Kelly performed the introductions anyway—and included the fact that Lenore had acted as a paid lady's companion for many years. Lenore felt certain she phrased the introduction that way to cause Lenore embarrassment. Was she offended because Lenore suddenly outranked her?

"So you're the poor girl who made a match with that unfeeling cad."

Lenore shook her head. "My husband is no such thing. He's a wonderful man."

The woman smirked. "You should speak to the families of the victims of his godmother before rendering an opinion on his character. Their daughters were murdered, and all because he pursued them."

Lenore blinked. "That is not true."

"Oh believe me, it is indeed the case. Lord Carmichael could and *did* have any lady he wanted. Those poor girls never stood a chance once he turned on the charm. Even my child fell victim to his scandalous ways."

Lenore lifted her chin. "He would never lead a lady on."

Lady Berry grimaced. "That statement just proves how little you know your husband."

"I've known him all my life."

Lady Kelly shook her head. "He has deceived even you, then."

"He has not. Lord Carmichael is kind and caring. A true gentleman."

"He's a scoundrel!"

A scoundrel would not wait for his wife to be ready for marital relations between them. He would not shield her from society until she'd adjusted to her new role.

Lady Berry squinted at her. "Do you think he loves you?"

Lenore balked at answering. He'd never said as much, but there were times when they were together lately when he'd look at her and smile in such a way that led her to hope he did care for her. Last night they'd made love, and he'd held her tight by his side, their fingers twined together. Surely he wouldn't do that if he felt nothing for her.

Lady Berry drew close. "He doesn't love anyone but himself, and the sooner you realize that the better for you. He is incapable of complete honesty. Why do you think he chose you? A paid companion, a servant to ladies of higher distinction who would never question him. You've no accomplishments of your own, no connections to recommend you, and no past worth speaking of in polite circles. You're forgettable. A *nobody*. He doesn't have to impress you because I'm sure you were grateful for his offer. A woman your age without prospects is easy prey to a charming smile and false promises of love and devotion."

"Think how easily you became smitten with Lord Thorne," Lady Kelly accused. "Scandalous."

Lenore gaped. "He did not charm me. He disgusts me! *He's* the scoundrel!"

Lady Kelly glared at her. "Thorne told me all about your failed attempt to seduce him the day you left my employ. You ran from that failure, and straight into another man's arms."

"That is *not* true," Lenore insisted, offended. "I left to marry my husband."

"How foolish of you." Lady Berry's expression grew hard. "You might have claimed a lofty title for your own and now you must live with the consequences. It's no wonder your name is not to be found on the guest lists of the best hostesses."

"I choose not to attend."

"You choose? Or is it that your husband decided for you? He must be embarrassed now to be wed to someone of so little distinction."

Lenore looked at Lady Kelly and saw her nodding. "You rushed off before I could dismiss you, but I certainly was about to for the shocking way you behaved with a guest in my home. And without a reference, too. And I wouldn't put it past you to have ruined yourself just to capture an earl." Lady Kelly turned to Lady Berry. "She was married barely a few days after leaving my employ, you now. I ask you, why the rush?"

"We were married within two weeks," she corrected. "That is not unusual when a husband is wealthy enough to afford a special license and we have known each other for years. And a marquess attended my wedding, so there's no scandal about the marriage."

"I highly doubt that the gentleman knew your name until it was too late to leave. Poor man. I doubt the man wishes to see you again," Lady Berry hissed.

Lenore gritted her teeth. Lady Berry was striking out at her because of the death of her daughter. "The Marquess of Wharton has called on me since our wedding. He was most agreeable and happy to meet me again."

"He sat down at your table for dinner, invited you to his?"

Well. "No. But we attended a picnic he hosted. A dozen of his closest friends saw me there."

"Just a dozen?" Lady Berry and Lady Kelly exchanged catty smiles. "Do you know Carmichael attends Madam Bradshaw's until dawn most nights? Wharton, Scarsdale and Carmichael are quite notoriously smitten with the place. Your husband is said to almost be a fixture and very popular with the courtesans who perch on his knee."

The wind gushed from her lungs. "No!"

She wished that cry back immediately, as the pair looked on her with fresh pity. "It's probably where he went last night."

"He was with me," she whispered.

Lady Berry shook her head. "He goes to Bradshaw's most nights with friends and obviously has never told you. No surprise why."

Lenore became very still. Price did go out, often with friends, and he never did say where he went. Gentlemen of the *ton* lived by a different moral code to respectable ladies, and frequently visited places where their vices could be indulged. She believed Price was different, but nothing she could say to this pair would prove it.

Lenore steadied her temper. The women were watching her, expecting her to fall apart at the news they'd imparted. She would not give them the satisfaction of souring her relationship with her husband with vile accusations. They were tying to undermine her marriage and her peace of mind. She would speak to her husband about Lady Berry and ask him if something can be done about the lies she was spreading. "I can't imagine why you seek to hurt me. It says more about *your* character, or lack of."

"Did he tell you then he professed to love my daughter?"

Lenore laughed, determined to regain the upper hand. This pair were making up lies on the spot now just to get under her skin.

Lady Berry smiled, though, and dug in her reticule. She waved a letter. "She believed every lying word out of his mouth. I found this after her death, hidden under her bed. He corrupted her, ruined her. Pretended to mourn her. As if he'd actually cared in the first place. He's been tupping strumpets at Madam Bradshaw's ever since the day she died!"

Lenore eyed the paper but shook her head. "He'd never behave like that."

Lady Berry shoved the letter at her. "Read it, and know the devil you married."

Lenore shoved it back.

"Ask him. Ask him about Angela and the others and catch him in his lies," Lady Berry demanded. "Ask him just how many of his godmother's victims died because of his carelessness and corruption."

"More lies. You need help, madam," Lenore declared before she turned on her heel and returned to her carriage, taking Hero with her.

Their walk had been ruined but she could not stay in the park with that pair around. The grooms had their backs to her but turned as she approached. She asked the door be opened.

Peter rushed forward. "My lady, is everything all right?"

"Take me home," she said, and the carriage door was finally opened, the step dropped to let her in.

Lenore stepped inside, pulled the door shut behind herself.

Lady Berry was unhinged and Lady Kelly was encouraging her. Something must be done about the pair before their reputation was harmed.

Although she'd prefer not to involve her husband, she had no choice. He had to know what they were saying about him.

Lenore suddenly found herself in front of her home again,

and she took a moment to collect her thoughts. She should be calm when she told him. He'd take the news badly.

She allowed a servant to take Hero and another to help her out. Lenore walked up the stairs and through the open front door. She passed her hat and gloves to the butler as if nothing was wrong. "Is my husband home?"

"Yes, my lady, but he has a visitor."

That gave her pause. "Who?"

"The Marquess of Wharton. They've been closeted in the study for the last hour."

How inconvenient. She'd have to wait. "Thank you. Humphries, could you take Hero to the kitchens for me?"

"Certainly, madam. When should I bring him back to you?"

"I'm not sure. But I will ring."

"Very good."

Humphries took Hero away, and Lenore debated the wisdom of interrupting their conversation. She wanted to see her husband very badly but with Wharton here it wasn't the best timing.

But perhaps they were almost done. Lenore walked slowly toward the study door. The rug beneath her feet muted the sound of her steps and soon she heard her husband's voice speaking. The door had been left ajar, and she could hear her husband and Lord Wharton talking together clearly. She knew she shouldn't listen in…but then she heard Lady Berry's name mentioned, and then Angela's, too.

Lenore risked a peek around the doorframe, wondering if he'd had his own encounter with the grieving mother. Her husband had his back to her, so too did the Marquess of Wharton. They had removed their coats, as men often did at home, but this was the first time she'd viewed her husband so casually attired. She skimmed her eyes over his broad shoulders, down to his trim waist and hips. He was sleek, her husband. Attractive and desirable. Popular with the ladies, it was said. He also looked very comfortable with his shirtsleeves rolled up. She stared at his arms…

A black band that encircled his upper right arm.

"We missed you at Bradshaw's last night," Wharton said. "Will we be seeing you there again anytime soon?"

"Not for the time being."

"Shame. The young ladies are missing you terribly."

Price chuckled. "I'm sure they are. You'll have to keep them entertained in my absence."

Lenore gaped. Her husband had lovers at Madam Bradshaw's who missed him?

He moved, and Lenore hid before she was seen, plastering herself against the hall wall outside the study as he spoke again. "As for that other matter, I'll have to go see her again."

"What will you say to Lady Berry this time? You already swore up and down that you were in love with her daughter."

"Exactly that, as I've always asserted. I do miss Angela and always will. But I must make her stop her senseless slander before my wife hears what she's saying about me. My marriage changes nothing about how I feel over the loss of her daughter. I love Angela even though she's gone."

Tears filled Lenore's eyes when his words sunk in.

He was in love with someone else, freely admitted it to his friend but never to her.

Was everything Lady Berry said about him true?

She peeked through the doorway again. Price wore a mourning band around his right arm. Was it for Angela? He was always touching that arm. Did he always wear it?

Had he worn it the day they'd married?

Lenore put her hand up to cover her mouth and turned away.

"Who's there?"

Caught loitering, eavesdropping, Lenore lifted her chin and forced her tears away. She walked slowly back to her husband's study doorway, though her heart was breaking. "Just me."

Gullible, unlovable me.

She looked up reluctantly. Price had pulled on his coat and had his hat in hand now. "I thought you might have been Humphries. I have to go out."

She studied his face, desperate for him to stay and talk to

her but what was the point? She knew the truth now of why he'd been so distant in the beginning from his own lips. To Wharton, he'd been more truthful than he'd ever been to her. "To where?"

"To visit a friend."

When he said nothing more, she could only nod and keep her misery well hidden. He was on his way to Lady Berry, then, and didn't care for her to know about it. How foolish she was to believe their marriage had been improving. That they were becoming closer. Falling in love perhaps. Their marriage was the same as the day it had started. Built on lies, it would never thrive. "When will you be back?"

Wharton appeared, clapping a hand over Price's shoulder. "Not for dinner. Your husband and I have some business to discuss and I'm hoping to lure him to the club for drinks later."

Her husband didn't attend his club. He went to a gambling den where courtesans draped themselves all over him every night. She looked for the lie in his eyes now and saw only his smile. How clever he was at deceiving her.

"I'll be back late, I expect, so I'll see you in the morning for breakfast." Priced kissed her cheek softly. "Don't wait up for me tonight."

Lenore stepped back against the wall and let Wharton stride past.

Price lingered, though, a frown line forming between his brows. "You look a bit pale. Is everything all right?"

"Yes. Of course. The same as ever." Except her heart was breaking.

"Forgive me," he said, then laughed. "I'm inclined to worry about you."

Lenore did not believe he cared about her at all now. All he wanted from her was to do her duty—invite him to her bed until she was increasing.

They would remain like this forever. Him with his life, hers always separate.

She watched him go with a heavy heart, and as soon as the door shut behind him, Lenore put her hands over her face.

She'd been fooling herself into thinking they might have been falling in love.

Only *she'd* made the mistake of falling for *him*.

It all made sense finally. The sudden proposal, their rushed marriage, him always being somewhere else. His lack of interest in taking her with him anywhere. She pressed her hand over her chest, struggling to breathe. She had humiliated herself trying to have a real relationship with the earl when all he wanted her for was to breed with, just like the cattle on his country estate.

Panic built inside her until she couldn't stand to be in the house a moment longer.

Chapter Twenty

Price darted into Wharton's carriage and took a seat. "Thank you," he murmured.

"For the carriage ride to Lady Berry's, or playing along with your deception by lying for you?"

"Both."

Wharton grimaced. "You need to tell her soon and put an end to this."

"I will."

"You must."

Price raked a hand through his hair. "It's just that everything is finally going so well between us lately. I didn't want to spoil…"

"The illusion. For God's sake man, don't continue this farce." Wharton crossed his arms over his chest. "Women always figure it out."

"What?"

"When we don't love them enough." He shook his head. "We all think we're the greatest liars until a man answer one question with a lack of care and bam, there are tears and china flying at you from across the room."

"But I do love her," he admitted.

Wharton sat up from his slouch. "What's that?"

"I do think I love her, after all."

Wharton nodded. "About time you let Angela go."

"It's not that I let her go. Not deliberately, anyway." Price glanced out the window, waiting for guilt but it never came. "It just happened."

A smile played around Wharton's mouth. "Did I tell you that I think she's good for you?"

"No."

He shook his head. "I wasn't going to mention this, you understand. I know Angela was very important to you...but she wasn't right for you."

"What do you mean?"

"You were too similar. The silver-tongued darlings of society marrying seemed too good to be true. You never argued, never fell out even once. You gave in to her every time she pouted. She was so very young, lacked the experience you needed in a wife for the years to come. I've seen unequal marriages like that go very wrong very quickly."

Price considered Wharton's point of view a moment, but failed to see a problem. "In time, she would have matured into the role of countess."

"Was that why you chose to marry Lenore then? Because of her age being closer to yours?"

"I don't know why I decided on Lenore." He winced. "I was drunk when I proposed, but don't tell anyone about that."

"Well, I already suspected that anyway. You were almost always drunk for a while there, especially at the time you must have written to Lenore. I took it as a good sign that you chose a wife outside of the *ton*, and someone you obviously admired for a very long time seemed a good choice."

Price studied Wharton, relieved there were no signs of disapproval. "We were friends as children. Her grandmother was employed on the estate. I used to try to get her to play when she should have been working."

"You know, she doesn't seem the type to play very often."

"No, she had a hard life before we wed."

"Then I suggest you do all you can to make it easy for both of you in the future. Purge the past and tell her of it all now, before it's too late. I'm sure if she feels any affection for you, she'll understand your reluctance to rehash the past. I'm not saying she won't be angry with you for lying to her. Most likely she'll throw something at you. Keep your eyes open and learn to duck."

Price couldn't imagine Lenore acting in a volatile fashion about anything, but he would keep his wits about him when he made his confession. Wharton was right, he'd have to tell her, and tonight, too. He couldn't let the truth remain unsaid between them anymore. The fresh start he'd been planning for began that very night.

Price exited the carriage outside Lady Berry's current residence, bid Wharton an enjoyable evening and rushed up the stairs, resolved to put the past behind him at last and then hurry home to his wife to pour out his heart.

Although Lady Berry's butler recognized Price, he seemed disinclined to let him in, though he relented when Price handed him a crown and promised he would only be a moment.

That wasn't exactly true.

Price would stay until the air was cleared.

Word had reached him today that Lady Berry had encouraged harmful gossip about Lenore, saying she was unfit to be in society, and the hostesses remaining in London had listened. He had noticed a decrease in invitations this past week but had thought nothing sinister about it at first, since many were leaving the capital.

But then Wharton had heard the same from his last mistress, too, and Price had to put a stop to it now before any more damage was done.

If his wife had heard, she was sure to be embarrassed and angry.

Price stepped into the drawing room, noticing the house was completely draped in the mourning colors. In the low candlelight, he could make out Lady Berry sitting on a settee, looking down at her hands.

He crossed the room and stood with his hands clasped

behind his back. "Lady Berry," he said.

"You always looked angelic in that pose," Lady Berry murmured. "It hides the truth of your true nature well."

Today he wouldn't be baited, and held his tongue.

The woman looked up eventually, squinting at him in the dim light. "Have you come to chastise me?"

"I have come to make peace with you."

"Peace? There is no peace for me or my daughter," she insisted. "I will never be happy again without my darling girl."

"People die, Lady Berry. People die every day, and those left behind must pick up the pieces of our lives and continue on."

"Well, you've certainly done so," she bit out. "Not six months since we buried her and you're married already."

He moved to sit beside her but she moved away, clutching a gold chain and locket tightly in her hand, before he could.

Price recognized it, as it had once belonged to Angela. She had worn it everywhere. It has been a gift from her mother, of course. A treasured keepsake that she'd foolishly believed brought good luck and security.

Seeing that necklace again made Price smile. Angela had loved that locket and could never bear to leave it off. "I had imagined Angela would be buried with that. She loved the gift you gave her so much."

Lady Berry clutched it tighter in her fist. "It's all I have of her."

He sat down finally and smiled sadly. "You had her love, and that is all we can ever have of anybody, when all is said and done."

"Do you think you have your wife's love? Does she help you forget the promise you made to me the night Angela died?"

"Yes," he admitted. "Marrying Lenore was the best thing I ever did for my peace of mind. She has helped me put the past where it belongs. No matter how much I wish things were different, I doubt I could have prevented my godmother from murdering her. But if she had not, where would Angela and I have been, anyway? You never approved of me before she died.

I doubt anything could have changed that, no matter how I tried to win you over. You would have insisted she marry anyone who possess a title greater than mine, and made her miserable."

Lady Berry bristled. "She would have done her duty to the family and made us proud."

Price arched one brow. "That is exactly what I have done, yet you condemn me for it. I married for the sake of my family. For the sake of my title, I chose a woman who would never bring dishonor on us. Lenore Griffin is no giggling debutant, but a woman of substance and good taste. She is caring, and she is kind, and she has more patience than any man could ever hope for."

"Spare me your gushing platitudes," Lady Berry hissed.

"She married me knowing that we were not in love, and she trusted me to take care of her and protect her. I would've done the same for Angela. But Angela has died, and I can't do anything to change that. I have a right to be happy again and fall in love too."

"Stop."

"No. Let us begin again and call a truce to this war you're waging against my reputation, and my wife's. She doesn't deserve to be ostracized because we don't like each other."

Lady Berry drew breath, her expression becoming murderous. "I *despise* men like you. You get everything you want."

"If that were true, Angela would still be alive, madam."

"You don't yet understand true loss!"

"You see only your own suffering, don't you? Angela never wanted you to be unhappy with her choice—and I *was* her choice, I assure you." He sighed. "I knew you would never really warm to me but I tried for Angela's sake. I offered to wait but Angela was an impatient, impulsive girl. She lived so full a life in so few years. I am grateful to have known her."

Lady Berry walked away from him to stare out the window. "You don't mourn her."

Price stood, removed his coat and showed her the armband

he wore beneath. "I wear this for all of them. For Angela, and for all the rest my godmother slaughtered."

Her eyes sharpened. "Does your wife know about the great love you claimed to feel for my daughter?"

"Of course not. I'm not as cruel as you would have me be."

Her eyes narrowed on him. "How like a man to claim lies as a kindness. Well, she knows now."

"What did you do?" He advanced on Lady Berry. "What did you tell her, and when?"

"I told her nothing short of the truth! I imagine you'll have a frosty reception when you return home today and expect to climb into her bed." Her eyes lit with triumph. "Did you know, too, that my good friend Lady Kelly swears that your wife tried to seduce an acquaintance of hers before you married? I'm sure it wasn't the first time. Women like that—"

Price grabbed her arm, intending only to shock her a little. "The scoundrel tried to seduce *her*. My wife told me all about it. She was innocent when she invited me to her bed. Believe me, I know the truth of that."

Lady Berry's face colored a little. "How dare you speak of your wedding night to me?"

"How dare you question my wife's integrity?" Price looked around, attempting to cool his temper. They were at an impasse. No good could come from arguing with her further. They would never see eye to eye about the past. He had tried one last time, but he'd more important things to do. "I see I've come on a fool's errand. I will bid you goodbye forever then, Lady Berry. I hope not to see you or speak to you ever again."

"I could only be so lucky," Lady Berry added.

"Good day, madam. I hope one day you can find the peace that you so obviously need."

He snatched up his coat and threw it on as he headed straight for the door, where he found the butler waiting with his hat in hand and a sour expression. "Take care of her, will you?" Price murmured to the man, glancing back at the woman who was weeping again behind him. Coming here had done no good. "Her daughter would have wanted that above all else."

He hailed a hack and paid them double to put a spring in the horse's steps. He cursed himself for holding back when he should have been honest from the start. Lenore had been a little quiet before he left her to call on Lady Berry. And now she might be at home, thinking the worst of him.

He may not have loved Lenore at all in the beginning, but he did now. He wanted to tell her everything he'd held back.

He flew up the stairs and let himself in with his own key. Hero rushed to greet him…but there was no sign of Lenore in the house, no matter how long he looked for her.

Chapter Twenty-One

Lenore pushed her egg and ham around her plate, and then shoved it aside, largely uneaten. She wasn't hungry. She was heartbroken. The pain in her heart was unbearable.

She stared out the window of her bedchamber in Albemarle Street without really noticing the view wasn't the usual one she had at home. She had left her husband yesterday, wearing only the clothes on her back. She hadn't even the funds for carriage fare, so she'd walked the whole way.

Lenore had turned her back on her marriage, believing she had no reason to stay with Price. She had not left word of where she was going or when she'd return. She could never return to live a lie with a man incapable of truly caring about her, until she had learned not to care about *him* as much. Price should have told her how things stood from the very beginning of their marriage, and not left her to find out the harsh truth for herself.

He could never return her love the way she'd hoped.

Yesterday, she had thought that taking charge of her life would make her feel better. Instead, the decision had just made her feel even more wretched. She'd come here to the Hillcrest cousins' academy, believing it to be the safest place for her to be while she took stock of her position and decided what to do. She was a wife, yes, but also a countess, with more money in her reticule at home than she'd ever had in her entire life.

She knew how to live simply if she had to, or she could be like every other member of the *ton* and live on credit.

All she had decided so far was that she could not go home, or stay in London. She needed advice, a plan, before she spoke to him again. Sylvia had been helpful in the past, Lenore hoped she would be again. So she had asked her friends if she might stay the night at their home without revealing her reasons for it. But she would have to explain herself today.

"Can I take your plate if you are finished, my lady?"

Lenore startled, and then quickly smiled as she remembered she wasn't alone. A servant had remained to straighten the bed she'd tossed and turned in all of last night. "Yes, please. I'm not hungry after all, although it looked delicious."

"I'll tell Cook you said so," the Hillcrest Academy maid promised as she repacked the tray and carried it to the door. She handed it off to a footman lingering outside and then returned. "Would you care to be dressed now, my lady."

Lenore glanced at her nightdress and nodded. "Yes, I suppose I should make myself ready."

The maid rushed to the bed, where her clothing from yesterday had been laid out in readiness to wear again. Each of the Hillcrest women had popped their heads around the door to bid her a good morning, but had left her when it became apparent her mood had not lightened overnight.

It was just so devastating to realize how far away from having a happy marriage she had always been.

She dressed with the maid's help, noticing a hundred things about herself that she considered unflattering. The length of her ears when her hair was pinned up. The odd gray streak in her hair, especially. Why would Carmichael care for such a sack of unattractive old bones? As Lady Kelly and Lady Berry had insisted, there was little to recommend her when it came to her looks.

All she had was her dignity and her pride, though both were sorely battered.

"There you are, my lady," the maid murmured. "Is there anything else I can do for you?"

"No, thank you."

The maid turned, and then picked up something from the dresser. "Your ring, my lady."

Lenore gave it a cursory glance and reached for the gold band. She put it on with reluctance, and only because it was the only piece of jewelry her husband had ever given her. She felt compelled to be careful with it until she was brave enough to return it.

Armed with wavering resolve, she left the room to seek out the Hillcrest cousins. The hall floor had no rugs upon it and her footsteps were very loud in the quiet house. At this time of day, the cousins would probably be in the parlor together. She went down the stairs and knocked on the door softly.

"Come in," they called.

Lenore stepped inside, and the moment she saw their expressions, instantly wished to cry. She could not do that yet. She wanted to explain herself first and ask for their advice before she fell apart.

Sylvia patted the empty chair beside her. "You are just in time."

"For what?"

"We are deciding what to do for the winter," Eugenia said sadly.

Lenore glanced at them all, her cares forgotten. "What do you mean?"

"We've emptied every pocket we possess, looked under every pillow, but our combined funds will not be enough to cover the lease for the winter, and we have no other clients," Sylvia advised.

"The Hillcrest Academy is in dire need of new funds," Eugenia announced.

"No!" Lenore cried, stricken on their behalf.

Eugenia pushed a penny around the tabletop. "We were foolish to believe we'd attract enough clients in our first year to fund the venture through the lean months ahead."

"But surely you have something set aside." Lenore glanced at each lady, horrified.

"We dare not dip too deeply into our inheritances. We promised when we started this venture that the bulk of those funds must remain untouched. They have to support us in our old age when we cannot work to support ourselves, too, you know."

Lenore's heart broke for them. "Can I not help you in some way?"

Eugenia covered her hand and smiled. "We knew you would want to help us, but we cannot beg money from a dear friend."

Sylvia smiled. "We have decided to separate for this winter and return to each other in the spring. Eugenia has been invited north to stay with the sister of one of our clients for the winter."

She looked at the other pair. "What of you two?"

"Aurora will remain in London as a companion to another client's elderly mother," Eugenia told her. "I am sure she will be quite comfortable there, and needed too."

"And Sylvia?"

"That is still up in the air," Sylvia replied with a shrug. "I'm sure I'll find something suitable soon."

"Stay with *me*," Lenore suggested immediately.

"Should you not discuss the matter with your husband?"

"I doubt he will object," Lenore decided. He'd probably not even notice, either. He was too busy running about London with his friends and mourning his one true love forever to care who she spent her time with. "We'll have a marvelous time together in the country. I can't wait to show you all my favorite places at Edenmere Park."

Eugenia's brow rose. "Are you going to the country?"

"With your husband?" Aurora asked.

Lenore wet her lips. "Yes, I'm going home at last."

So she had decided her course of action, after all. She would return to the place she'd felt safe all her life—without her husband or his permission. She didn't know what he intended to do with his life, nor did she need to concern herself with his feelings anymore. He hadn't thought much of hers.

Sylvia tugged her sleeve. "Are you really going?"

Lenore forced a smile to her lips. "Absolutely."

"When?"

"Very soon."

Sylvia picked up her hand. "I would love to visit your home for the winter, if I did not think going there would only make matters worse between you and your husband."

Lenore looked between the three women. "I never said—"

"They already know, my dear. They guessed. You can trust us all to keep your secrets." Sylvia gave her an encouraging smile. "We only want you to be happy."

"Dear lady, you didn't have to say a thing to alert us," Aurora murmured with a smile of understanding. "It's easy to see you're not happily married."

Tears threatened but she forced them away. "I *was* happy."

"Nonsense," Eugenia declared. "But there's no surprise or no need to dissemble. Arranged matches are rarely without challenges."

Lenore turned her attention to Sylvia, who smiled. "I swear I said nothing to either one. It's our job to be observant. You haven't been happy in a very long time."

Eugenia nodded. "Not since you were a companion to Lady Kerr before she died, I think."

"She was my first employer. Lady Kerr made me laugh," Lenore admitted. "She used to play tricks on everyone who hadn't called on her for a while—pretending to be deaf or blind to see what they'd do. How loud they'd shout at her."

"And your husband doesn't make you laugh, does he?" Aurora frowned. "Because nothing short of complete misery would ever have compelled you to leave your beloved Hero behind yesterday and stay the night with us. I take it you reached the end of your tether?"

Lenore concentrated on tracing the pattern of the tablecloth with her fingertip. "I couldn't stay. I was too upset with him for deceiving me."

"How has he done that?"

"Did you discover he has taken a mistress after all?" Sylvia asked.

Lenore sighed. "If only it were that simple."

Aurora patted her hand. "You don't have to tell us but if we don't know what's happened, we can't plan for his demise. Something grizzly," Aurora declared hotly, rubbing her hands together. "Something equal to his betrayal of you should be in order."

Lenore laughed bitterly. He'd be reunited with his beloved Angela in heaven if he died now. "Dying would only make him happy."

"Well, then we won't chop him up into little pieces and feed him to the crows on the commons. Though I'm sure he wouldn't be happy to be fodder for carrion."

Lenore lifted her face and met Aurora's animated expression with a frown. "I'd forgotten how bloodthirsty your imagination can be sometimes."

She winked. "The thoughts are always there. I just rarely express them out loud, or have reason to lately. Scares away the clients. But I would commit murder for a friend if there was a chance you might smile the way you used to again."

A tear fell down her cheek. "He's in love."

The three women gasped.

Lenore put her head into her hand. "If only I'd known before we married, but he didn't say a word."

"Are you sure he loves her?"

Lenore nodded miserably. "Sure. Certain. From his own lips too. I'm just a sorry replacement for the woman he really wanted to marry."

"I don't believe that could be true," Sylvia declared. "There's always a chance you're wrong about him."

"You're always looking for the bright side, but my marriage is utterly unfixable."

There was silence around her, and she let the knowledge settle over her. She had been willing to be a wife, mother, lover, and a companion without the love of her husband. She'd known they might never fall for each other, but being second fiddle to a dead woman was too much to bear.

She looked up suddenly. "Does my confession make me a client of the Hillcrest Academy now? I can pay you well to put me back together so he can never hurt me again. Perhaps then, you wouldn't need to close your business and could stay together."

"That is a discussion for another time," Eugenia murmured. "Lets talk about you for now."

They could not fix her marriage, but she'd let them try. Perhaps somehow she'd find a way to endure her marriage with their help and support. Talking to them about what she should do next with her life, she hoped, would lessen her pain.

Sylvia slipped her arm around Lenore's back and squeezed. "Everything is fixable."

"Not this," she whispered. "My husband probably hasn't even noticed my absence. He never came to find me. It shouldn't have been too hard for him to suspect I might be here."

The women withdrew to confer just outside the room, and Lenore didn't mind being left alone with her thoughts. She did wish that she hadn't left her Hero behind, though, wondering where she'd gone. She would feel better if she had someone who loved her without hesitation by her side right now.

The ladies returned, smiling happily. "Well then, you're in luck. You have just become the final paying client of the Hillcrest Academy this year. And we are determined to prove you wrong about your marriage, too."

"That would require a miracle," she murmured morosely, and then smiled. "But I am willing to give you a chance."

"Good. Now just you keep that heart of yours open to all eventualities a little longer."

Aurora excused herself suddenly while Sylvia urged Lenore to stand. "Let's take our discussion to the library, shall we?"

Lenore tripped along, willing to let them try to make everything all right for her. She hadn't the faintest fear of starting over now, of living alone for the rest of her days. She may have become used to having a husband, but she supposed she had never really had Price after all.

Eugenia sat behind a large desk and brought out paper and wet the nib of a quill. "Name, please?"

Lenore took a chair facing them and folded her hands in her lap. "You know my name," she chided.

"I ask all clients to say their own name out loud."

Lenore sighed, willing to play along. "Lenore Wagstaff, Countess Carmichael."

"Age?"

"Old enough not to answer that question."

"She is six and twenty," Sylvia answered for her. "She's recently married. Just the once."

Eugenia set her pen aside and folded her hands on the desktop. "How can we help you, Lady Carmichael?"

"I need help with my husband."

Eugenia clucked her tongue in disapproval. "Love potions, if such concoctions actually existed, are beyond the scope of our services, my lady."

"I don't want you to make him love me. It wouldn't be real." She shrugged. "Besides, he's already in love, and has vowed never to forget the woman."

"I see," Aurora murmured. "What do you want us to do about that?"

"Nothing, really. I just want…" She rubbed her brow. "I suppose I just need advice on how to live with knowing that about him. She's dead, you see."

"Dead, you say?"

"Yes, she was murdered," Lenore admitted. "Six months ago."

"So, no chance of resurrection," Aurora added as she slipped into the room and took a chair.

Lenore glared at Aurora for being flippant. "None, of course."

"So if she is dead, how has he betrayed you?"

"He mourns her still and never told me! He wears an armband over his right shirt sleeve under his coat. He hides that, too."

The cousins exchanged glances. "How else does he mourn her?"

"He keeps his feelings to himself," Lenore answered. She didn't want to mention he had lovers at Madam Bradshaw's. That was even more humiliating. "Isn't that enough?"

"That is a problem with many men. Talking is not their strong suite, and they do not wear their hearts on their sleeves. They keep that part of themselves well hidden." Eugenia sat forward. "Does he visit the grave of this woman and place flowers upon her resting place, perhaps?"

Lenore frowned at that. "I don't know. He goes out a lot without me. He never says where he's been."

"Do you know her name?"

"Angela. Angela Berry."

"I know that name," Sylvia murmured, ruffling through some newspaper clippings on a side table. "Ah, here it is. Angela Berry was murdered by Lady Scott, Lord Carmichael's godmother. The young woman was supposed to be buried in the county. Carmichael does not leave London, so I cannot see how he could have visited her grave since the marriage began."

Lenore's heart twisted painfully at the news. "You investigated my husband?"

"The murders, my dear. We had to know what was going on in society. Some of our clients lost sweethearts, too."

Lenore nodded slowly. "I cannot compete with a shade, and I won't."

Eugenia sat forward, her hand clasped on the table. "Why do you feel that way? You do have an advantage over a dead woman."

"Yes," Aurora agreed. "He can reach out and touch you anytime he wants."

"He has other women apparently, too," she blushed, looking down. "He visits a scandalous place almost every night with his friends."

"But surely he's shared your bed."

Lenore nodded. "If only I believed it was more than duty guiding him toward me," Lenore said bitterly, and then she told them the truth of how her marriage had started, the misunderstanding that had brought her to London, and how, after seducing him, he'd fled her bedchamber and the house. She couldn't go home to face that situation again.

"Men often love more than one woman in their lives, you know," Sylvia said gently. "Women do, too."

"I just wanted one man to think of me first for the rest of *my* life. I just wanted to love someone. I wanted *him*."

Eugenia smiled. "Well, that is a relief."

Lenore laughed bitterly. "But it doesn't matter that I fell in love with my husband."

Eugenia started to smile. "Are you sure it is love you feel? I know he's handsome, and rich, but so many men are."

Lenore nodded miserably. The Hillcrest cousins would never repeat what she told them today. More importantly, they wouldn't tell Price. She'd have to pretend forever, and never let him see how she felt. But just this once, she wanted to unburden herself. The days ahead were going to be empty and so very cold. Loving Price in silence was the only decision she had no control over. The only real option she had was to learn to hide how she felt and never let him know how deeply he'd hurt her. "Yes, I love him. I just don't know how I'll bear it."

"Many husbands don't love their wives, and they get along just fine without it."

"But doesn't she deserve to have a husband who puts her happiness first? He should put her on a pedestal, too," Aurora declared.

Price had been so easy to love, and she had promised to devote herself to him until the end of her days. He'd pushed her to accept his proposal, and she really had not put up much resistance. "I don't want to be on a pedestal. I just want to be the person he dreams about."

A floorboard creaked behind Lenore as someone entered the room. "I think, personally, *dreams* of love are not enough to sustain a marriage. *Actual* love, though, is another matter…and worth fighting for," Price said suddenly. "Especially yours, wife."

Lenore froze as her husband settled his hand lightly on her shoulder and Hero jumped up on her lap to lick her face. She clutched her dog, but she didn't dare turn around at first.

Her husband had come after her, but all he'd heard were her complaints that he could never love her.

Chapter Twenty-Two

———◆———

Price felt the shock that rushed through his wife's slender body and clenched his jaw to keep in an oath. Hearing his behavior described by his wife in such defeated tones after the horrid night he'd just experienced brought shame crashing over him.

He'd hurt his wife.

Not deliberately. But by omission, he had undermined her trust in him and faith in herself.

In his battle with his conscience, with his own lust, he'd failed to reveal to Lenore just how essential she had become to his life.

He did not want her to only do her duty to him.

He wanted her to care about him as much as he'd come to care about her.

Perhaps more than that, too.

He had always shied away from making comparisons between Lenore and Angela. But he doubted that Angela would have put up with him the way Lenore had if their situations had been reversed. Angela had *demanded* to be on her pedestal. Lenore never would.

It was time for him to face up to the truth—his heart had quite thoroughly shifted allegiance. He thought of Angela out of guilt, not love.

He loved the woman he'd married, more than he'd thought possible.

Ignoring the stares of her friends, he released Lenore, caught hold of a chair, and dragged it to face hers. He sat beside her, concerned by her pallor and stillness. It was clear to see his arrival had surprised her. Startled her.

But she had no reason to be afraid of speaking her mind to him directly. It was a relief to hear the dissatisfaction she'd obviously been hiding so well. The fault was his. "Look at me, please, Lenore."

She swallowed and glanced his way quickly. Her jaw set and her lips pressed together tightly. There was mutiny in her eyes, and the certainty that she was finally being honest filled him.

It was time for him to do the same.

He reached out and brushed his thumb across the tip of her chin. "I apologize."

Her eyes narrowed slightly. "For what?"

"For letting you down. For not telling you everything."

Her glance dropped away.

"Yes, I was in love, and I had intended to marry Angela Berry."

Her eyes closed.

"I was heartbroken for a long time," he admitted. "My godmother killed Angela so I couldn't marry her, someone she deemed unsuitable."

Lenore shifted in her chair.

"And yes, I do still mourn Angela, but I also mourn all the innocent women my godmother killed for the same reason. That's why I wear the armband under my coat and don't show it. I grew tired of hearing people promise that it wasn't my fault, when I know damn well it was."

Lenore's eyes flew to his.

"No, I wasn't in love with them all, but it quickly became obvious to me that I had stolen a kiss from many of the victims at one time or another. My godmother died before I could discover if there was any other reason that she had singled out those poor girls. Can you imagine the guilt I felt, knowing that I'd put them all in danger?"

"You said you didn't know about your godmother," Lenore whispered.

"I should have. We were close." He winced. "I believed I'd never love anyone in any way again, after her betrayal. I told everyone I wouldn't. And then you came."

"You sent for me," Lenore reminded him.

"Yes I did," he freely admitted now. He glanced at her friends briefly. "I'm relieved that you told your friends how our marriage began. It wasn't fair of me to expect you to keep that to yourself forever."

"It was a most unique proposal," Eugenia Hillcrest murmured.

"A proposition from a drunkard," Price said to correct her, then looked at his wife only. "Badly done of me and completely unworthy of you. I'm quite ashamed I even wrote to you that night instead of paying you a proper call. I knew exactly where to find you, and there was nothing important keeping me in London. I should have courted you. You deserved so much better than me. I should have given us time to get to know each other before any marriage began, before proposing even. But given your stay overnight in my home might have become known, I thought it best to head off any scandal and marry us quickly. But to be honest, I just wanted the matter settled so I could pick up a glass of spirits and continue living in a daze."

Lenore's brow furrowed. "At Madam Bradshaw's."

"Yes. I hate drinking alone, so I became almost a perfect fixture in her parlors. But for the record, there hasn't been another woman but you since Angela."

Lenore met his gaze and seemed somewhat relieved by that news. "Why me?"

"I have been asking myself that same question since I re-read my own letter. I don't really understand it myself still, but I'm not sorry we married."

"Why?"

He picked up her hand and held it lightly. "When I realized you were not at home when I returned yesterday, I waited up for you all night. I even sent a footman last night to enquire if you were here. They said you were long gone."

Lenore glanced at her friends. "Why didn't you tell him where I was?"

Eugenia huffed. "When a friend comes to our door, obviously near to tears, asking to spend the night here, what are we supposed to do? Send you straight back into the arms of the husband most likely to have upset you?"

Price nodded. "By morning's first light, I was frantic with worry. I was consulting with Runners when Sylvia's note arrived, explaining you really were here after all, and that if I wanted to save my marriage, I'd better get over here immediately. I didn't wait for the carriage. I ran to you."

"I sense a change in the air," Eugenia mused with a pleased smile as she stood. "Perhaps we should give this pair a bit of privacy now."

Price nodded. "Thank you for looking after Lenore for me."

"Anytime, my lord. But I shouldn't like it to happen again too soon."

"It won't ever happen again."

The door closed silently behind the trio and Price bit his lip. He had to tell her everything now, or she might never trust him. "I've been making this up as we go along, fumbling the change between us very badly, haven't I?"

Lenore nodded. "It's not all your fault."

"Don't you dare let me off lightly, Lenore. I deserve a good shouting at."

Lenore wet her lips. "I've been thinking of going to Edenmere soon," she whispered.

"Edenmere?"

"I'd like to arrive at your country seat before winter sets in."

"We don't need to go home for the winter," he said slowly.

"But I want to go. I can barely remember the place, and now it's my home again. I'd like to take long walks through the grounds before any snow makes it too difficult."

"I suppose we—"

She put her finger over his lips. "I'm not asking you to take me. I know you have a life here in London."

He evaded her finger. "Lenore, surely you realize I'm never letting you out of my sight for this long again." His heart gave a strange lurch that he might have lost her forever when she didn't react. "Admittedly, I'm not doing or saying the right things to prove I'm falling in love you, but if you just give me a second chance to prove it, I—"

Lenore pressed her hand over his lips once more. "Say that again."

"Which part?" he asked around her fingers.

Her brows furrowed. "The love part?"

"I believe I am in love with you," he said, tightening his grip on her hand. "You have to believe me, I didn't know."

"Oh." Her shoulders sagged. "I'm sorry."

"I know our arrangement didn't have anything to do with this sort of thing, but sometimes love just happens without warning."

She caught up his hand again and pressed it to her lips. "It does," she whispered before kissing his hand again.

He searched her gaze, wondering if he understood her correctly. Did she really love him as she'd assured the Hillcrest cousins she did? She was smiling at him, her blue eyes soft and full of tenderness. "Why didn't you say something?"

"I was just as afraid as you to say what was deep in my heart. I thought you wouldn't *want* me to love you."

He let out a breath of relief. "Of course I do."

Her gaze dropped to his mouth, and a shy smile played across her lips. She put her fingers out to touch his chest, and then cupped his face. "I love you, Price."

He kissed her hard.

Although Lenore seemed a little more subdued than she normally was at first, the strength of her embrace when she wrapped her arms about him banished his every doubt.

They loved each other, and together they would figure this out.

He rained kisses over her face and neck until she giggled and squirmed in her chair. Price pulled her onto his lap and held her close. She'd lifted his spirits the moment they'd married, even if he hadn't realized that at first. "We'll be going home together," he decided. "But after we've been at home for a little while, we're going to make a trip together, too."

"To where?"

"The Duke of Exeter's estate."

She stared at him steadily.

"Ah, you already knew about the party, didn't you?"

She nodded, her jaw firming.

"I won't ask you to reveal who spoiled my surprise, but I think you'll really enjoy the opportunity to mingle with some of the nicest people of the *ton* before we return to London again for the season."

"So we're not going to stay in the country and make babies together?" she murmured.

"We can make babies anywhere and any when you like, my darling."

Lenore slid her fingertips across his chest. "Now?"

The caress, meant to be seductive, stirred him only a little. He was not really in the mood for lovemaking when there were probably three sets of ears pressed against the door still. He kissed her cheek and whispered, "As soon as possible, darling. I imagine your friends will want to return to this room soon, so we'd better wait until we won't be interrupted."

"I wouldn't want that," she whispered back.

He grinned. "Oh, my dear woman. I am horribly in love with you. Every time you move, speak, smile, my heart soars with the most incredible happiness. I knew it the night that woman died. When I saw her, and then you standing safely on the pavement, I gave thanks that I had you in my life. You make me feel so very alive."

Her lips trembled. Price had never expected to make that sort of declaration when he'd married Lenore, but he meant every word.

"I was afraid it was just me who felt that way," Lenore whispered, pressing her head to his.

"Now we both know the truth about us." He chuckled softly as Hero wormed his head under their hands. "How on earth did you put up with me that first day, week, month of our marriage?"

"Everything was so new to me that I just thought ours a normal *ton* marriage," she explained with a fond smile. "I wanted so much to make sure you never regretted marrying me."

"I never could." Price sighed and pulled her closer. Regrets and doubts had almost ruined their marriage before it had truly begun. The only way forward was to lay bare his heart and soul, and protect hers at all costs. "Do you realize this is a love match, dear wife of mine?"

Lenore's smile was immediate, and she wrapped him tight in her loving arms. "I see that now, husband," she whispered. "I feel it, too."

Epilogue

Lenore rubbed her gloved fist against the foggy window of their traveling chase and peered out at the dreary white landscape. It was bitterly cold outside, but the snow had stopped falling an hour ago. She felt bad for their grooms, who had to endure the worst of it on the outside of their conveyance. There was nothing new to see outside, just miles of unending white-shrouded fields. It made playing their game to pass the time problematic.

She glanced over at her dog, or what she could see of him under his blankets on the opposite bench. He was curled up as close as he could get to Sylvia Hillcrest, attempting to keep warm. They were a cozy little group, keeping each other amused and excited about their trip together. Sylvia and Price had reassured Lenore that the house party they were traveling to would not be torture. It was to be as gentle an introduction to the *ton* as was possible.

If it wasn't for the cold, or the endless rocking, Lenore would be quite happy to go on traveling forever. But she couldn't, of course. Sylvia was only to spend the winter with them, and then return to London and her cousins as the season began. Hero would probably miss Sylvia as much as Lenore would. "I spy with my little eye—"

"Hero," Price declared with a laugh.

"No. Just wait a moment," she cried.

"You were looking right at him, love," her husband insisted.

"But I wasn't about to repeat myself."

Price heaved a sigh and pulled Lenore close, covering her up again. He nuzzled her ear, and a blush heated her cheeks. "What letter then?" he whispered.

They had been playing games for hours as they traveled toward their final destination. It was a long way from London to the Duke of Exeter's estate. Hero had borne the confinement better than they all had. Sylvia had chosen to sleep for most of the trip. A feat Lenore had not mastered at all. "I spy with my little eye, something beginning with H."

"Hero!" Price cried out again. "Every third H has been him."

"It is not our dog," Lenore promised.

Price stared around the carriage. "Handle? That bunch of holly you just had to bring along from our last stop?"

Lenore smiled, loving how hard Price tried to guess each and every time. "No, to both."

"Well, I hate to say it, but I must give up. I've no idea what this one could be."

She looked up at his face and smiled. She had gotten so lucky when she'd agreed to marry him. "Are you sure?"

"Yes, you win." He waggled his brows. "This time."

"Husband."

"Yes?"

"*Husband*," she said with a little more emphasis.

"But that was much too obvious!" he cried.

She laughed softly. "Happiness, then?"

His arms tightened around her, and he bent down to kiss her lips lightly. "Happiness indeed," he promised, whispering in her ear.

Lenore loved it when his voice became husky and deep like that.

Sylvia suddenly unwrapped herself from her blankets with a groan. "Are we there yet?" she cried. "You two really need to be alone for a good long while soon."

"Sorry, Sylvia," she apologized with a laugh.

"My deepest apologies again, Miss Hillcrest." Price said too. "It's Lenore's fault."

Lenore gave him a playful shove. "It's your fault, too."

Sylvia stretched. "It's love," she declared with a smile. "Proof undeniable."

Lenore kissed her husband again, and then settled against him, pulling up the blankets to her chin. "How much longer?"

"We're close now," he promised.

She looked up at him. "Do you think they will give Sylvia a room close to ours?"

"I don't know yet."

"I'll be fine wherever they put me," Sylvia promised. "As long as I can be warmer than I am now, I'd be happy anywhere."

"Poor Sylvia. You should get yourself a husband," Lenore suggested. "They make excellent warmers."

"I'll have to mention that advantage to future clients," Sylvia replied dryly. "If my gentlemen clients made sure to mention that first off when they go down on bended knee, they'd never be refused and would not need my help."

Price chuckled at that. "What about a husband for you, Miss Hillcrest? Ever felt the urge to tie the knot, too?"

"Not in the least," Sylvia insisted with a disdainful huff.

"I'm surprised by that. Please don't take this the wrong way, but you've the sort of managing disposition many a gentlemen need in their lives." Price squeezed Lenore. "I have my perfect partner in Lenore."

"Thanks to poor penmanship and a barrel of gin," Lenore teased.

"It was cider." Price trailed his fingers across her cheek. "I'll forever be grateful for your patience, though," he whispered, and then she could feel him leaning down to kiss her.

"Are we there yet?" Sylvia wailed.

The kiss never happened because they all began to laugh. Their ease together had been apparent all along.

"Oh, look!" Price cried out suddenly. "There is Grafton Park."

They all tuned to stare out the foggy windows, rushing to clear them for a better view. In the distance, a mammoth structure rose from the foggy landscape into the clearing sky. Lenore blinked and gaped at the size of the ducal estate. Beneath the fog, the rest of the building was merely a shadow under the pearly whiteness. It seemed to Lenore to be almost a mile long.

"I really thought it would be bigger," Sylvia said sarcastically.

Lenore giggled.

"Please don't let the duke hear you say that," Price warned. "He'd start building a new wing just to impress us all."

"He wouldn't," Lenore said, her eyes fixed on the looming structure. Surely it was already big enough for a duke. "Didn't you say he was working on the landscape?"

"I heard he intended to completely transform the park, but I doubt he'll begin until us guests have gone," Price explained.

More of Grafton Park became visible, and Lenore was in awe. She bit her lip. Most likely she'd get herself lost on her first day. Thank heavens she wouldn't be alone. She had Price and Sylvia to mount a search for her. Hero, too.

Her nerves returned, and when Price caught hold of her fingers, she realized he knew what she was thinking without her having to explain. "It's going to be an adventure," he promised.

She nodded. "That it will be."

They finally arrived beneath a towering pillared portico. Footmen swarmed out of the house as soon as they came to a complete stop, and Lenore reluctantly moved away from her husband's warmth in readiness to exit.

The cold outside was bracing, and she shivered before she even reached the front door. They were quickly ushered into a reception room where a roaring fire burned in the hearth. Lenore's cheeks tingled.

"Oh, I may never leave this room," Sylvia whispered as she nearly climbed into the hearth to warm herself.

"Be careful your skirts don't catch," Lenore warned.

"I am," Sylvia promised and did draw back a little. "Can I have one this size at home?"

"You'll need a bigger house," Price advised, as he too joined them by the fire and rubbed his hand before the heat. "The duke has married now, so is off the market, but maybe you could find a gentleman with one of similar size somewhere."

"He'd have to be rich," Sylvia said absently as she turned to warm her other side. "Obscenely rich, and blind, too."

"Well, there you have it. We'll have you settled with a hearth this big before the month is over," Price promised, laughing.

Sylvia was about to reply when the doors cracked open again. An older gentleman strode into the room with a handsome woman of similar age at his side. "Finally!" the man cried. "I was just considering whether it would be necessary to mount a search."

Price bowed. "We ran into bad weather, Exeter."

His grace nodded, and then he smiled warmly at the woman by his side. "Kitty. This is the cur who stole our chef."

"And you have him back," Price protested.

"Just as well." The duke slipped his arm around the woman's back and grinned. "Carmichael, this is my wife Kitty, the Duchess of Exeter."

Lenore hurried to curtsy to the woman, and so did Sylvia.

Price bowed deeply, too. "Your grace, it is an honor to finally meet you. Congratulations on your marriage."

"Thank you, my lord," the woman murmured. "Welcome to Grafton Park. I hope you enjoy your stay with us."

"I'm sure we will." Price drew Lenore forward. "And this is my wife, Lenore."

"A pleasure."

The duchess smiled kindly on her, and then at Sylvia. "You must be exhausted after your journey."

"Cold," Sylvia murmured, and Price hurried to introduce Sylvia, too.

"You'll soon thaw once we get you upstairs," the duke promised.

The duchess ushered them to her side. "Let's get you settled in and changed out of those damp gowns before you catch a chill. Most of the ladies have gathered around the great fire in the west drawing room."

Lenore reluctantly followed the duchess, but noticed that Price was trailing after them at the duke's side. The pair seemed to be very friendly and informal as they started to talk.

"So you finally married," Price noted.

"So did you," his grace replied with a smile. "You look happy."

"So do you, too," Price replied, and then chuckled. "So how is my chef enjoying his holiday with you?"

"He is *my* chef, and he's very happy, thank you very much," the duke insisted. "Don't you dare try to steal him away again."

"I didn't even try very hard the last time," he joked.

The duchess ran back to the duke and slipped her arm through his, pulling him along. "Now, now, darling. Don't squabble over the poor chef on the first day. There will be plenty of time for that later, after he's served up the feast for your party."

The duke quickly kissed her cheek. "As you wish, my love."

Price put his arm around Lenore and pulled her close, too. The duke and duchess of Exeter grinned and led the way, whispering to each other like a pair of young lovers. Like she and Price often did when they were alone.

As Sylvia followed after the duke and duchess, Lenore grinned up at her husband, her anxiety fading away. "This is going to be a very good Christmas, isn't it?"

"The very best," Price promised as he hugged her close before hurrying her along to their chambers where they could finally be alone again.

—◆—

The Distinguished Rogues will continue . . .

MORE REGENCY ROMANCE FROM HEATHER BOYD...

SAINTS AND SINNERS SERIES

Book 1: The Duke and I
Book 2: A Gentleman's Vow
Book 3: An Earl of Her Own

REBEL HEARTS SERIES

Book 1: The Wedding Affair
Book 2: An Affair of Honor
Book 3: The Christmas Affair
Book 4: An Affair so Right

THE WILD RANDALLS SERIES

Book 1: Engaging the Enemy
Book 2: Forsaking the Prize
Book 3: Guarding the Spoils
Book 4: Hunting the Hero

MISS MAYHEM SERIES

Book 1: Miss Watson's First Scandal
Book 2: Miss George's Second Chance
Book 3: Miss Radley's Third Dare
Book 4: Miss Merton's Last Hope

And many more...

About Heather Boyd

USA Today Bestselling Author Heather Boyd believes every character she creates deserves their own happily-ever-after—no matter how much trouble she puts them through. With that goal in mind, she writes steamy romances that skirt the boundaries of propriety to keep readers enthralled until the wee hours of the morning. Heather has published over 40 regency romance novels and shorter works full of daring seductions and distinguished rogues. She lives north of Sydney, Australia, with her trio of rogues and pair of four-legged overlords.

You can find details of her work and writing at
www.Heather-Boyd.com